Toothsucker

Kaden Love

Svetling Press

Also by

Also by Kaden Love:

Paladins of the Harvest:

Beastcall: a Paladins of the Harvest novella

Elegy of a Fragmented Vineyard

Duet of Pernicious Eels

Contents

For Sonya and Igor, we love you.

For all the refugees and immigrants who endured senseless difficulties.

Let your stories be heard.

Glossary

And: Androids, often used as servants.

Bite: Term used by Deleon's crew to describe their hypothalamic implants that give them their abilities and a hunger for teeth.

Exos Sapien: Boneless human remnants of a body that survived techbone, also known commonly as Jelly Fiends.

Finian: Dolphin cyborg.

Fix: Cybernetic drug.

Glowbones: Glowing skeletons held together by flesh, another remnant of poorly treated Techbone

Haven Health: The pharmaceutical company that is currently the president of the Republic of Capital, produces Okrepinate.

Memoryrunners: Ruling party/company that produces memtabs.

Memtab: Fix that fills the user with nostalgic bliss.

Mindshow: Film experienced in the neurospace.

Light: A substance measured on the spectrum from red on the bottom to violet on the top. Used for currency, power, fashion, and many other aspects in modern society. Most modern civilizations are sorted into districts based on the light that powers them, with Red being a wasteland and Violet being society's elite.

Neurospace: Computer implant in the human brain.

Okrepinate: Drug produced by Haven Health that led to their success. Treats symptoms of Techbone and requires lifetime usage. Does not treat the disease itself.

Osteolyte: Pharmaceutical company run by Deleon.

Republic of Capital: The country formerly known as the United States of America, including parts of the former Canada and South America.

Ruling Parties: The corporations that make up the government of the Republic of Capital.

Shac: Stands for Synthetic Human Advertisement Citizen. Androids used for advertisement purposes. The term "Shac" is also used as an insult.

Socitab: Fix that fills the user with social gratification.

SocStan: A Ruling Party. What were once referred to as "blue-collar" workers who gained value in society as the rise of AI eliminated many jobs that were once luxurious.

Techbone: A disease that causes bones to degrade and eventually dissolve. Caused by certain individual's reactions to cybernetic implants.

Chapter One
Enamel

I never expected to become addicted to eating teeth when I immigrated to the Republic.

You get used to the enamel after a few days. It's like an orange peel hiding the sweet pulp inside. Just below the dentin, the innervated pulp was more addictive than heroin, even more than memtabs.

I wiped the blood from my chin. Sanguinous drool covered my shaking hands. Neon blue lights in the night made the blood look like black ichor. The blue District wasn't easy on the eyes, but the wealthy liked it enough to fake admiration.

I pulled some more teeth from the man's mouth, savoring them but not taking too much time. After a moment to digest, my hands stilled. My strength had returned.

"Hurry up, Petya!" Tevon beckoned as he wiped the blood and bone dust from his mouth. Eat too fast and you look like the monster you are. I preferred to take my time, making the uncivilized act as civil as possible. It was a futile gesture but helped to soothe the guilt. Regardless, I lost the guilt after the first few months. If you need to eat teeth to survive, it's best to not get hung up on the morality of it.

"I'm almost done." I crunched the molars with my own. My teeth were unbreakable, but the guard's molars were still tough to crack.

"Please," Ali whispered.

I waved him away, taking a final look into my victim's mouth to make sure I would leave my plate clean. "They won't hear us. Deleon ran the checks and blasted an EMP on their neurospaces. I've been watching the time and we have a good three minutes left until they reboot."

"Only three minutes?" Ali shook as he popped a few teeth from his pocket into his mouth. I can't stand teeth if they've been out of a mouth for more than an hour, but Ali wasn't as picky. The skinny kid always had them on hand. *Kid.* Zeg, I'm just a few years older than him and just as gaunt, but his timidity makes him feel like the baby of the crew. *I was just like him. Give him a couple more weeks and he won't be as skittish.* I pushed my hair back up into its wave, sides shorn, making it look like a skunk sat on my head with the bleached stripe in my gray to match. Tevon thought the stripe was juvenile, but I wanted something after the hypothalamic implant tainted our hair color. Mine had gone from brown to a dark black, while the others had a variety of greys. At least I didn't have Ali's buzz cut that made him look so young.

Ralia leaned down and kissed Ali on the cheek. The three of us laughed while he squirmed. The print of her red lips remained, though no one could tell if it was from blood or her ever present lipstick. Her parted, ear-length gray hair looked teal under the blue neon lights. "Which is why I'm here to make sure their emergency signals aren't broadcast inside. Three minutes? Pssh, all the time a girl could ask for."

Ali's face remained red. "Did the master hit the guards' neurospaces inside the facility?"

"Master?" Ralia laughed, her eyes flashing as she pressed her finger against one of the guard's temples. "Zeg, you'll have to ditch that '*master*' thing soon."

"Respect is good," Tevon added. "It'll keep him safe."

Ralia jumped to the next guard's temple. The flashing returned to her eyes. "But not sane."

"Deleon said there were a few inside, but he couldn't see them all. Their walls are breach blocked."

"Then how does he know what's in there?" Ali asked.

"'*Master* knows all," Ralia chided, as she finished wiping the last guard's neurospace. "Signals have been killed. Nothing more than corpses now."

I walked over to Ali and nudged him. "It's all good. Deleon cleared it so we know it's possible. Most of the guards were out here, we know that much. Zeggin' bastards left a feast to fuel us before going in."

Ali stared at the ground.

"Everyone had enough?" Tevon asked.

We all nodded.

Tevon sent out a message to our neurospace group chat with Deleon and Doctor Cut.

Tevon: Heading in.

Deleon: Take out the first one you see inside. Have Ralia send me the data from his neurospace and I'll get a rundown for the facility.

Ralia: Sure thing, daddy.

We all chuckled, knowing the disgruntled middle-aged man would be squirming behind his desk.

Tevon walked ahead of the group and we followed in tow. Though our feast of teeth fueled us with inhuman strength, he was the only one with a build fit for such power. He was a true giant among us. I still didn't know the extent of our abilities from eating teeth. Some questions were best left unanswered. I already found myself less human by the day.

"Ralia," Tevon said, "we need you at the door, too."

"Should I be surprised?" She winked at Ali as she strutted past. At least her jacket wasn't as flashy tonight. The blue fit the lights and her style well, but she wasn't my type. Maybe because she flirted with everyone, so who knew if she was into anyone? We tried not to worry about those things. We had a job, one forced upon us, but it helped sustain us. Maybe if we made it out of Deleon's grip, we could think about the more mundane things in life.

Ali kept his distance but watched Ralia work on the pad next to the door. Her eyes flashed as she touched it.

"You watching, Al?" she asked. "Tell Del you want to learn and he can mod your Bite implant. Is it that or–"

My attention fell away as her self-aggrandizement rambled on.

Tevon looked down at me, a head taller than all of us. His emotions were hard to read with the metal band over his eyes. The implant claimed to improve upon human eyes, but I had found tech promises to be less reliable by the day. I would have refused Deleon's hypothalamic implant if it hadn't been forced into me. We all had our reasons to fall into Deleon's trap. Despite our differences, we were unified in our suffering.

Tevon breathed through his nose, his nostrils flaring, but a lack of wrinkles on his forehead gave a hint to his mood.

"What's up?" I asked. I wanted my fix. Socitab, memtab, either cybernetic drug sounded nice. Would I have enough time to leave and hit it?

Tevon scratched his head. His hair looked like blue turf sticking straight up. I wondered how close turf was to the grass that had long gone extinct.

"Can I... cut your hair?"

Ralia laughed. "Zeggin' Tev! You made me lose my focus. I'll have to start over again."

"Can I?" Tevon asked me.

"No! Again, you zegging creep. What is your problem? Stop asking me!"

"Ah, come on, Pet. He's just trying to show his love."

"Get back to the code, Ralia. He doesn't care about me. He asks everyone and who knows what he does with all that hair."

Tevon was at a loss of words.

"You have weird interests, Pet. You can't get off of those socitabs."

"It's not the same. How long are you going to be?"

"Two minutes."

"Two?" Ali quivered. "But you said we only had three before their neurospaces reactivated."

"More like half a minute, hun."

Ali groaned.

"Don't worry, I've got it under control."

I tapped into my neurospace and sent a message.

Petya: Deleon, give us another blast. Ralia needs more time.

Deleon: On it.

"That was fast!" Ali breathed.

Fast to do what he needs to get what he wants. Slow to actually care. "I'll be back in a minute, Ralia. I need a fix."

"No prob!"

I stepped away, tapped into my neurolink, and threw on some music. Tevon and Ralia knew that I preferred to do jobs with my mind in my own space. Distraction and annoyance free. Ali seemed to think it was odd. Frankly, I wouldn't care except that I liked the new kid. He was into the same art-house surreal mindshows that I liked and had shown me a couple of decent ones in our downtime.

I scrolled through my playlist in my mental interface, hovering over *Punk Runner*, but decided to go with something that made me feel happier. My mind had been set on melancholia for months. It was rare for me to step outside of the mood. Ever since Deleon took me in, I found it soothed the pain to romanticize my dwindling happiness. Ali liked the same style of music too, but even his taste ran too depressing for me, just like his favorite mindshows. I should have been worried about him, but he seemed happy enough, only a bit nervous.

I tapped on my guilty pleasure playlist that I chose not to name. The songs still had a melancholic taste, but they were more focused on love and longing, if not lust. The first song began with synths that shook my mind, placing it into a new sphere of consciousness. I had listened to it enough for it not to disrupt the jobs. Finian technology had transformed music into a new cerebral experience.

Let's Eat by Naoma played, giving my thoughts their own sound-track. Naoma, the '*Neon Idol,*' pop singer worshiped almost solely by young girls who longed for love and heartbreak alike. I hated that I liked some of her songs so much. They were catchy and hit the mood right. Regardless of the factory-produced lyrics, I liked to listen to her and similar artists whenever I used socitabs.

Memtabs were my favorite fix, but they were expensive. They were almost a mindshow, letting one relive the purest nostalgia. My generation had been trained to become nostalgia addicts by marketing schemes and the idea that the past was always better, making memtabs a lucrative business. If not for us, the memtab manufacturers–the Memoryrunners–would have never been a part of the government. What a mess our actions had put us in with that.

I checked on Ralia, making sure she was still working on the system. It looked like I still had some time so I pulled up my consumable files and tapped on a socitab, my cyber-drug of choice, letting Naoma's lyrics take me for a ride.

If not for you, I would have been empty.

Because of you, I am once again.

Again.

Again.

Play me again.

Connection. Love. Belonging. Physical touch along my spine. Appraisal. Respect. Every shade of admiration, anything that could make one feel important, rushed through me alongside Naoma's ballad. The socitab experience was concentrated social gratification. The whole world followed, liked, and worshiped you in the social neurospace for a mere moment. None of it was real, but the sensation was.

I turned off Naoma's song and reverted back to my synth ambience playlist as the feelings of gratification dissipated. I felt immediate withdrawals, but did not have time for more as the door opened before Ralia.

I told myself that I could have another fix after the job, knowing that I would need it. As long as it was available, I'd use. If it wasn't, I would get more. Deleon was a zegging shac, but at least he kept my supply full. I wasn't happy that I'd developed the habit but told myself that it was better than the insatiable need for teeth. We all had that problem and would for as long as Deleon's zegging hypothalamic implants remained.

Just another excuse to tell myself that there was no problem with using fixes. Using them was like when artificial sweeteners were the big hit, until someone whistle-blew the fact that they were some of the earliest substances linked to mental-tech manipulation. Enough companies had their excuses as to why fixes were "unhealthy" and "unnatural," but every organization had a motive. Corporate benevolence was a thing of the past. How else would the government have finally given up the guise of politicians, admitting that they were corporations? Life seemed a lot clearer since the ruling parties became companies, CEOs no longer needing to hide between politicians. Then again, life was never clear.

Technology birthed lies.

I waved for Tevon to lead the way. He touched my hair as I passed and I slapped his arm. Ralia's smile was huge, but she bit her bottom lip to contain it.

I patted Ali's shoulder and moved him to the back. He gave me a faint smile. I nodded and turned down my synth ambience to hear the others.

"The zeg are those?" Two guards pointed their light rifles at us.

Tevon stepped before us with a blue light shield the size of his body. He charged them both and knocked them down, not giving him a chance to react.

Tevon retracted the shield, and Ali dashed forward. His metal hands transformed to blades with an indigo lining as he decapitated their helmeted heads.

"Pulse! That's what we need, Ali!" I whispered as I stepped forward to look around. The hallway went on for a few meters before splitting in two. The walls were lined with blue plating and artificial light with a holo of a naked human that spun in place at the end of the hall. Nudity had lost its shock-value in the present light era, but even in the past, it was not uncommon in medical facilities. This was the third Deleon had sent us to in the last month, but none of them had what he *"needed."* Whatever that meant, we could only guess. We eliminated the threats, sent him their data, and he would direct us from there.

"Sorry I used indigo light," Ali said.

"Why?" Ralia said with her arm around his shoulders. "Don't worry about expenses. We've gotta rely on the high end of the spectrum. You saw they had blue energy shields and you did what you needed! Tevon should have used something else. If they had indigo rounds, they could have pumped us fulla' light!"

"I know, but–"

"Al, baby, don't worry about the price of the light. This is all on Deleon's bill."

"But–"

"She's right." I said. "We live poorly and hesitate to use even green light, but you need to realize that *everyone* in this District is using something better than that. Pray we don't have to use violet to counteract their light attacks. A little indigo is no problem. You did well."

Ali nodded. I wondered if he was using too much light back at the hub. Deleon kept things strict like that. The zegging bastard molested us with his systems, except on missions like this when we needed to be as technologically silent as possible.

Still, there were times when it was needed.

Petya: *Any reading on the inside?*

We waited a minute before receiving a response.

Deleon: Take the left.

We all made eye contact and nodded. Our attention shot back to our neurospace as a new message arrived.

Deleon: Plenty of guards and a lab on the left, but I can't read what is inside. Petya, take the right. There's a large warehouse. Roaming guards, no one focused on a single point. Made just for you. Everyone else, take the left.

"Aw, Pet doesn't get to see this girl in action." Ralia ran her finger down my face as if it was a tear.

"Make sure Ali stays focused and confident." I whispered to her.

She winked, and I knew she would take care of him. Despite her chaos, she knew when to be serious.

I nodded at Ali, then looked at Tevon. "Keep your zeggin mind off of my hair, or *anyone's* hair, for the sake of the light."

Before I could hear his response, I turned up my synth ambience and walked ahead of the group and turned right. With music in my mind, I cast aside my other concerns and focused on my duty. I pulled my neurospace up and put on my Punk Runner playlist. The synth ambience drained away and the melancholic tech-heavy music took over. I would save Naoma and the happier music for later. *Punk Runner* was *pure* music, not the Finian mind-experience 'new stuff.' I needed focus if I was to do what Deleon referred to as my specialty.

No guards stood before me in the hallway, only a staircase. What lay beyond, I could only guess.

Punk Runner blasted into my consciousness, and I ran.

The staircase led to a door and continued to ascend on the right in a switchback rise. I took my chances and climbed. If Deleon wanted me to use my specialty, so be it.

I felt the teeth that I had eaten burn within, fueling me as I soared up the stairs without the pace of my breath changing.

I reached the top after five flights, not finding a single guard along the way. A simple access pad locked the door at the end of my path. I was nowhere near as skilled as Ralia, but this door was nothing compared to what she had faced at the entrance.

I reached for the handle and ripped it off, then reached through the hole with a small indigo blade in my hand. Using the light implant in my neurospace to spend the indigo light, I ignited the blade and cut the door's bolt. Much to my relief, I pressed the door open without any alarm.

I stepped through to see a guard walking away from me, a light rifle secured against his right hip.

I dashed with silent footsteps. I could hear everything, even with the music blasting in my mind, but I did not need to listen to know I ran no louder than as a spider.

With hands faster than a light shot, I spun the guard's helmeted head three hundred and sixty degrees. The pop of their neck was muffled by their energy shield. Sure, it would have protected them from a light shot or strike from anything lower grade than indigo, but close combat was not their typical threat.

I felt a slight hunger as I burned the tooth storage that powered the agility mod of my hypothalamic implant and knew I needed to satiate it before going too far. I pried the helmet free and ripped the guard's jaw from his head. As I gnawed on the lower jaw's teeth, I threw the helmet back on him.

The gore and dead eyes weren't a problem. They were an unpleasant sight and would be for anyone who discovered him. It was an odd thought, caring for someone's macabre discovery, while ignoring the murder committed by my hands. It wasn't murder, was it? Does a predator commit murder as it feasts upon its prey? It's nature, and I had become a part of it. I had no problem with death. I told myself this and made sure that I lived by it. Deleon held me with a promise. If I complied, so would he. I could not relent. I suffered and slayed so others would not have to.

My mind drifted back to the task at hand, my hunger satisfied for a moment.

As I ran onward, there was no longer a wall to my right, but an opening. I slowed my pace and stepped up to the railing to peer out into a room five stories tall. Guards patrolled each floor, many of them stood with another at their side, presumably chatting as they looked out over railings like mine.

I tried to look down for anything unique on the first floor and recounted the levels below, seeing now that my count was wrong. This new ground level was two more floors below what I had thought was the first level. A thin blue light, like those used by the guards for energy shields, covered the bottom floor, rather the *top* of the new level. Regardless of what was happening on the ground, I knew we had to make it there. The people I saw below the light wore hazmat armor rather than the guard armor worn by everyone we had seen throughout the facility.

How many guards did the facility usually have? The Pharma market had exploded more than ever before since techbone became such a common condition. With a shot at a seat in the ruling parties, the corporate competition for power in the Republic of Capital became as intense as any mob war in the so-called virtual era before *physical light* changed the world. Sure, the Tech and Entertainment competitions were intense, but nothing compared to Pharma. People killed for the knowledge used to heal. Thinking of Pharma as philanthropic was laughable. It was a business and, as far as I believed, always has been. Even more than that, it had evolved beyond business. Its lucrative nature meant power. Today, that power meant a government seat. After the SocStans lost the last election, Pharma regained power.

Power in Pharma meant presidency. Deleon was shallow. He wanted what every other Pharma wannabe hoped for. Market domination. In our neo-capitalocractic nation, that meant government sovereignty.

Ralia: Almost done, Pet?

I was relieved to see that she had sent a personal message. I knew Deleon could tap in if he wanted to, but I would rather not have him push me. He knew I hated it. I was fast but could only do so if left to focus on the job and not a time.

Petya: Zeg. You're done?

Ralia: Just wrapping up. Lettin' Al do his thing. Boy needs more practice.

Petya: Stay back. Let me do this on my own.

Ralia: Whatever.

Petya: Please.

Ralia: I'll try. Tev will probably get bored. Haven't found anything so far.

But I have.

Petya: I won't be long.

Ralia: Stay safe, babe.

She sent a kissing sound that played in my mind with her last message. Zegging girl. At least someone can keep the light on in the group.

I hopped over the railing, hanging on to the edge to peer down to the floor below, and swung onto the next level. The acrobatic skills programmed into my Bite were top-tier, but they couldn't prevent an injury from a seven-level drop. Regardless, I doubted I could cut through the blue light shield below. Even if I could penetrate it with enough indigo cuts, I had to approach the people below with caution. Deleon was interested in their research and I didn't want to throw myself unprotected into an area that required hazmat suits. My immunity was superhuman, but nothing living could be completely invincible.

Deleon: Watching you.

Zeg, that would never not be creepy. I hated the man and was glad that I could in my mind. At least he couldn't reach me there, as far as I knew.

Petya: And?

Deleon: You've got a lot around you. Send me a shot.

Thank the light he couldn't see through my eyes. We allowed–or were forced to allow–our current level of observation with every mission. At least we knew there was a choice, even if it had been taken from us.

I let him in for five seconds, showing him my surroundings. No guards had found me on the sixth level yet. I looked over the edge and showed him the blue shielded bottom level.

Deleon: We need them eliminated. You've found it, at least I think you have. Can't have any witnesses.

"Can't have any witnesses." That zegging phrase never left us. It was as tied to our hypothalamic implants as our need for teeth. He held that confidentiality with the hope of curing techbone. If his future implants turned people into fiends like us, that shac was going to kill his zegging self before we could.

Petya: on it.

Another message came in.

Ralia: I'm not telling you to hurry. I know that bothers you. I'm just informing you that Tevon is veeeeery interested in seeing what Deleon sent you to do. Love ya, Pet. Don't hate me.

Tossing the image out of my interface, I blasted my music in my mind and ran around the sixth floor. I ran into two guards, killing them as I had the guard above, but took no time to eat their teeth. I continued to repeat the process, killing like a shadow and pouncing on my enemies. The process repeated, two guards per level, until I stopped three floors above the base.

Ralia: Coming in. Figured I'd warn ya. Blame it on Tevon.

Zegging Tevon. His impulses are probably all screwed up from using his supply of illegal fixes back when he dealt. Who am I to talk? At least mine are legal.

I skipped ahead a few songs until the right one hit. The name and artist escaped me, but it was one of the perfect songs for a night drive. Fast, but still melancholic, with a synth wave to seal the mood. Concerns aside for a moment, I descended to the next level to do what I could before they arrived. Not knowing how big the facility was, I could have a few minutes or seconds.

To my surprise, the next guard I met while running was walking counterclockwise, unlike the others who kept to a distinct pattern. I had ways to sneak around those who were stagnant, but facing someone in a head-on sprint was a different game.

Before he could shout or trigger an alert, I shot a neuromuffler from the gauntlet on my right wrist. The needle hit him in the chest with a spark of violet. It was an expensive shot, but Deleon loaded me up for the job. With the others about to barge in, I likely wouldn't need the rest. Regardless, a few more moments of silence could mean the difference between five targets remaining and ten.

The guard grasped his helmet. A ringing headache now pulled his arms and mind off of any weapon. Having your neurospace become a deafening and blinding static was far from pleasant. I was sure he was screaming, but no sound would escape his throat for another minute.

I picked him up as I slammed into him, saving him from throwing himself off of the edge, only to be killed a second later as I broke his neck.

"Zeg, no!" Tevon shouted as he entered.

"But why not?" Ralia added to their conversation that I did not care to follow.

"Because!"

I shook my head and completed my circle around the floor, relieved that no one remained. I peered over to the edge and saw the open door Ralia and Tevon had entered from a floor above me. Blue light shots from below blasted into steel crates behind which they hid.

Ralia laughed with Tevon next to her.

I moved closer to the edge. No one seemed to have noticed me. Tevon probably thought his shouting could help distract any guards. Sure, it would for a moment, but moments before, no one else had been aware of any threat in the room.

Petya: Deleon wants us to hit the bottom floor. Work your way down and take out any guards. No witnesses.

Ralia: As usual.

With the edge next to me, I turned and swung down a level without stopping to look for a guard. Ralia and Tevon could take care of them. I continued down to the bottom floor, dodging a few shots as I swung down the railings and gaps in between floors. Once I reached the metal rim around the blue light floor, the shots ceased. I clung to the wall, sure that someone would spot me soon enough.

Tevon shouted back and forth with the guards, but Ralia was tempered enough to keep silent. None of us had any range weapons. Deleon said that we were "above" things like that. He had our bodies and the so-called "gifts" granted to us by the hypothalamic implants.

A few guards cried out, but they were on the opposite side of Tevon's shallow blurts. I was quick to judge Tevon, but it was well deserved. He was usually lazy and when he chose to act, it was impulsive. Otherwise, he just pissed me off. Still, I loved the guy. I couldn't feel otherwise. It used to be the three of us until Ali joined us. We'd lost some allies much worse than Tevon, which made me appreciate him.

Still, he really knew how to piss me off.

Feeling that the guards above were sufficiently distracted, I circumvented the blue panel in search of some entrance. Looking down, it did not surprise me to see that those in hazmat suits were stirring in a panic, their eyes looking up at the light rifle shots.

They pointed at me.

Zeg.

Half of them ran into another room while the other half ran to a wall, pulling light rifles from a rack hidden from my view.

They pointed their rifles at me but did not fire. They couldn't. Their shots would either be sub blue or they couldn't transverse the light without breaking it. Were they expecting me to break it? Light used to be such a simple phenomenon. Ever since its physical form was discovered, its usage became more complex. I could step right through blue, break it, or it could be impenetrable. Every guess was as good as the last.

Nerves hit me again, noting that they were a step ahead of me until I figured out what the light was. Zeg, I didn't even know what they were doing and why I wanted it. What would happen if their isolated area was opened? Deleon was thorough with his planning but never let us know *exactly* what we were doing. I assure, you sir, we're not trying to steal your research or lack thereof. We're just trying to survive.

I felt for something I could toss onto the light to test its durability. Tevon beat me to it.

With a primate's call, the zegging behemoth jumped from his floor into the center of the blue panel. Just because our implants could take such a fall, did not by any means it was a wise decision.

His impact shook the light as if he landed on elastic water that rippled from his landing point. He bobbed up and down a few times until the light found its equilibrium once again. The people below turned their rifles to him, some gradually turning to face me after they had a moment to calm themselves. I can only imagine that their fright matched my frustration.

"Tevon! The zeg are you doing?" I shouted.

The rifle firing above had ceased, but I still heard grunts and shouts as Ralia and Ali finished off the guards.

Tevon pulled out a pristine cleaver with a slanted top and flicked on the violet edge. "Gotta move, Pet. You've been dickin' around for too long while we took care of business."

"You see their hazmat suits?"

He shrugged and crouched. "If you get sick, eat some teeth. It always works."

"I know, I–" I had been doing this longer than him. I wasn't in the mood to argue. Let him screw up the job if he wanted. We had nothing to protect against every pathogen, but I put some hope into my mask. The masks were in no way intended for medical protection, but it would be better than nothing.

I tapped into my neurospace and activated my mask, though it was more of a helmet. The black chord that hung around my neck opened and covered my head.

The metallic shell had a thin sliver visor that was supposed to act like Tevon's optic implants. Who knew how close it came to his false eyes. It was completely black with clear lines traced throughout that would accept any light color I chose to fill it with. We rarely needed to conceal our identities. We were low life criminals that would have suffered with the rest of the poor in the orange district, would it not have been for Deleon giving us the hub in the blue District in exchange for "service."

If anything, the masks could help save us from a direct shot to the head. Violet or blue, it did not matter. The mask's system could detect a shot before it hit. If we were focused enough, dodging would be no problem, at least when facing a single opponent.

Tevon plunged his blade into the blue beneath him, burning the violet for a second. Rather than shattering or retracting, the blue light melted and stretched thinner. I jumped atop the light with Tevon as it brought us down with the speed of dripping honey.

He threw a blue shield up as they fired indigo rounds.

"Zeg!" he shouted as a shot flew through the shield right into his shoulder.

I stepped out from behind him and shot two neuromufflers at the frontmost enemies. The others held back from firing for a moment as their allies shook and clenched their heads.

"Now, Tev!" I shouted as I ran. I jumped atop my first target, almost gliding in the air for a moment as I kicked their body down hard enough to crack their head on the ground. I jumped onto the next one.

Tevon charged in with arms spread wide to knock down three enemies.

Our instincts worked twice as fast, helping us take out anyone aiming at us before they could manage a shot.

Their hazmat coverings provided no throat protection as I hit them with quick strikes, feeling their bones crunch.

I finished my job, for that is all that it was. Tevon completed each kill with a grin, even laughing as he did so. Regardless of how numb I felt, killing was never a joyous thing, just an obstacle. Was Tevon's joy a byproduct of his past career or something that spawned from Deleon's assignments?

I raked my fingers through my hair, sure that I would leave blood streaks in it, then scratched my eyes with my wrist. Tevon bashed the heads of his final two targets against each other well past their death.

"It's not bad here, Pet. My throat doesn't hurt, and it smells fine."

"Lucky for you, carbon monoxide is no longer used." My neurospace connected to my mask, and I tapped in for it to run an air reading.

ENVIRONMENT CLEAR. NO THREAT DETECTED.

My mask retracted. I sent a message out to Ralia and Ali.

Petya: Bottom is clear. Come down when you're good.

"On it!" Ralia shouted from above.

I heard her running footsteps above us. Ali shouted a complaint.

"How are they going to get down?" Tevon asked. "Can't jump like us." He tapped the back of his neck, the hypothalamic insertion point. "They aren't as good as we are."

"I'm the only one with the acrobatic mod," I said. "Keep jumping like that and your legs will break. I don't care if your mod makes your bones thicker. Gravity–" I ran after Tevon as he moved over to the bodies and kicked them over for inspection. "Whatever. Just be cautious. They had protection for a reason."

"Whatever it is, there's bound to be a cure for it."

"What about techbone?"

"You can't catch it without an implant."

"I know, I'm just–" Leave it alone. I looked around the lab, ignoring Tevon after he had already put my prattling out of his mind.

The lab was lit by the same blue light used by the city, though it was a touch darker, still not quite indigo. Three rows of four long tables filled the area with cabinets against the wall. The tables were empty, though fallen canisters and metallic tools littered the floor and had been shoved in disorganized ways into the compartments below the table. They cleaned up in haste once they saw us coming but still did not have time to remove a large tank of violet liquid that took up most of one of the table tops. Three tubes connected it to the ceiling.

I moved closer, noting that there was something inside the tank resting on its base.

My attention shot back to Tevon as the ringing clash of metal hit the floor.

He held a cupboard door open, looking at the floor as a few more fell. They looked like large syringes, but none of that mattered to me next to the large tank.

A door beeped to my right. Ralia and Ali exited from a green-lit passage that soon turned blue.

"Whatcha find?" she asked.

I pointed to the tank, and she ran to it.

"Zeg me!" she shouted!

I looked through the illuminated liquid. A naked humanoid laid prone with a mask attached to its mouth. It was hauntingly gaunt and its head was a depressed lump, as if air had been let out of a balloon. Three syringes connected to tubes covered each limb. Its feet, though they faced up, did not hold their shape. The being before me was completely boneless, yet it lived.

I almost vomited. "It's a zegging jelly fiend."

"Huh." Ralia placed her hands on her hips and shrugged. "Interesting. Well, we can take that back to the hub. I need a pick-me-up. All this work is tiring. Let's eat some teeth, boys. We've got plenty of bodies!"

Chapter Two

The Hub

"Firstlight is using Exos Sapiens?" Deleon paced back and forth across the white tile, though it looked blue under the light of the city through the window behind him, taking up the whole wall. The only other lights were a strip of indigo along the floor where it met the wall. A useless waste of light to flaunt a wealth that only existed in his mind.

"What is that?" Ali whispered to Ralia. "What was the point of that assignment, anyway?" They sat to my right with Tevon on my left.

Deleon raised an eyebrow at Ali. He turned to me as he tucked his sleek, neck-length black hair behind his ears.

"None of us know what we're ever doing." I whispered. "Deleon's lack of clarity is one of the shining features."

"Care to say something, Petya?" Deleon asked.

"I was just telling Ali that 'Exos Sapien' is the scientific term for what we call jelly fiends on the streets," I explained.

"'On the streets.'" Deleon shook his head. "You should be above that, Petya. You have a nice home here at Osteolyte. For the light's sake, you even live in the blue district. Don't pretend to be one of the orange lowlings."

I would rather be in the orange District if it meant freedom. His home came at a cost, one that took a toll on us more mentally than physically. Zeg, I wanted a fix. A socitab would feel really nice right now. The false reassurance that all was well. I bit the inside of my cheek. Come on, Petya, teeth aren't enough so you have to rely upon another addiction?

"I am afraid I do not understand," Ali said. His Eastern Arabasian accent became more prominent under pressure. At least we had immigration as common ground, though I knew our stories would differ.

"You saw what was in there, right? Those boneless skin sacks?" Tevon asked.

Ali nodded.

"And?" Tevon said.

"I–I–"

"Give him a rest, Tevon." Deleon stopped pacing in front of Ali. He tapped the back of his own neck to pull some blue light that sat on the tip of his finger like a small sphere until he tossed it into the air. The light expanded into an interface from his neurospace with an image of a pile of human flesh without bones. It extended a hand forward to crawl slowly in place.

"That!" Tevon pointed at the projection.

Deleon nodded. "I think he could gather that much, Tevon. Do not fret, Ali. Exos Sapiens, or 'jelly fiends' as they are sometimes called, are uncommon outside of the Red District. If seen, they are deported there."

"I'm still lost as to why you don't know what these are?" Tevon blurted.

Ralia smacked Tevon's shoulder, though he made no reaction. She rested her hand on Ali's back. "Don't forget that he came from an institution that sheltered him from the outside world even more than Deleon does."

Deleon glared at her.

She looked afraid for a moment but winked to cut the tension.

Deleon smiled. "You'll see more of the Exos Sapiens soon enough."

My nerves ran cold at the thought of the Red District. The lowest light in the spectrum and the lowest point of civilization made up that hellish wasteland.

"I sure like it here," Tevon said.

I turned to Ali and whispered, "Techbone kills you."

Ali nodded. "Yeah, I know."

"Bones disintegrate, but some people survive. Their bodies live on without their bones, but they lose most of their brains as well."

He furrowed his brow. "What causes that to happen?"

"An excellent question, Ali!" Deleon said as he stepped towards us. "Pay attention now, *all of you*."

I heard the guards in the back of the room take a step forward. Deleon rarely had to use them on us. Since we lost Keiro, we were more compliant.

"What causes the Exos Sapiens to survive while the others who suffer from techbone perish? The fact that I do not have the answer makes me even more glad that you–*we*–took out Firstlight's headquarters. While their research may not be as fruitful as my research into the cure, it warrants our attention."

He stood straight with an expressionless face and straightened his buttoned black shirt with a circular collar, eyes still flashing with lights in a dead stare, one that told us all that he was using his neurospace.

The doors opened behind us, but we kept our attention forward. Deleon had sent a message to call someone in.

Cut entered the room and stepped between our seats and strode towards Deleon, stopping a few feet away from him, and stared out the window.

I did not need to ask the others to know that they, too, felt goosebumps in the presence of Doctor Cuttrin, Osteolyte's chief medical executive, whom we referred to simply as "Cut."

A moment of silence held them all still until Deleon spoke. "I just relayed the information from your successful raid on the Firstlight headquarters to Doctor Cuttrin for him to become aware of our circumstances."

Even Cut did not insist on his full title being used. Deleon tried too hard to make his business sound official, when we all knew it was just a front to deeper desires, though what they were remained a mystery. We *were* the street folk, contrary to his previous statement. Rats implanted with technology to execute his will.

"Received." Cut said. He did not move from his position, wearing a blue lab coat that stopped at his waist. His parted brown hair looked even greasier under the blue light of the city.

"Any insights, Doctor?" Deleon turned to him.

"Is this it?"

"Ralia?" Deleon stepped towards her. "Surely you have something besides a few mindshots."

"Of course!" Her eyes flashed with a variety of colors. "Sending the pictures over now. Sorry, I couldn't dig up too much. I pulled what I could from the lab. They didn't keep much in their net. Most of what I could find beyond the firewall couldn't be downloaded."

Cut and Deleon nodded.

"Anything?" Deleon asked.

Cut held up a finger and sighed, letting a minute pass until he spoke. "Too little to draw any conclusions about their intentions with the Exos Sapiens. This is the middle of their research, with no clear end or beginning. They—wait... here we go."

"Yes?"

"Who told you this was the base of their operations?"

"Why?"

"You were mistaken. This was a mere outpost. Rather, let me begin again. Yes, you succeeded in eliminating Firstlight, but they are an appendage of a greater parent company."

"Zeg, does the President's company own them?"

"No, Haven Health does not, as far as I can tell. Still, the President has her hands in every pharma power in the Republic of Capital, especially here in Zingang. What is more interesting is that Firstlight has ties to many of the other ruling parties that make up the Republic's government."

"Which ones?"

"Entertainment? Pharma? The SocStan laborers? Perhaps all of them, though I cannot draw any conclusions."

"Zeg. Well, what now?"

"This is your company, Deleon. That is your decision." Cut started towards the door. The blue light on his glasses hid his eyes. "Let me know if you learn anything else that applies to me."

The doors opened and closed, our gazes remained forward.

"Well," Deleon held his hands behind his back and resumed his pacing. "I suppose you should head out for another investigation."

"Uuuuh, I can't be the only one that doesn't get what we are investigating?" Tevon said.

My pride made me reluctant to agree, knowing that Deleon would clarify anyway, but I needed to be a better teammate for Tevon. Ali and I nodded. Ralia shrugged, then nodded.

"We need you all to work your way into the other governing parties to see where this company stems from. If we here at Osteolyte are to ascend the pharma ladder to the top of the market, we cannot allow the research conducted by Firstlight and their parent company to continue."

Tevon offered up another challenge. "But I still don't see why *this* company is so important. What is it about their research with the jelly fiends that has you so concerned?"

Deleon stared at him for a moment before speaking. "I don't know why they are interested in the Exos Sapiens, but it must not be permitted to continue."

I furrowed my brow and was quick to relax my glare. Deleon knew something about the jelly fiends that he was not sharing. Who was I kidding? Most of Deleon's missions were blind quests for absurd purposes. Deleon wanted Osteolyte to rise. When his company rose, so would his power. Outcompeting Haven Health for the presidency seemed too simple an answer for Deleon's desires. I had learned when he first took me in to be compliant and not ask questions. That delayed curiosity was wearing on me.

"Sir," Ali raised his hand. "Might we have some time to recuperate before we begin this next assignment? I think my comrades would agree that we are all exhausted."

Deleon looked at Ralia, who nodded.

"We need it," she said.

"Very well, but if you go out to see the city, do not exhaust yourselves with leisure."

"Thank you, sir." Ali stood and bowed.

Deleon offered an awkward smile and dismissed us.

I trudged after the others from Deleon's office. Despite my time under his service, I could never figure out how much freedom we had in the city between assignments. I had never seen any sign of Deleon's observation but was not naïve enough to think that we were left unsupervised. Even Ralia kept cautious, only going out to eat something other than teeth and the factory produced guk that Deleon fed us, or to take a walk. Even if I wanted to exhaust myself with the city's debauchery, Deleon gave us too little pay for any sex houses. Sticking to neurolove was hardly close to the real thing, but it was cheap and the exhaustion was not physical. I would be a little zegged up after the night, but Deleon could go zeg himself if he wanted to keep me from living my night with any fix I wanted. He knew about my addiction and wouldn't give me enough money to pay for the kinds that didn't harbor as many risks. I would risk the consequences of the cheap stuff because of Deleon's persistent ignorance. Still, what else could I expect from someone who *gave* us an addiction to eating teeth?

Zeg, I craved some molars.

"Ralia."

She turned around as we walked down the hallway. "Yeah, babe?"

I grinned but lost it as I spoke. "Wanna *feed* before we get some actual food?"

"You're speakin' my mind, brother!" Tevon said.

I took a bite of the imitation meat from my wrap and thought about what real meat would taste like. Everything I ate was artificial or grown in a lab. It would always be the same unless I ascended to live in the indigo or violet districts. I couldn't imagine such a life, let alone one outside of Deleon's grasp. The hot sauce tasted so mild next to the memory of eating teeth a few minutes before. The sweetest dessert. Sushi from Arabasia's finest chef. A glass of water after a week of thirst. Sex for the tastebuds. Compared to teeth, all other food lost its glory.

"Mmh!" Ralia hopped up and down on the bench across from me. She wiped the green sauce from around her mouth and licked it from her hand. I couldn't tell if she was sincere. Her spirit, regardless of the circumstances, was always elevated. I would have tried to bring her down to my realistic melancholy if she hadn't been so effective at elevating us. We could all learn something from her.

Ali looked around at our surroundings, having only taken two bites from his wrap. The taste of teeth was probably the only thing on his mind.

I followed his gaze. The skyscrapers rose all around us with shades of blue lighting them up with advertisements. Drones flew in every direction, delivering every convenience. The stars looked beautiful, as they always did, since they put more constellations in the night sky. One could no longer tell which ones were real, or even if the sky itself was. The area was filled with people dressed in the indigo of affluence and even some poor wanderers dressed in yellow with their heads hung low. Not everyone wore the colors of their home district, but it was definitely the style, even if it was a guise. None of us wore any colors, per Deleon's request, but I feared it attracted more attention than it deterred. All black was not the fashion in any district. I held that hope, telling myself that it caused the attention and not our identities.

"Zeg me," Ralia said. "Al, is this your first time in the city? Like actually *out* and about?"

He nodded.

"We're a bunch of shacs. Three months without leaving the hub? Sorry, my guy."

Ali shrugged, eyes stuck on the man dressed in a tight green jump-suit who approached us.

"Hihow!" He greeted us with a wave and put his hands on the edge of our blue-rimmed table.

We all turned to look at him. Not even Ralia responded.

"Nice weather tonight, right?" he said.

We continued to eat.

He scratched his throat. "A lot better than it has been. Any of you been outside of Zingang recently?"

We had, but he didn't need to know.

"Why?" Ali asked.

"Oh, you better be careful pal, what's your name?"

"Ali."

Ralia smacked his wrist. Tevon and I ignored it.

"Well, Ali, you need to check the air quality. Some industrial winds are blowing from the west. Say, have you had a cough recently?"

"A month or so ago." Ali said.

The man inhaled through clenched teeth, hissing. "All too soon. Let me tell you, my friend." He waved for us to make some space for us on the bench, but no one moved. He nodded. "If you don't protect yourself, your lungs will suffer from those fumes. Tell me, have you ever thought about respiratory smart filters? They are an implant that you will *never* notice–"

"Ah, get away!"

"Zeg off!"

We all shouted and waved him away. Ralia even tried to kick him.

The man lifted his hands and hunched as he walked away, stopping at another table with the same pitch.

"Zegging shac!" Ralia groaned, quickly returning to her cheery mood as she continued to eat her wrap.

"Wh–what was that?" Ali asked.

"A drawback to the city," said Tevon, "that's what it is. Not all lights and fun."

Ali turned to Ralia with a furrowed brow.

"That's an actual shac," I said. "Ever wonder why we call people shacs? Now you know. Synthetic Human Advertisement Citizen—SHAC. Walking advertisement bots that are ten times more annoying than the ads all over every screen."

Ali took a reluctant bite from his wrap. I still couldn't tell if he hated it.

Ralia wiped her mouth. "Now that you've seen the guk of the city, is there anything *good* that you would want to see?"

Ali shrugged, a confused glare lingering on his wrap. "I don't know what there is to see."

Ralia lowered her fingers as she listed. "Shops with guk we can't afford, neurolove hubs, the entertainment District if you want their propaganda—"

Tevon held out his hand towards Ralia, his eyebrows furrowed towards Ali. With his ocular implant, it was difficult to follow his focus. I doubted that was the sole drawback. "Before we take you out, just *how* much can you take?"

"He's not a child," Ralia swatted his hand away.

"But he didn't know what jelly fiends were," I said.

"You see what I mean?" Tevon said. "Ali, we've known each other long enough. Come on, tell us how you got here."

"Only if he is ready," Ralia said. She looked at him.

He pushed the wrap out of the way and looked at us.

Ralia leaned in. "Do you want us to tell you how we got here? Will that make it better?"

Ali nodded.

My breath shook as I inhaled. I suddenly found the city a lot more interesting than their conversation, though my ears and mind remained attentive.

"I have no problem sharing my shame. Don't care who hears it." Ralia looked around, contradicting her confidence. "I ran with some of the high rollers in the entertainment party. Musicians, actors, influencers that do nothing more than broadcast, I knew plenty of them. Want me to name drop?"

Ali shrugged. "I do not think I would know their names even if you did. But forgive me, I do not understand. If you were so affluent, how did you end up... working with us?"

"Funny thing, hun. *I* wasn't affluent. I lived in the green district, a humble enough apartment on the fortieth floor of some skyscraper. Make friends in the right places and they'll take you with them. Made some stupid decisions and along the line, I spent my nights crashing in violet penthouses. The problem is, if you leech long enough, your victims start to pick up on your behavior. Some of those entertainers are so shallow that you suck all they have out of them too soon. They tossed me out. By that time, I had stopped paying for my apartment. They took all my belongings in the eviction. I was living fast and didn't care about what I had at home until everything before me disappeared. No more fancy food, no more food at all. I was prideful and left all past relationships behind when I hung with the entertainers. After them, the people in my life were gone, and I needed quick credit before I would die. Take too many fixes and you forget to eat. Just ask Petya."

She giggled, and I made no note of it. I didn't offend me. It was the truth. Ralia was not for the faint of heart, but I figured that was a given with our job position.

"The world wants you to produce, Al. It's always taking. If you have nothing to give, it will toss you away for the next best thing."

"So that's why you joined Deleon?" Ali asked. "Because you could 'produce' with him?"

"Baby, what are you sayin'? I joined Deleon because I *couldn't* produce. I sold myself to his experiments and ended up with a zeggin' appetite for teeth just like you." She scowled at his confusion. "Al, you didn't sell yourself to him like us, did you?"

He shook his head. "I thought you were all handed to him like me."

Tevon laughed. "Zeg no! It was my stupid choice to give myself to his medical trials for some quick credit. Worst decision of my life!"

"You would have been dead in the yellow District without it," I remarked.

Tevon laughed as he clapped. "Like I said, worst decision ever! Let's get back to you, Ali. If you weren't as desperate as the rest of us, how *did* you end up with Deleon."

"A change of ownership."

"Al, babe, what is that supposed to mean?"

"I–I was owned by another company that did things similar to Deleon, except there was no–um... hunger associated with the implants."

"I get it," Tevon patted the table. "You went to them first in need of some credit?"

"No," Ali said. "I was... my home was destroyed in the Arabasian and Medislavia war. Merchants shipped me here to some company to become a tech test subject. I developed techbone after a while and someone in Osteolyte took me from them, I guess to test me like they are testing you. Every other company refused to take me, so they were ready to trash me into what they called the 'Red.'"

"Zeg me, I'm so sorry, hun."

Tevon grumbled. "No wonder you love Osteolyte. But you actually *had* techbone? Zeg, so Deleon's implants actually worked! Guess I don't need to worry about getting it with future implants."

"Don't be so sure, Tev. At least you're here with us, Al. We might not have the best life, but it's still something!"

"Still don't know if it's better than the Red," I said, turning back to the group. "We have to kill people here daily, but in the Red, most of what you kill to survive can hardly be called human."

"What is that?" Ali said. "This 'Red' that they threatened me with?"

"The Red District." I replied. "Pray you never see it."

"You know what, Ali, Pet also came over from that same war, but he just called it the Arabasian war, said the Medislavs were tyrants and don't deserve glory."

"But you two don't look the same," said Tevon. "No offense, but Petya is an eerie pale, while you have some color to your skin."

"You zegging idiot," Ralia slapped his shoulder. "That's because they are from different sides. Ali is Arabasian, his country was destroyed. Petya is–"

"Medislavian," I cut in. "That's why I know they are zegging tyrants."

"That's right," Tevon said. "You are a refugee, just like him."

I shook my head. "No. He's a victim. I just had enough sense to leave my corrupt government, but that didn't make it any easier for me."

Ralia smiled with one corner of her mouth. "Why don't you tell Ali how you–"

"No. I don't want to talk about it." I stood. "You all go see the city. I think I need some time to just... let my mind go."

I looked at Ali, wanting to apologize for the atrocities committed by my people against his, but the guilt was not mine.

I had already made a scene and didn't want to deal with the awkward repercussions. "See you all in the morning." Stepping away, I waved them farewell. I would make things better with Ali later. I was too dumb to make the connections in our pasts before he explained it. Zingang was a big enough city to attract all races, but I should have known what brought him here.

"What about you, Tevon?" I heard Ali ask as I walked away. Ali seemed to be as eager as I to avoid the tension by ignoring its presence.

Tevon's characteristic deep chuckle almost pulled me back. "I sold fixes. Helped make them a bit, modded 'em."

"What's wrong with that?"

"Just like any pleasure, pushing it too far pushes beyond what is *legal*. Got busted. Lost my empire, lost a few years of my life in prison, then wound up crawlin' to Deleon like the others."

Tapping into my neurospace, I selected the *Punk Runner* playlist and turned up the volume. I needed some melancholia to turn off the trauma of that eternal war.

Chapter Three

Neon Idol

I turned my music down as my surroundings grew louder. Joyful pop replaced my melancholic synths. I kept my head down while walking through the mindshow district, not wanting to distract myself with the advertisements for the latest tenth or eleventh edition of some formulaic action movie. Anything with a predictable plot and the latest actor idol was beyond my... zeg, I sounded pretentious even to myself. My taste in mindshows was *unique*, but it was nothing to the selection of foreign shows that Ali had shown me.

Was he going to hate me when we saw each other again? If his people had destroyed mine, I would be furious, regardless of who he was. I left my old home behind because of their actions. That was enough, right?

Maybe talking about my past would clarify my position. I had no secrets, rather only memories that pained me to revisit.

I knew I had found the place when all the holos and ads shined with violet and indigo; colors beyond my worth for the sake of bringing me to contribute to their entertainment empire. I wonder what life would have been like back when entertainment was a mere corporation and not part of the government. Society fed actors enough attention, given to be idols so much that we made them into the powers that ruled us. Entertainment hadn't held the presidency since the time before the SocStans, and now Pharma, but they were never far from influence.

Some holo-projections cast blue images of classic bands, still holding on to the strings and horns of the past. I enjoyed jazz and orchestral music from time to time, but electronic waves had a deeper hold on me. Synths were nice, I thought as I passed the row of masked DJs, but they were nothing compared to the Finian music that held our generation.

How the dolphin cyborgs had worked their way up to swimming in violet wealth was astounding and unbelievable until one heard the music their kind produced. Though they still relied on humans to stand as the musicians, the Finian production was unmistakable. Finians were never the performers. Their impact was more influential in the music's creation.

Indigo and dark blue shone around me as I walked further into the projected concerts and dancing holos of Finian pop. The sonorous voices and electronic beats went beyond my imagination to paint pictures in my vision as if I was hallucinating. Maybe that was the secret to their ethereal music magic. I never tried the puffer fish toxins the Finians loved to get high on–hearing that it was even more destructive to the human body than it was to theirs–yet I continued to use fixes to my pleasure.

I wanted a fix. Alone because of my tendencies towards isolation, I needed the warmth of a socitab. As I walked, the need diminished as the hypnotic voice of the most famous pop idol in the Republic of Capital soothed me.

I stopped before a stage upon which a holo concert was projected. The star was bigger than her actual size, large enough for all to feast their eyes upon. Rather than the company spending their full violet light, they added a stylistic visibility, bleeding rich violet with the worthless red and yellow lights for a bright pink that reflected off of the faces of each spectator.

The Neon Idol walked across the stage, singing one of her more intimate pieces rather than the power anthems that earned the devotion of every youth who would spend all their light just to see her in person.

I almost thought she stopped to look at me, thin legs crossed atop blue platform heels. Blending light was a common trick, one made much easier since light became *physical*. Our money, ammunition, and the world's power all came from the spectrum of light.

She leaned down with her head sideways, chin-length teal hair floating down to expose small blue earrings on her pink ears. Multi-colored strands of hair framed her face, but left the sleek eyes to bask in. Her short skirt and sleeveless top shined in bright pink.

Her eyes caught mine.

Naoma.

My heart shuddered. It was just a projection of a pre-recorded performance, but I felt the light violet of her eyes pierce my cynical glare. Her projected eyeliner was blue with white eyelash accents, just like the pink that made her. Violet fingernails of a vibrant holopaint, likely the same light paint she actually paid to wear, danced near her pink holopaint lips.

Light was power. Why not adorn yourself with it to show how wealthy you were? With such extravagant style, would the wealthy eventually identify as the colors they live in?

I turned away from her lustful lyrics, rejecting the allure she used to prime the youth for the adult products and entertainment her parent-company would sell. Mindshows, music, virtual reality, it didn't matter. Throughout human existence, sex always sold. If a company could hone into a human's hunger, they made them into an animalistic consumer.

I was no better, reaching for my fix. I told myself to resist it out of principle. Had the Finian music not been so distracting, I would have failed.

I walked away to let my mind destimulate itself with something simpler. Perhaps some jazz would help calm my demons of addiction.

The Finian music was still plenty loud as I left Naoma's performance. The mind-projected images of pulsing magenta and pink followed me. Faces of reluctant lovers floated in my vision until they kissed with utmost passion before dissolving like mist in the wind.

Naoma's lyrics followed me, banishing any other thought until a deeper addiction kicked in. Unheeded fix addictions were but an itch compared to the *hunger* that seized me. It hadn't been too long since I last fed, but that hadn't been enough. I burned more energy touching the evolved senses that came with my curse. Deleon's gift granted power with a vile cost.

My eyes widened and my chest pounded. Each breath was loud and shaky.

I was in the middle of Zingang with countless civilians walking around me. Many were focused on their neurospaces, but I was still open to their attention.

I needed to eat teeth.

I held onto the wall of the alley as stars danced across my blackening vision. Zegging idiot, why did you have to leave the others to live out your melodrama? If I passed out, no one would be able to help me. I had never let it happen before, but Tevon said that doing so would turn us into rabid predators with a loss of control until we satiated the hunger. We had no reason to believe him, but even less reason to test his theory.

Laughter ahead told me to veer right when the opportunity arose. I had to feed.

It had to be a living victim. Living teeth were pure. Dead teeth could satisfy the craving for a second, but *living* teeth were needed to power our Bites in full.

If anyone saw me, I prayed it would only be my victim.

I stopped for a moment and let myself free from leaning on the wall. My vision was clear, but weak.

Even though the blue District was affluent enough, those from the yellow, even orange, District still found themselves lost in the blue heart of Zingang. One had to make enough blue light to pay for life. Some people, like Deleon, chose to earn that light in less ethical ways. When fixes are too expensive for an orange dweller, blossom would do. It was simple to make with the right tech. Cannabis and methamphetamine were common enough in the yellow Districts and were even worse for addicts when made into the blossoms that were the drug. If you weren't caught, you could make a living in the blue just by selling to visitors from the lower Districts that couldn't afford to pay.

These thoughts hung in my mind as the smoke of the blossom lured me to the right. I never sunk so low to use it and hated the smell, but it was sure to leave someone inebriated. Vulnerable. Even if a blossom smoking vagabond had companions, they would all be zegged out of their minds.

I turned right, drawing farther from the light of the city, as if Zingang ignored the dark underworkings within its cracks. The sky to the east looked more teal than blue. The Green District was close in spirit, yet it was a fairly distant ride.

The alleyway was littered with broken bottles, a variety of upload chips with who-knows-what varieties of fixes that fell all along the spectrum of legality. Countless blossom buds and ashes filled the cracks and corners with a lingering stench to match.

Continuing down the alley, I couldn't find anyone hiding behind a dumpster to sleep and did not want to risk the group talking a few alleys behind me. Cursing myself for the horrid aftertaste that would follow, I turned left towards the lingering stench of freshly lit blossom.

Dead eyes turned towards me, though the bum's gaze never landed. His disheveled hair fell to his shoulders onto a torn jacket with some Pharma company logo. While healthcare couldn't save him from his addiction, he continued to advertise their brand as a sign of societal failure. A silver arm powered by lines of yellow light held what remained of a burning cigarette with another fresh one between the next two fingers.

He took a pull on his cigarette, coughing with a metallic scraping as he scratched a metal neck. While the glowing neck implants were likely the only thing keeping him alive, techbone would take the rest of him eventually, now that cancer was no longer a threat to society.

The human body was not meant to be upgraded by artificial means. Pride, greed, and convenience argued otherwise. How long could humanity go? Who was I to speak? I was as much a part of the problem as everyone else.

I glanced around, my patience expiring like a weak bladder.

"Wahyu wanna from me?" Drool fell as the bum spoke.

He's a victim, just like you. He doesn't deserve this.

No one does. I could never allow sympathy to reach my shrinking soul. I thought about starving myself when the hunger first began, but Deleon had a promise to fulfill. Others would suffer, but I would uphold my side of the deal by living through until the bitter end.

He held out an unlit blossom cigarette with fingers stained yellow. "Light?"

I couldn't tell if he wanted me to light it, if he was offering it, or merely asking for some spare light to spend to get him through to his next pack of smokes.

I crouched before him and held his head between my hands. Even looking into his eyes I found no present soul.. I could consider this a mercy, but that was just another excuse. I knew what I was doing, hated it, and yet continued.

Using the speed modification "gifted" to me by Deleon for my hypothalamic implant, I pulsed my hands with a violent vibration. The man's eyes drifted further apart and pink ooze drained from his nose after a few seconds. Turning someone's brain to mush was unpleasant, but better than the alternative.

I reached my hand inside his mouth, pleased to find that most of his teeth remained and pulled my hands apart with a speed-enhanced jolt. His mandible popped as I broke his jaw and ripped teeth from pale gums.

I tossed out the few metal replacements he had—five in total—then began with the incisors. I wanted the heartiness of the molars, but had spare resolve left to keep them until the end.

Energy shot through my spine, pulsing out to each limb with restorative strength. Breathing was easier. Clouds cleared from my mind. Each thought was birthed from a clear mind compared to the feral addict that I had been moments before.

Moving past the frontmost teeth, I relished the pleasure that was the molars. Each bite was greater than the juiciest and most tender meat, though its texture argued otherwise.

I wanted to run across the entire Republic of Capital, swim across the oceans, fly above the layers of pollution.

Teeth were greater than any drug one could create. They became my idol, my very life. My hunger was satiated to keep me mentally and physically stable, though it would return to me most unwelcome.

As blood pooled and drained from his broken mouth, I became aware of his blood that coated my mouth and hands. I leaned down to wipe it away with the edge of his holey shirt, not bothered by the mix of body odor and brush smoke that filled my enhanced sense of smell.

Staring down, the man had become to me like discarded fishbones. It had not been a rich feast, as it would have been with a healthy indigo citizen. This man was the equivalent of microwaved fish. His teeth were worn and unkept. It was a poor meal but quenched the hunger.

Ready to leave, I turned and found myself caught by the stare of a man and woman in *violet* suits, their eyes hidden behind an implant or covering. I could not tell. I could not think straight. They had seen me feast. They knew what I was. I had no reason to hide.

I ran up the wall and jumped to the other before I could slip. My speed modification burned the few teeth I had eaten. I would have to eat soon but now was not the time to reserve what I had.

They walked towards me, not rushing as I did.

Deleon was going to zegging kill me.

I prayed to the lights that he wouldn't dig into my neurospace memories. There would be no reason for him to unless I returned with warranted suspicion.

Hands firm enough to dent the edge of the metal roof, I hauled myself atop the building and ran. If the violet-suited pair was following me, I had other matters to worry about than merely being seen.

I hopped along the uneven rooftops of the light blue residential district. The bright neon of the blue center shined to my right and subtle green colored the horizon to my left.

There was no reason for violet-wearing elites to be strolling through the poorest parts of Zingang. Had I been followed? Did my feeding solidify the evidence of some investigation?

I tried to calm my anxiety, but it was difficult not to be paranoid in my circumstances.

I approached the edge of the district. I slowed as I landed on a rooftop with a high wall around the edges and a closed latch rather than a door for anyone to enter or leave it.

I rolled as I landed atop it and moved to the wall, sitting in a slouch as I caught my breath.

Zegging shac, you're better than this.

Deleon's past reprimands replayed in my mind. *"Never let your hunger endanger you. If you feel hunger coming on, make sure you make plans to eat in private."*

Zeg him. What did he know? What did he know about *any* of this? What was our *owner's* goal? Would it be so bad to be caught by some violet elites? Let them experiment on me. It couldn't be worse than Deleon's jobs. It would be better for our victims whose vengeful souls increased tenfold daily.

Such a surrender would nullify Deleon's promise. I betrayed humanity by serving him, but there were those who needed justice through fulfilling his oath. No matter how much I hated the man, he never broke a deal. Those who broke his, faced his wrath. They faced us.

I stood, the energy from the teeth kept my mind clear. The few teeth I had eaten from the vagabond helped the hunger pass, but it would soon return.

A message appeared in my vision, though it was only visible to me. I checked it in my neurospace.

Deleon: Be careful the next time you eat. We don't want any unwelcome followers.

All thoughts of appetite vanished. My heart felt as if it pumped ice through my mutant veins. There were no cameras. Deleon had upgraded our neurospaces to detect them. I never granted Deleon permission to view through my eyes. Even if he bypassed the allowance, I would have known.

No one had seen me.

No one except the couple in violet suits.

No one working for Deleon's Osteolyte was a violet resident. His whole plan was to climb the societal ladder to reach that point.

Who the zeg are you, Deleon? What do you *actually* want?

Chapter Four

Expiring Innocence

I was glad Deleon kept his focus on the city through his office window. Morning was coming onto Zingang with a red sun shining through the dense pollution, and I could not keep my glare off of him. I hadn't slept the whole night, worrying about his message.

He turned to some unfamiliar kid whose chair leaned against the wall. Deleon's eyes stopped on me for a second. Though he spoke nothing of it, I knew he was acknowledging last night. Words need not explain that knowing stare with an all too confident smile.

Deleon winked at the boy, who nodded along with some unheard beat. I thought about turning on some of my own music but couldn't allow the emotions those songs carried to alter my focus.

Deleon checked his watch, a relic of style in our evolved era. He whispered something to the boy, who looked at me for a second before returning to his nodding and chair rocking.

I did not ask who he was. Deleon liked his large introductions and anything that flaunted his sense of power. Still, the boy took my attention away from Deleon, so I followed the path my mind took.

I was only twenty-eight. The kid had to be half my age. He didn't have any open neurospace connections, and I was not in the mood to pry. His hair was a pale blue and cut in the shape of an upside-down bowl. He looked down, yet it still looked as if he held his chin and nose high, his lip protruding with condescension.

He noticed my stare, furrowed his brow, then flipped up the long collar of his silver jacket with reflective panels and *living* indigo light. It was *living* wealth, real physical light, and not an LED counterfeit. It would have surprised me to see such a young and wealthy guest in Deleon's office, but my expectations had changed after seeing his violet watchmen. Was this kid tied to them?

I had to ask about them. Perhaps my worries were unfounded.

They could be new members of his organization, but even that was unlikely. Deleon was not quiet about his new tools. If he found some indigo boy, surely he would have spoken about *violet* level associates. Indigo light was a luxury, but violet was godly.

My life would be easier if I didn't ask questions.

Deleon clapped and put on his characteristic grin. "Finally! I hope you all slept well."

I turned back to see the others enter. Tevon's arms hung limp as he strolled to his seat, scowling at me as he sat. Ali grinned and Ralia kissed my cheek. She could have woken up on her way into the room and still not lost her spunk.

"Who's the kid?" Tevon blurted out.

Ralia smacked his arm and Ali chuckled before hiding his smile and lowering his gaze.

"Be nice, Tev."

"She's right to reprimand you, Tevon." said Deleon.

Tevon scowled at Deleon. "Huh?"

Deleon placed his hand on the kid's shoulder, earning a flinch. "This, respected Imps, is a gift."

'The Imps,' a term coined by Cut that didn't stick until Deleon started referring to us as the Imps. I hated it, even more so when Tevon and Ralia decided they liked using it, as if Deleon hadn't dehumanized us enough.

He patted the boy's shoulder and walked away.

"And?" Tevon sighed.

Deleon shook his head with a smile. "This is Devóne Eclaine, the newest addition to your party. Does his last name–"

"Devin?" asked Tevon.

"Day–vown," the boy annunciated. His skittish countenance quickly turned to bite. "Ee-clay-nnn, get that? Heard it yeah, you better have, you zegging—"

"Now, now," Deleon chuckled.

Tevon looked as if he did not know if he should laugh or fight the kid. "The zeg is that supposed to mean?"

Deleon shot Devóne a glare, earning silence. A feigned smile returned to face us. "I presume some of you have heard about the recent tragedy with the Eclaine estate?"

"Never heard of 'em."

The kid guffawed.

I shook my head with Ali, but Ralia was sure to speak.

"Such a *tragedy*. I'm surprised you aren't aware of them, Al."

"I am not well informed concerning celebrity families and names. Forgive me."

Despite his awkward phrasing, he had a nice grip on Amerikese. Perhaps it was close to his native tongue, but I couldn't tell which side of Arabasia he came from. I was born learning Amerikese. All the best entertainment came from the Republic of Capital. When I was growing up, I knew that I was destined for a better place. That same hope told me there was a better side of the Republic that waited for me beyond Deleon's grasp.

"Oh, Al, they're no celebrities, but a *very* influential family that runs an anti-war campaign alongside their company. They come from high up in the SocStan Party of the ruling parties."

Ali nodded but looked no closer to understanding.

"Don't worry," I told him. "I've never heard of them either. The news today is depressing." All of it speaks of our homelands tearing at each other or drama generated by the Republic media to make our lives look difficult. Still, I found it interesting that the boy came from a SocStan background. Usually the Societal Sustainers dressed in humbler clothing, but what did I know? Since the blue-collar workers of the past gained importance after artificial intelligence took many of the high-paying jobs, the humble gained pride with power. The farmers and mechanics became staples to society in the virtual era and had only grown in power since their last three terms in presidency.

Ali nodded with a smile. It was enough to let me believe he held no grudge for my past nationality.

Our attention reverted back to Deleon as he spoke. "The Elcaine tragedy occurred a short time ago. Some rogue automaton explosion reduced their property to rubble, or something of the sort. The investigation is ongoing. Devóne was the only survivor of his family of seven. A tragic accident, though one most timely for our needs. "

What a saint you are, Deleon. You saved a rich orphan from a life of mediocrity by forcing him to become—oh please, tell me you didn't do it to him, too.

"What are you doing to him?" I demanded.

"Zeg me, Del, you didn't buy the kid, did you?"

"I'm not a kid!" Devóne shouted. Red rings surrounded his eyes. The red light from the sunrise reflected off of wet cheeks.

"No, of course I did not *buy* him."

"I can speak for myself." Devóne said. "After... it happened ... I had nowhere else to go. I wandered, took trains and rides to get as far as I could from the people who killed my family."

"Now, Devóne, we discussed that it was a mere accident. Nothing you could have done could have saved them."

Devóne ignored Deleon. "I could not let them catch me. I don't know how I made it so far without anyone hurting me. Deleon found me when I was lying in an alley with some bums from the Orange District. He took me to get some food and offered me a place in exchange for some work." He looked at Deleon. "Thank you again."

"A pleasant coincidence. We are pleased to have you, Mr. Eclaine."

Coincidence, my ass! I almost blurted. I used to trust Deleon, but my naïvety decreased by the day. After last night's encounter, I would have bet half of my lumens that Deleon had followed him ever since the accident to utilize the single heir of a massive fortune. I almost wanted to accuse him of orchestrating the fall of the Elcaines, but even Deleon had his boundaries. Deleon was an opportunist. If he had orchestrated their deaths, we would have been the ones to carry it out.

"So what is our lil' prince doing?"

Devóne scowled at Ralia.

"An opportunistic coincidence," Deleon repeated. "One indeed timely for our next assignment. You all recall Doctor Cuttrin's assessment of the Firstlight discovery, right? Firstlight is connected to multiple ruling parties who are researching the boneless Exos Sapiens. In order to slow their progression for the sake of our—Osteolyte's—success, we must locate those who owned Firstlight. Who better to help us than a former Indigo resident? You will be working with him as your newest Imp to infiltrate the ruling parties and destroy those tied to Firstlight from within. With their research out of the way, we can move towards eliminating the President's company for the next election. Let us Replace Haven Health with Osteolyte."

"And what will you do then?" Ralia asked.

"Oh, you know, my dear."

No, we didn't because he gave us the same zegging answer every time.

He looked at me and I knew my frustration was visible.

"Cure Techbone, of course! It is the purpose of Osteolyte and I cannot make our research change the Pharma market as long as Haven Health continues to pump people with their ineffective drug, but everyone knows that Okrepinate entails a lifetime subscription for mere symptom management. We will cure it, stopping bone degradation, instead of relying on their drug that only treats its symptoms."

Cure everyone like you have cured us?

"Did you treat Devóne?" I asked. The kid's pale blue hair almost confirmed my suspicions without having to ask. If I was right, it would be as gray as the other Imps in the next few days.

"I upgraded him, fit to work among you."

Zeg you, he's just a kid. Even though I didn't speak, I know Deleon could read the seething disapproval in my glare.

"Zeg yeah, feels fantastic!" Devóne's grin was as wide. It was as if his parents had bought him a new tech implant.

"When did you do it?" Ralia asked.

"We finished up just before you came in to join us."

It shows. Devóne would lose that grin as soon as he realizes the cost of such an implant. I only hoped he wouldn't lose it forever. I struggled as of late, but most of us still held firm to the little joy we had in our poor excuses for life.

"Gotcha. So tell me, Del, how do you expect us to do this?"

"I will divide you to infiltrate the ruling parties. I have tailored each of your assignments to your specific fields of expertise. Ralia–" she smiled and looked side to side with a shrug as if it was a complement "--you will naturally infiltrate the Tech party, utilizing your hacking prowess to dive beyond their elite security, extracting any relevant information related to Firstlight's parent company or companies."

She chuckled. "Hold on a second, I can't just *hack* a political party, just as you can't speak to a country. The Arabasian war would have ended long ago if someone could just write a kind letter to a country itself."

He smiled and shook his head. I had never seen him upset at Ralia. She was smart enough to know his boundaries.

"Of course not. Neither will the others assassinate a political party itself."

Devóne's leaning chair fell forward. What a shame. The kid really had no idea what he was getting into. His attention was stuck on Deleon like a child to their mindshows after their neruospace is finally implanted.

"My secondary intel department has organized a list of targets for each of you, at least three each, should you face any dead ends. If they need to be eliminated, so be it. I trust your discretion, but do not burn an end before you have explored it thoroughly. You in particular, Ralia, have been assigned to visit the estate of Rovik Sibirk. Does the name sound familiar, Petya?"

I nodded, keeping my hatred within. I had no problem with Sibirk. He was human filth obsessed with lucre. I accepted that. What I could barely stand was Deleon's snide allusions to my past as if I was some undercover Medislav loyalist.

"Who, sir, might that be?" Ali's hand shook as he raised it.

I spoke up, not wanting Deleon to twist the reality any more than he could. "Tech mogul from Medislavia. He made a living here in the Republic selling tech intel to his home country until he was busted. His reach was too wide and they couldn't contain it, so they did what any perfect justice system would do. The Tech Party bought him out and hired him to do the reverse, providing the Republic with the best innovations from his people in Medislavia before they could capitalize on it."

"A tech emperor indeed," Deleon said. "His reach is the reason Ralia will be focusing there."

She nodded. Her smile looked weak.

"Sibirk is just an example and frankly, the only name anyone will probably recognize, except for one of your targets, Petya."

Zeg you.

"Now for you, Tevon, I intend to use your expertise, though not the brawn mod to your hypothalamic implant."

"Okay." A faint orange light danced across Tevon's vision implant.

"To touch on your past, I want to utilize your familiarity with the fix market. More specifically, the Memory Runner party."

"I didn't really specialize with... *those* ones, yah know?"

"Of course I know, but I don't plan on using your expertise with illegal fixes while I'm trying to manipulate the legal system."

"But, Deleon, I—"

"This isn't a comfort assignment, Tevon. Are you compliant or not?"

"I am compliant."

The room was silent for a few moments.

"As I assumed. Now, the Memory Runner Party has a fix monopoly because their memtabs are more popular than any other product on the market. Nostalgia sells, especially when you can revisit those memories. Maybe your past is a mess, but other people want to enjoy theirs. You feel the same, don't you, Tevon?"

"I feel the same."

"I'll send you your list soon. Ali, I would like you to join Tevon. You've followed Ralia around long enough."

They nodded at each other.

Deleon steepled his fingers and pointed at me, then to Devóne. "Now for you two."

No.

Please don't make me the one who shows him how zegged up this world is. The indigo haze still blinded the kid. Soon enough, he would see the world as red as we all did. Even my negative outlook was blinded by the walls Deleon had built before us.

"It's about time you take on a new member. Ali has spent plenty of time with Ralia and now he is learning from Tevon."

I looked at Devóne, then back to Deleon. "Has he fed yet?"

"I ate an hour ago."

I shook my head, eyes still glaring at Deleon. "Has he *fed* yet?"

"That will have to be one of your first lessons. By my estimation, he should be ready for his first taste following this council."

"Yeah, I could eat."

I ignored the kid.

"Petya, you will comply, won't you? If you want more people like you to suffer as you did before meeting me, go ahead and cut your end of the promise."

"No. I'll take him."

"You will remain compliant?"

"I am compliant."

"Then let us continue from where we left off. Do not worry about handling three parties. I will manage the Pharma party. While I take care of the intel, our research teams will continue at a tireless pace to find a cure, or a proposal for one, available by the time Haven Health falls."

I kept my mouth shut. I never believed in a cure, let alone one from him. Tevon was probably too simple-minded and believed Deleon. Ralia was just optimistic enough to buy into Deleon's claims. When this would all end, would he be kind enough to free us from the curse he placed on us? If he were ever to bring his company to the top of the market, what other tyrannical goal would he pursue?

"Should any of you find your trail fruitless, I will utilize your help with Pharma. The president must fall, but she is far from vulnerable. To take her out now would be a mistake. Only with Osteolyte's success will we defeat her in the next election."

"But that is in two months."

"Great observation, Petya. Now you understand how pressing this is. I am assigning the last two ruling parties to you. Devóne will work with you, utilizing his knowledge of his family's prestige to reach certain targets within the SocStan party. This should come after your first assignment to best prepare him for those more intimate matters. Your selected targets belong to the Entertainment party.

Tevon chuckled.

"What do you want?" A smile broke free from my grimace.

"While we handle the things that run society, you'll be gawking over neuroshow stars and zegging influencers. What kind of an assignment is that?"

"Zeg you," I said.

"I would have laughed with you before," said Deleon, "but we all know how society bows to celebrities. The virtual era had it bad, but now they are *literally* our politicians."

"I know… but, it's still… sorry, Petya."

"What am I doing with them?" I asked. "You said I had a prestigious target? Who is it?"

"We will get to her, but your primary target is the Finian producer Anton Jackson. He has a hold on nearly *every* leading musician in the market. Without him, you cannot get to any of the public idols."

Tevon busted out in laughter. "It's–it's–" he pointed at Devóne. "Oh, zeg, it's just too good. He'll blend right in."

I sighed and tried to keep my focus on Deleon. Devóne was not as strong willed as I was.

"What is that supposed to mean?" The kid's anger was split by confusion.

"Come on, anyone? Can't you see it? Love in Touch?"

"That terrible boyband?" Ralia said. "You listen to them, Tev? You know their lyrics are written by companies to make psycho fans out of teenage girls."

"I–no, zeg no, but look at him. He looks just like that one that they put on the fast food ads, right? Come on, I know you've seen their videos on your neurospaces. He always jumps in front of the group and has a higher voice than the rest."

"I got yah, Tevon." I said. I hated that I knew it from mindless wandering on the neurospace social programs, but the group of five boys was everywhere.

Tevon laughed and clapped. "That's it! That's your name from now on."

"What?" Devóne guffawed.

"Do you even know that one's name, Tev?"

"No, and I don't care. Our new friend is Boyband. That's his name and I'm not giving it up."

I chuckled. I hoped the kid wouldn't take it too hard. Tevon needed something to keep him happy if we were going to succeed. A downtrodden Tevon is a lazy Tevon. Deleon's convoluted scheme would only work if we all did our parts.

"I like it," Boyband said, as if he was trying to prove himself. "You all have names like that?"

"Nope, just you." I grinned at him.

His smile fell.

"Can I have a *second* of your attention?" Deleon pleaded.

We all nodded. I wanted the meeting to end. I needed a socitab fix. Feeling empty and alone, I needed artificial love and praise. Thank the light technology allows us to skirt reality.

Boyband's hands shook and he looked pale. He clenched his face and squeezed his stomach.

Perhaps prolonging the meeting would not be so bad. The more time Deleon took, the longer I could delay teaching the kid what it meant to satisfy the violent hunger that was eating at him. Could I push it off long enough for Deleon to do it for me?

No. If Deleon could defer responsibility to someone else, we would with pleasure.

"Thank you. Now, I will send you your lists and any information I have regarding their presumed locations and any precautions you should take before investigating via neurospace. Petya, take Devóne out to feed, then return to me for a modification. Everyone else can follow me after this, unless you need to feed as well."

They shook their heads.

He started towards the door and waved for them to follow. "Then we'll take care of your additional modifications now."

"What kind of modifications?" Tevon asked as he stood from his seat.

"Upgrades for your hypothalamic implants."

"Upgrading our Bites, huh? Cool. What kind of modifications?"

"Tevon, please, can you wait and see? And you know I do not like you referring to them as *Bites*. Perhaps I should add patience to yours."

"Okay, okay, but one more question?"

Deleon stopped as the doors opened for him. He spread his arms and sighed. "Yes?"

"Who is the other target Patya and Boyband are going after? You said it's a big name and I wanna know who it is."

Deleon laughed, breathing out his frustration. He looked at me. "Naoma. The *Neon Idol*."

CHAPTER FIVE

The Shared Suffering of Prey and Predator

Let's Eat - Naoma

I eyed my coveted guilty pleasure song on my neurospace interface, my mind trembling with disgust and fearful anticipation. I thought about playing it, perhaps one last time, before it became tainted by my assignment. There was no use. It was already too late. All Deleon needed was for me to show the kid how to feed. Didn't matter how or where we did it, so I chose a route that would lead us to a private enough feeding spot.

Boyband grunted as my shoulders hit his.

"Hey!" He scowled at me.

"Sorry. You would have thought that by now, someone would have figured out how to make a smooth train ride."

"I've been on ones that aren't this bad."

"Yeah, but any in the sky? How great of us to sacrifice practicality for novelty, right?"

"What?"

I smiled and shook my head. "Nothing."

"So, where are we going?"

I looked at him, but he avoided me. If everyone hadn't been staring at his indigo-laced clothes, I doubt he would have sat so close to me. I wasn't worried about him just yet. After his first assignment, he would learn that his Bite made him a lot more powerful than anyone glaring at him on the skytrack.

I pointed to the map above the windows across from us. "We're on 3A."

"Where's 3A?"

"It's not a place, it's—oh, come on, kid, aren't you familiar with the skytack lines?"

He pointed to the indigo light on his jacket. It would burn out soon enough without his parent's money to pay for it. "I don't *need* public trains in the Indigo district."

"Right. Rich parents."

"Oh, so you think because you've had it tough that you are so much better than me? I lost everything. I know how hard life can be, and don't call me kid."

You don't know the least of it. You'll get a taste of your new life at the end of this ride. *Taste.* I almost laughed at the sick joke. "How old are you?"

"What does that matter?"

"If you don't want to be a kid, how old are you, *buddy*?""Zeg you!"

"Kid has a mouth on him, huh? Learn that now that you're living with rough people like us? We're just trash to you violet citizens, right?"

"*Indigo.* We weren't *that* rich."

Boy, you and I are worlds apart.

"I'm nineteen." He grumbled after a moment of silence.

"Checks out."

"I'm an adult. How old are you, twenty?"

I chuckled. "Twenty eight."

The sound of rushing wind beyond the cabin walls filled the pause in our conversation. The light on the map showed that we had a fourth of our journey left.

"No kid, alright?"

"Alright, Boyband."

He laughed and shook his head.

I scrolled through my neurospace and prepared to tap into one of my five remaining socitabs. I would need to download more before we left for—zeg. Was Deleon going to send us into the heart of the Violet District to pursue the Entertainment politicians? Where else would we find Naoma? How did he expect us to blend in? How could we even *get* in? Boyband looked rich, but the Indigo residents were still worlds apart from the affluence of the Violet residents.

Boyband pointed at the map, and I stopped myself from turning to a socitab to forget my concerns.

"So where is 3A taking us?"

"An Orange district."

"Why out there?"

"It's not too far from where we were in the blue. Deleon's hub is on the western edge of Zingang. Take this line twenty minutes west of that and we are in an Orange district."

"But *why*? Just for some food? If I wanted to eat trash made by the poor, I could have found it in Zingang. I have before."

Food. Is that what you told him, Deleon? You sick shac. "You're familiar with Zingang? I thought the Blue was too poor for you."

He shook his head. "Most of my schooling was in the center of Zingang."

I nodded.

"I've just never been to the orange, let alone the green."

"Let me guess, your parents warned you about them? Told you the poor will jump you and steal any light they find on you?"

"No, they were more liberal than most on that topic. I got into a couple of fights with them after telling them what my friends said. I hear horrible things about the Yellow, even worse about the Orange and Red."

"The Red District *is* terrible. I wouldn't take you to Orange just yet, but Yellow isn't too bad."

"You've been to Red?"

Incarceration after crossing the border. A voice echoed in my mind. *"Zeggin' slav, if you don't like it here we'll toss you to the glowbones in the Red. Get it? One bad move and you're their food."*

"No, but I've been close." I neither wanted to talk about that or his feeding, but I was caught between the two. "What do you think about Deleon?"

"Why? Does he have something to do with the Red?"

I wish I could toss him in there. I shook my head. "No. Just wanted to know how he treated you when he found you. Has he explained what we do here?"

"He fed me, gave me a home after I lost mine. I *kind* of understand what we are doing here—not now, but with the ruling parties and all that. He didn't explain much else." He shrugged. "Seems like a nice person."

Seems like. That's your problem. "But he put the Bite in, right?"

"Huh?"

I tapped the back of my head. "Hypothalamic implant. You've got one?"

"Oh, yeah, that. Didn't really explain that part, but he said it would help. I don't know with what, but I felt like I had no choice. He took me in and–"

A voice spoke over the intercom. "*Now arriving: Old Trenton - Orange District East station. Please gather your belongings and prepare for your stop.*"

He looked at the worn crowd of laborers who neared the doors, then at me.

I nodded and waved for him to follow me towards the exit.

No one kept eye contact with me. I was glad. My distinct violet eyes tended to lead people to believe I was from Violet District, despite my similarly poor appearance to theirs. My sleek white athletic jacket had its fair share of cuts and burnt out light patches.

I traced my hand along words cut into the wall by the doors.

Zeg Farm.

Poor spelling, but it made its point by speaking how we all felt. I heard their reign began with insulin, that was until diabetes was cured. New diseases *somehow* arose and their origin was too convenient to be considered a conspiracy. Medicine will find its income no matter what. I believed in the natural origin of techbone, at least. Perhaps the light gods were punishing us for cutting away our bodies in place of artificial constructs. Did the kid have any implants besides the bite? It was likely. I would have bought some at his age if I had the money, but I had other problems at nineteen.

The flashing lights through the window slowed, becoming advertisements and buildings instead of blurs.

"*Arrived: Old Trenton - Orange District East station. Please mind the gap. Thank you for using Republic Skytrack.*"

I stepped ahead, looked side to side, then waved for Boyband to follow me to the left, away from the orange lights of the city's center. Only a few of the commuters exited with us.

"Where to now?"

I checked back over my shoulder. Two people were behind us. Both of their heads hung low. The orange street lamps still glowed, even though it was midday.

Deleon could have picked a better time for us to feed, but the kid would have to get used to day hunting eventually. He had grown shakier by the minute. He was already grinding his teeth. When the *true* hunger calls, delaying only increases the risks.

"Don't worry, you'll feel better a lot sooner."

"I ate some 2-real sausage and a slice of bread before the meeting. I'm not usually hungry around this time."

Every second I delayed, I only made it worse. I clenched my fists, digging my rough fingernails into my palms. It would be better to break our prey's jaw and lay the feast out for him before he could run away.

I prayed to the light that his first feeding would go better than mine. If Keiro hadn't been assigned to me, maybe Ralia wouldn't have made my first target a kid just like I was. I never wished death upon anyone, except for Deleon, but maybe Keiro's had been an act of the light's justice. Life had been much better since he left us. Still, it struggled to believe that it was a life worth living.

Deleon's promise held me.

Now, maybe giving this kid the best life he could have would be another thing to keep me afloat.

"Pet?"

"Only Ralia calls me that. Petya is fine. She's a little too—she's her own type. You'll figure her out soon enough." I turned back. Only one person followed us. "And don't get too excited if she kisses you. That's just who she is."

He laughed a little, his face slightly grimacing, though I couldn't tell if it was from disgust or the growing hunger pains.

As we neared a bench, I pointed to it and sat. "Wait here a second. I need to check something."

He nodded and sat next to me.

I looked up as if staring into my neurospace, but kept the person behind us in my periphery, only looking at him as he passed.

"Are you using a fix?"

"What? No, who told you I–"

"Deleon said you had a problem with them."

"I don't." By the light, I did. Those zegging socitabs pulled me away from the thrills of social contact. I told myself I was becoming better, but I knew that was just another excuse. "Don't use them. Waste of money." I held my next thought back. *Even when you are tempted to escape our somber reality, don't lose touch with it.* I looked at the man down the street, trying to decide if I should pulverize his mind to make it easier on the kid.

No, I couldn't. He had to see it for what it was. The screams of our victim kept us in check. They were torturous to the psyche but taught us to always remember the cost of our labors. Never take a life for granted. I wondered if I would have eaten *real* meat if I had the money to do so. Maybe I wouldn't, knowing that each pleasurable bite came at the cost of an animal's life. There were other things to satiate the gut's appetite. Teeth were the only choice for our implant's hunger.

"I've had plenty of them."

"What?" I looked back at him.

"Fixes."

"Oh, yeah, right. So you weren't a perfect child, huh?"

"I'm nineteen. The guidelines only say that you should wait until eighteen until using. Still, I had a lot as a kid."

"So your parents were more lax on it than others?"

"Zeg, no," he chuckled. "Rich or poor, teenagers will live. They only rotted my mind a *little.*" He elbowed me.

I smiled back at him. For a moment I forgot our feeding. His shaking hands quickly reminded me of our duty.

"I don't care for them anymore. Why live old memories while I'm in my prime? Why pump my mind with false feelings? They're too distracting."

"I wish I was like you." I was only a little sarcastic.

"You can be."

Our prey crossed the street and entered an alley just after a foreclosed restaurant.

I stood and waved for him to follow. We crossed with no cars in sight.

The alley opened up to another busy street on the other side, but our prey still had time before he finished his shortcut. Trash littered the ground and luckily there were two large green dumpsters on the left side. A fire escape rose on the building to the right, with some light shining through the upper residential windows. If I didn't have the kid with me, I would have climbed up to eat at the top. The alley wasn't optimal, especially for a first feed, but I felt confident we could stay hidden. In the end, it *was* the Orange district. Two levels above the low Red, random acts of crime were common enough.

A full set would keep him full for a couple of days if he didn't spend too much Bite energy, especially if the teeth were clean. I would take a couple, holding me over until I could take out a quick target alone at a later point.

"Where are we going?" he whispered right behind my shoulder.

I stopped for a second. "Link with my neurospace."

He touched me and a request popped into my neruospace interface. I accepted it and sent a message.

Petya: Don't say anything. Follow me and do what I tell you. This is going to suck. Don't freak out.

I felt him stumble and cursed myself for intimidating him.

Petya: You will be safe. This will help stop your shaking. But please, if you can't stay quiet and by my side, we are going to be in big trouble.

Devóne: What is happening?

Petya: Baptism by fire.

"Hey!" I shouted and ran a few steps forward. "Excuse me?"

The man ahead of us turned back and spared a glance.

"We're lost. Can't seem to find a restaurant."

"Did you look at your map?" he grumbled. He looked cleaner than most I had seen in the Orange districts. Still, his tie was loose and his suit had plenty of stains.

Probably a hard-working husband off to provide for his family by what humble means he had. Zeg it. These are the kind of thoughts I had to keep out of Boyband's mind.

I continued to walk towards him. "The problem is, we don't know any good ones. We're from out of town and could use a suggestion."

He waved us away like the pests that we were. "Just jump on some neuroforum. I'm late as it is."

"I prefer a recommendation I can verify. I'll send you a few lumens for your time."

He sighed loud enough to ensure that we were aware of the inconvenience. "What kind are you looking for?"

"Just a second." I acted as if I was pulling something from my jacket pocket as he approached. I kept digging, though I had nothing in it, until he was a step away from me.

Petya: Don't do anything. Just stay here.

"Really, pal, I gotta–"

I pounced on him like a rabid ape, throwing him to the floor with the speed of a lightrifle shot.

He didn't scream, but a choking sound came from his throat as he smacked against the ground. Blood pooled from behind his head.

"Wha–what are you–"

I grabbed Boyband's arm before he could run away. "Stop and keep quiet."

I let go and crouched, relieved to see that the impact was enough to do the duty. I reached my hands into his mouth, turned back to nod at Boyband, then moved my prey's head close to me as I broke his jaw wide open, away from the kid's view.

He let out a whimper as I lowered the silently screaming head back to its pool of blood. Strength filled my fingers as I burned the essence of my Bite. With a grip strong enough to crush a rock, I ripped the bottom molars from his skull and separated the gums from the teeth before offering them to Boyband.

"Eat these." I demanded.

"What is zegging wrong with you, you sick bastard? Get that away–"

I grabbed his arm, squeezing it tight enough to bruise before loosening my grip. "Your arms are going to keep shaking and you'll pass out if you don't. You wonder why I hate Deleon? This is why. That little thing in the back of your head? It made you one of us. You're an Imp now. If you don't eat teeth, you'll die." Worse would come before that, but I didn't need to tell him.

"What are you *talking* about?"

I thought about slapping him, but I needed his trust. I put one of the molars into my mouth. It popped like a grape against my charged bite. Zeg, it tasted better than anything I had eaten in days. This man had taken care of his teeth. I tasted a cavity, but the enamel was well cared for.

"The molars are the best." I handed him one. "Just do what I did. Please, Boy–Devóne. Just do it and we can head back to the hub."

"Why the zeg would I want that? If Deleon is the shac that put you up to this, I don't ever want to see him again!"

His shouts were all too familiar.

"I'm going to shove it into your mouth if you don't. Wait any longer and you'll lose your mind, killing anyone to eat teeth."

"You can't be–"

I didn't shout but spoke with a distilled somberness as I stared into his eyes. After a few more days, they would be violet just like the rest of ours. "I am serious. This is it. This is your life now."

I grabbed his hand. He initially resisted but gave in and opened his palm. I dropped the molars in. "I'm begging you. Eat these."

He tried to force a mocking smile but lost it with a few gasps. His eyes welled with tears as he shook his head at what he held in his hands. "I–I can't. My teeth will break. I can't *eat* teeth."

I grabbed his hand and crushed the teeth with our grip together.

"See that? *Feel* that?" I tapped the back of my head. "The Bite has changed you. Your teeth are stronger now, as is your jaw among the other muscles. Try the dust first, then I'll pull out more for you to try."

His lip whimpered, but he sucked up the dust into his mouth.

I crouched and pulled out some more molars as I heard his pleasured moans.

"It's good, right?"

He tried to force a disgusted face, but his eyes shot to my hands with a hungry glare.

"You want more? Wait until you try the real thing."

He snatched the three teeth from my hand before I could even fully open it.

His chewing sounded like he was eating raw pasta. I took some of the incisors, only three to hold me over while I pulled out the rest.

He acted like a hungry child, clawing at my hands for more teeth until he gave up on formality and ate the rest from the man's mouth without even pulling them loose. The gums were not bad, but rather a distraction to the taste, like the pieces of lettuce in a salad without dressing.

Boyband opened his mouth, contorting it with his tongue picking out any remaining pieces of teeth.

Our victim's mouth was a mess of torn flesh, but small bits of tooth roots remained inside. I crouched and picked them free, eating them like crumbs. "This is why we pick them out. You ate it like a child eating corn on the cob. Order in everything. If we take a life to satiate ourselves, we cannot waste a single piece."

"I was so zegging hungry. Once I started, I couldn't stop."

I sucked the last few pieces from my hand and used the man's tie to wipe his blood from my lips. "What did I tell you? You cannot let yourself get this hungry. The longer you wait, the less control you have over your appetite. Next time we'll be sure to be a little more delicate."

"Next time?"

"Yes." I sighed and shook my head. "Zegging Deleon should have taught you to feed right after he put your Bite in. Come on, let's head back."

I started to walk away, only stopping for a moment to wait for Boyband to catch up.

He was staring down at our prey. I thought I heard him whisper an apology.

"Come on, Boyband. It gets easier."

Though that was true, I hated its implication.

All sin requires to thrive is the right amount of justification.

He left an empty seat between us on the way back. I didn't blame him. I had done the same with Keiro when he took me out to feed for the first time.

I had a duty to the kid, one bound by my honor and not by Deleon's assignment. Part of me wanted to avoid any attachment. Our business was not designed to lead us into a leisurely retirement. Regardless I could already see him becoming like a younger brother to me. The others were my family. Why not include him? He was cocksure and condescending, but everyone had their problems. Especially me.

It was my turn to break the silence. He would have plenty of time to think about teeth, but now did not need to be that time. "Tell me about your parents."

He scowled at me, though I could see the sorrow in his protruding lip.

I was a shac to bring up such a touchy topic, but I needed one bold enough to distract him from self-hatred. "Deleon said they were some anti-war social justice type of people. Is that right?"

"Not like that."

My gaze passed between him and the floor. He was slow to blink and did not move his stare from the other side from the skytrack.

"What kind–"

"Do we have to do this right now, Petya?"

I moved to the seat between us. "You don't have to talk if you don't want to, but it will make it easier. The quicker you accept what we are, the easier it will be."

He wiped a tear from his eyes. "They weren't like those... you know... they had a purpose."

I turned to him, and his eyebrows were arched.

"What?"

"They didn't like your–the Medislavic–government."

I smiled and chuckled. "Glad to hear. They probably didn't hate them as much as I did."

"You–"

"A story for another day. But I would be glad to hear yours."

"You'll tell me yours later?"

I hesitated, then nodded. "Deal."

"Well, they were pro-Arabasia. They wanted the war to end through an Arabasian victory and utilized our influence in the Republic to support their side, especially in agricultural shipments, based on our farming monopoly. My parents visited the peninsula, had some meetings with the King. I wanted to go but had other obligations."

"Couldn't take you on vacation? Must be tough."

"It's not like that. I felt like I could have contributed. A lot of misinformation has skewed the public view of the war, which in turn harms the Arabasian stance. It's tragic."

"So you are *really* invested, huh? Boyband, I think you and I might have some common ground."

"What do you know, growing up in the Yellow?"

I glared at him, but he couldn't hold back his laughter. We caught a couple of stares as we laughed together.

"I'm glad you can take a joke." he said. "You seemed gloomy on the way here."

I shrugged. "Now you know why. How would you act if you took a kid to–" I looked around, noticing our loud speaking had attracted a couple of stares. I softened my tone. "To do what we did."

He lost his smile.

I gave him a moment before speaking. "What kind of 'misinformation'? Stuff related to the war?"

He raised an eyebrow.

"Come on, Boyband. I want to know. This old Slav needs more reasons to hate his government. His *old* government."

"You? Old? *Come on,* we're like the same age."

"A lot can happen in nine years."

He looked around, waiting until the people he stared at looked away. "You ever heard of *'Neon Essence*?'"

I furrowed my brow.

"If you listen to the news, any neurosocial forums, they say that the war is over Medislavia's hold on Arabasia joining the United System Conglomerate. Is that what you were told when you were back in your home country?"

I nodded, but it wasn't as sure as I would have liked it to be. "My people were tyrants. That's why I left. They had their excuses. I believed none of it."

"'Power, control,' yeah, they all sound like simple reasons to go to war, but that's not it."

"How sure are you?"

He shrugged. "I might sound like I know what I'm talking about, but this is just what my parents told me, or rather, what I overheard them telling other people."

"Fair enough."

"You know how the former United States conquered China and established a republic there?"

I nodded.

"That's where we found the physical light. With that, we bought Chinese loyalty. That is why they came to join us in the Republic of Capital. Light is power."

"I've been in your Republic for quite a while now, Boyband."

"Yeah, sorry, what I mean is that the light was discovered in *Asia*. China had a lot, but I guess the substance in Arabasia is something even better."

"That Neon Essence you mentioned?"

"Exactly. That's what your people want."

Not my people anymore. "What makes it different from the light we have now?"

"I don't know."

"You don't know? Did you ask your parents?"

"I don't know if they knew either."

I smirked.

"What?"

"Sounds like a conspiracy to me."

"Nah."

I shrugged, knowing it would antagonize him.

"That's what everyone said about the ruling parties back when they were mere corporations. I bet everyone that didn't believe they were going to become the government feels stupid now."

"Life was nicer when all conspiracy theories weren't so believable."

"Right, but this isn't–" He swatted his hand in the air. "Nevermind. You don't get it."

"No, I do. I'm just saying you need more information. If Neon Essence is related to physical light, it's already beyond my comprehension."

"I guess you're right. Why should we worry about some foreign war?"

"Right." It was easy to agree, but I knew I would never distance myself from it.

CHAPTER SIX

The Anti-Spectrum

"Devóne. I expect Petya treated you well."

Boyband looked at me, keeping calm as he had promised. He still couldn't maintain eye contact with Deleon. I couldn't blame him. I hated looking at the rat, and Cut's laboratory was an odd spectacle of intriguing objects, each with their own convoluted explanation. All I needed to understand were the two operating tables with white cloths over their tops. Cut stared at us from the corner of his room. Four of his associates, all dressed in lab coats, spoke amongst themselves as they stood behind him.

He looked at me.

"He did well."

"Well then, I'm happy to hear that the team synergy continues."

"Where are the others?" I asked.

"They've already left to fulfill their assignments. Are you ready for yours?"

"After... whatever this is?"

"Of course. Doctor Cuttrin and his associates have been waiting for you."

I shrugged, walked over to the operating table, and swung myself on it.

Boyband furrowed his brow.

"Come on." I waved him over. "The sooner we finish, the sooner we can get back to your rich part of the Republic."

He continued to stare at me. Having seen what the Bite had done to him, how could he ever trust Deleon? I didn't, but I knew his modifications were worth a limited trust. He had bought us with the Bite—rather, stolen us—but each modification was an addition to his investment. I had the agility, Ralia had her hacking, and Tevon had his strength.

"We're both getting a new one, right?" I asked Deleon.

"Yes. It comes at a high cost, but we need to ensure your success."

"Trust *me*." I told Boyband. "It will only help."

He sighed, then moved to sit on the other table.

Cut approached with his associates. "On your stomachs, please. We'll use anesthetics before doing anything invasive."

We both did as told after removing our shirts. We faced each other as we lied prone. I smiled at him as I asked Deleon another question. "What is it this time?"

"Something not quite what you would expect based on your previous modifications. By that I mean that this is more of an update to your system, rather than an addition to it. Your agility modification gives you an advantage, so we will provide Devóne with a unique talent of his own, but both of you will receive the systemic upgrade. I know it is early for him, but I need you all at the same level."

"What do I get then?" Boyband asked.

He touched Boyband's cheek. "Your charm can easily deceive us lower-classmen, but you will need a little more to weave your way through the Violet District. I considered downloading musical talents into your mind to give you an easy approach to Anton Jackson, but even we should not toy with downloading information and talents."

Boyband looked relieved. The experimentation of doing so in the virtual era had created too many emotionless humans by downloading information that eventually corrupted any human mind they had left.

Deleon continued. "I am giving you a coercion modification. Nothing as magical as it sounds, but a way for your hypothalamic implant to send impulses into other people's minds, making them more susceptible to trusting you, among other added bonuses. You will not be as hypnotic as you might hope, but if you learn to hone this talent, you will be a master manipulator."

He nodded. I wasn't sure how he took that.

"What do you mean by the upgrade for both of us?" I sneezed as they put a nasal cannula into my nostrils and started an IV.

"The light spectrum has found its way into everything that we do. In the natural world, ultraviolet light is the most powerful, for this reason the wealthy use it for all they do, but our minds are too compartmental when it comes to such spectrums. While wealth, power, and most of our society relies upon the energy of the higher colors, red and orange still have their uses. They are not without power. Your hypothalamic implants run on this opposite spectrum. As you may have noticed with the violet glow in your eyes, that they run on violet light. The strongest in terms of natural power, but not as strong as indigo in the *anti-spectrum*."

I furrowed my brow.

"Your hypothalamic implant no longer needs the energy we rely upon in violet light to power it. Now that your body has grown with it, it supplies some of its own energy. We are alternating it to run on indigo light, on the anti-spectrum. Plan on advancing down the spectrum until you reach pure red. If you were to ever reach that point, you would be at your maximum state."

"State of what?" My words slurred, and I felt my eyes start to roll back with a wave of somnolence.

"You will see in time, Imp. Welcome to the second stage."

I lost consciousness.

I sat up from the operating table, heart pounding and breaths fast. I shook the side rails.

"Settle down, Petya." Cut approached and tapped my wrist as he turned to look at my vital signs.

Blood pressure: 100/60

Heart rate: 40

Oxygen saturation: 100%

He nodded and removed the cords and electrodes from me.

I swung my legs down as he lowered the rail. Cut's associates were still working on Boyband on the table next to me.

"Couldn't Deleon have given me time to wake up on my own? I hate that adrenaline rush right after a nice nap."

He shook his head. "It is not restful sleep, anyway. Deleon requested your presence in his office while we finish with Mister Eclaine."

"What time is it?"

He handed me my shirt in exchange for the gown. "Eleven PM."

"Will we have any time to sleep before he sends us out?"

Cut stared at me with bored eyes. "You know well that I do not have that answer. I just–"

"Work here, as do I. Maybe someday we can both make it out."

He raised an eyebrow and returned to his colleagues.

Honestly, our circumstances were not even close. Even if Cut detested Deleon, only the five of us were victims to his Bites. Perhaps Deleon had other means of coaxing them. I couldn't understand how anyone could work for the man, knowing what he had done to us and what he would do to rise in the Pharma market. Maybe the benefits outweighed the unethical methods. For all I knew, Cut was as much a criminal as our master.

I shook my arms and steadied my breathing as I walked out of the laboratory to Deleon's office.

I entered to see him staring out the window overlooking the blue cityscape, as usual.

He looked over his shoulder, then back to the city. He had a focused gaze, letting me know that he was not in the neurospace.

"Everything went well, I presume?"

Like you weren't monitoring us as it went through Cut's updates? I would never believe for a second that he turned back his surveillance on us when allowing his people to touch our most delicate hardware.

I walked towards him but kept an unfriendly distance. "I suppose so."

"Can you feel the upgrade yet?" He walked towards me.

I shrugged. Energy burning within me screamed for release, as if I had taken an energy shot before a workout, but that was expected with the rude awakening from my surgical slumber.

"You will." He turned on a spotlight in the center of the room with the snap of his fingers. He lifted my chin and looked into my eyes. "Indigo as sure as I can see." He nodded, and the spotlight turned off, leaving us in the darkness of his room only lit by the city and subtle blue lights around the base of the wall.

"What does that confirm?"

"That they got the concentration right. The anti-spectrum is a delicate one. You'll feel the difference soon enough."

"I'm afraid I do not understand."

"Forgot what I said before the operation?"

I hadn't, but it was convoluted and argued the laws of light.

He smiled. "You are the antithesis of the known spectrum of light. I hope this shows you how valuable those hypothalamic implants are. Sure, they have a cost, but a small one compared to what you will become."

There was no use in arguing with him. Anyone who can justify murder has thrown human laws out of their conscience.

"Are you a–I mean, were you ever a fanatic of video games before your employment?"

"I was born after the virtual era had passed."

"Yes, virtual reality was all the craze then, but you can still find them today."

"In nursing homes and among the poor who would rather live a virtual life than their sorry excuses for one?"

"No need to dampen the mood. There is more than the old virtual reality."

"I never touched the ones in the neurospace, but I played some on screens as a kid."

He smiled as if to thank me for finally being willing to hold a conversation. It was difficult to bring myself to hold one with him but pleasing him was the best way to get what I wanted. "Role-playing games allow you to upgrade your character, correct"

I nodded, thinking of the monster training games I still had a longing to return to if I had the privilege of leisure. Had seen glImpses of them in a few of the memtab experiences I had.

"Think of yourself as leveling up. The indigo, rather anti-spectrum indigo, now powering you grants you new opportunities, those inaccessible to the anti-spectrum violet level."

"Like what?."

"You will learn in due time." He continued to stare at me as I held my attention on the cityscape. My peripheral vision seemed wider. Perhaps that was a new perk.

"Now that we have some time away from the Eclaine boy, how do you anticipate he will fare with you Imps?"

He's a coward that lived too far above the poverty line to understand how vulnerable we all were when we joined. Cocky. Condescending. Naïve.

I liked the kid.

"Young, but just as malleable as we all were when we joined. He struggled to take his first bite of teeth, but I couldn't stop him once he started. He needs to learn control, but I don't see a problem with him adapting to a tame appetite."

"I am glad to hear."

"Should I trust his admiration for his parents?" I wouldn't trust Deleon's opinion, but I had to see both sides. I never wanted to speak about the war. My poor life was an escape from my past. It was a sorry alternative, but one that could help resolve matters if Deleon held to his promise.

"Awfully tragic, wasn't it? I hate to capitalize on his loss, but it is too great of an opportunity. Regardless, his parents were radicals. Like the old hippies of centuries past that you see depicted in mindshows. They spend most of their fortune campaigning against the war rather than against our country's involvement. If the war is ever to end, someone has to push one side towards victory. Enough of that. Business is our focus, not politics. Do you have everything you need for your departure?"

Business is politics. I trusted Boyband's retelling much more. Deleon's impulsive change of subject concerned me, as if he was going to speak offense. He couldn't be an advocate for Medislavia, could he? If Deleon wanted power in our government, why not support those who wanted the same on their side of the planet?

"What do I need?" I had learned early on not to complain about the timing of his assignments.

"Nothing more than a few personal items, not including clothing. I have that all taken care of. Living in the Violet District requires that you appear like a natural resident. I am sending you to the center of the Indigo District via skytrack. Once you arrive, I have a ride to take you to the Violet District to your temporary residence just outside of the entertainment hub. Jackson's studio is a ten-minute walk from the station, though the other targets are not quite as close. I'll relay all the information to you in a file after you depart."

"Do we have access to their skytrack or a bus system?"

He scoffed. "You have a whole new world to awaken to. Even Devóne will be surprised by the gross wealth in the Violet District. Everyone you meet in the entertainment hub will be wealthy enough to buy their own District here in Zingang."

"Are the others in the Violet District as well?"

"No, most of their targets are in the Indigo District or lower. We aren't going to assassinate any figureheads while we can eliminate the key gears in their systems."

"I thought we were investigating the connections to jelly fiends?"

"Oh, you are, but we won't leave any trails. While the parties will notice if any of their key players are eliminated, the whole world will notice if a music idol or mindshow star is eliminated. The entire Republic will eventually see what is happening, especially when we are so tight to those connected to Firstlight, but our goal is to be above scrutiny by the time people begin to point fingers."

"Are you sure we can do this? None of us are detectives."

"Which is why your leads will be along with the other files. I've scrupulously researched these paths and only need someone to complete the course. Trust me, Petya. All is in good hands."

"Even if I do, we are talking about the whole Republic's government and the leading Pharma party."

"I am more than just a single man with a discrete company. As you do what you are told, perhaps you will recognize how wide my reach is."

I nodded, doubting his confidence until I recalled his unknown associates in violet suits.

"Read through the files, start with Jackson, and utilize the Eclaine kid's coercion modification."

Scratching my eyes, I agreed.

"I get it. You need some rest. Take four hours, the kid will have about three if he is not yet finished. Catch the 3:30 AM skytrack. It'll have you in the Violet District at a good time to get to work and blend in with the traffic of the area."

"Thank you, sir."

"You'll notice that you need less sleep now that you are on the indigo level of the anti-spectrum."

I turned back to see him looking over his shoulder.

"Perform well, Petya, and I will see that you ascend to blue and beyond soon enough."

Chapter Seven

Hunger

I felt more comfortable riding beside Boyband, having the secret of the Bite behind us. We would have to feed again before we took a ride to the Violet district. I doubt I had to tell Boyband that. He could feel it in his body as much as I could. How we would manage to take out prey in the Violet District with their advanced security was beyond my present capability to plan.

"Did you open the files yet?" he asked.

I shook my head. "You?"

"Should I?"

"You can once I do, but don't worry about the load. Deleon did a brilliant job in organizing his company, but the man doesn't do it all himself. His notes in the files will reveal how little he cares to spend time for clarity."

He chuckled.

"I'll skim through it a bit on our way to the Violet district, but let's just enjoy some time to relax."

He bounced his legs and rubbed his fingers together.

I smirked. "Or maybe it would be a pleasant distraction."

"Yeah, I'd have to agree there," he said.

"Don't worry, you'll be able to control your hunger better after some time. Maybe the indigo upgrade will help." I wondered why he had given Boyband the upgrade so soon after receiving his bite. Why hadn't Deleon upgraded us earlier? Useless questions for a senseless man who thrived on the tension of a mystery.

He shrugged, turning to look at the woman sitting a few seats away. His eyes were stuck on her.

Zeg.

I should have accounted for the stress the surgical modifications would have on our bodies. We should have had at least two sets of teeth each to keep us held over for a few days. If Boyband lost control of his appetite, it would be my short-sighted fault. "Don't think about it."

He smirked with a challenging glare. Whatever childish innocence he had was hidden behind a bestial hunger. He looked the other way, seeing another man asleep with his mouth mode open. Only these two people were with us on the three-thirty train.

"Devóne," I demanded.

He stared at me with a clenched jaw.

"A distraction is what you need. Open the file."

"I can't focus. My mind is buzzing."

I sighed and wiped my face.

"Tell me about how you got here," he said. "A story might help distract me. I can't focus on the assignment until I feed."

"Now isn't a good time for that."

"*Tell me,*" he hissed.

I felt his words grasp my soul. "The zeg was that?"

He furrowed his brow in confusion.

"You shac! You tried to use your coercion modification on me, didn't you? Don't think Deleon is stupid enough to let you boss your superior around. Zeg, now I don't know if I can ever trust you with my story."

Anger fell to vulnerable fear. "I-I'm sorry, Petya." His eyes shot to the woman, then to the man who slept with an open mouth. His eyes widened. He shook his head and looked back at me. "I don't know how long I can hold it in for. Fine, read from the file. At least that's something."

I almost reprimanded him for burning energy by using his Bite modification, but he needed more love than condemnation. I was better at the latter.

I opened Deleon's instructions in my neurospace and spoke as I read from the file.

First target: Anton Jackson - Finian producer, well acquainted with many Entertainment executives, but not one himself. Despite this, he is one of the elite Finians and is closely tied to all they do in the entertainment party. I have a meeting set up a few hours after your arrival at one of his studios. He believes you are coming to introduce a new cochlear implant that can improve general human reception for Finian music. The Finian outlook on tech is quite unique. Their existence relies upon its success. Let this serve as a natural transition into gauging his interest in Firstlight.

"Even if he isn't an executive," Boyband asked, "how did Deleon land him? He produces for zegging Naoma."

"You listen to her?"

"No, but I bet you do, you poor shac. Everyone falls for her music. It's all–"

"Factory produced? Made to attract? Yeah, I know. You want some niche music? I'll show you."

Boyband shook his head. "Doubt it. You ever heard of Docile Caribou? Blinchik?"

I laughed. "You're joking, right? Those are the musicians people listen to when they want to sound like they know music. Give it a few more years and you'll know music. I'll send a playlist over after this, though I doubt you'll like it."

"Zeg, you sound so pretentious right now."

We shared a laugh. Mine grew weak as he stared at the woman a few seats away. "Let's stay focused on the assignment."

"But that doesn't explain how Deleon landed a meeting with him. Deleon looks like your typical Blue District executive wannabe. I doubt my parents can...I-I doubt my parents could have landed a meeting with him even though we were elite in the Indigo district."

"Deleon claimed to have a wide influence and a large corporation, but none of us ever see beyond our assignments. The business side of Osteolyte is a mystery. Frankly, I don't care to know."

"How can you not?"

"I have no belief that he is doing good. What he has made of us gives me little reason to believe that he actually wants to cure Techbone. I just do what I'm told."

"Then what? Do you think it will ever end?"

"I hope so." My hope was a frail thing. If I thought too much about the repetitive cycle of labor, I would start to panic. It was best not to pass it on to Boyband, but I didn't want to lie to him. A distraction would better serve its purpose.

"Let's stay focused on the file."

He nodded as if shaking free a headache.

Firstlight has connections to Reef Records. Whether that connection is more than a mere investment is for you to discover. Reef Records is the label attached to most of Jackson's clients, namely your second target.

Second target: Naoma.

Boyband smiled with a gaze fixed on the ground. I dismissed it as another withheld insult from him but soon learned that assumption to be a poor mistake.

I went further into my neurospace, looking for any online mention of Reef Records having a history sponsoring Firstlight, but searched to no avail. Firstlight was hardly mentioned online. I was searching from the wrong point. As Deleon had suggested when we first exposed their research, Firstlight was likely a small branch of a large conglomeration. Jelly fiend research was probably a mere tenant of their overall goal, just as it was with Osteolyte.

What I could find about Reef Records was little more than advertisement—and with links to the Entertainment Party propaganda.

Deleon had too many resources—namely people—to spend on some large web of corporations just because one of them was a competitor in his research. It was easy to believe this was true, but I had learned from my distrust of society that I could not believe his intentions were so simple.

We would soon learn more than ever that entertainment for purposes of joy had long expired.

Capitalism killed art.

I faded out of my neurospace too late. Boyband was mid-sprint down the train car towards the woman.

I dashed towards him at twice the speed, pulling him back just as he grabbed her shoulder. I ripped his hand from her, leaving deep gashes in her semi-translucent sleeves.

She screamed. I held him back, but he continued to reach for her like a starved hound, teeth bared ready to eat her entire jaw.

"Stop!" I shouted, pulling him back and burning a little of my Bite reserve without enough to exacerbate my hunger as well.

"Come here!" he shouted at the woman. "*Now!*" His urgency spoke with an inhuman power, depriving him of any civility. He was going feral, wasting his entire Bite reserve to satiate a single feeding.

The woman stood from her seat and walked towards him. Bereft of emotion, she tilted her head back and opened her mouth as if trying to catch food.

As soon as she came within his reach, he shoved his hand into her mouth, ripping out half of the bottom row of teeth with one hand while his other hand wrestled with mine around his waist.

She dropped, moaning with a dead stare as he ate the bloody teeth he had taken from her mouth. I couldn't tell if she had lost consciousness or was still under Boyband's coercive spell. Blood pooled from her mouth, soaking into her pink jacket.

I spared the man behind me a second of my attention. He hid behind a seat, now wide awake with bulbous eyes staring at us from over the top of the head cushion.

The cameras were fixed on us, likely sending out a silent alert to alert the next station that a cannibal and his distracted companion were arriving. Luckily, the next station was our destination. Even if it wasn't, Boyband's lack of control would have forced us off to fight our way through Republic officers. With each rising District giving more power to law enforcement, I expected the worst outcome.

I let Boyband go. He dove at the woman and broke her jaw, once again finishing his feeding as messily as a starved child. As he chewed and came to himself, he looked back at me. Anger dissipated as shame filled worried eyes.

I shook my head. "Just finish her. We have no choice now."

"What do you mean?" His mouth was full and he spit out a crowned tooth.

"We are going to have to face a whole squad of enforcers at the next stop. I'll take the other guy. We're going to need all the reserve we can manage to avoid arrest, if they are patient or survive an execution."

The man ducked down behind the seat with a whimper.

"I'm sorry, Petya."

I shook my head. "We'll talk about it later. Finish eating and have your belongings ready. We're going to have to run."

He nodded and picked at the remains of her broken teeth.

I sighed as I strode towards the cowering man. I couldn't see him, but I heard silent prayers and heavy breathing.

"Please, please, please," he cried, staring at me through the crack between the seats.

It was best to be done with him. There was no point in torturing myself over whether I was going to feed on him. I hated feasting on anyone who saw me coming. Not giving my prey time to agonize over what was coming made it easier for me to bear on my conscience.

I dashed forward, broke his neck rather than burning any of my reserve to scramble his mind, and broke his jaw open to expose my meal.

I had little time to think about savoring each bite. I was hungry enough but could have gone another day without needing to feed. His teeth were well cared for, but my mind was too occupied by Boyband compromising our assignment.

I heard moaning and grunts among the pounding of fists against the floor and looked back. Boyband was throwing a tantrum, reminding me how young he was. I laid the corpse of my prey on the ground, his bloody face facing the floor.

I licked the blood from my lips as I walked towards Boyband. I would never drink blood on its own, but its metallic taste was a nice compliment to a fine set of teeth.

"What is it?"

He turned back to look at me, eyes red with tears.

I sighed and checked the map on my neurospace. We had a few minutes. Even if I had thought of a solution to cover up our feeding, we wouldn't have the time to do so.

"You're going to have to learn to control yourself soon enough, Devóne. I'm not going to be able to cover you each time."

"Wha–" He sniffed and smeared blood across his face. "What are we going to do?"

I tapped into my neurospace and messaged Deleon. He was going to learn eventually, if he hadn't already.

Petya: The kid lost it. Make sure the ride is close to the station. We'll be off in a few minutes, and I expect to run into plenty of enforcers.

"Did you at least finish the teeth?" I asked.

"Yeah."

"If you are that desperate to feed, I need you to make sure you keep something around to hold you over for a while. If you lose control like that again in the Violet district, you're done."

"You'd get rid of me that easily?"

"I'd have no choice. Deleon would do it for me. This is delicate stuff."

"Okay, I get it."

"I sent Deleon a message. If we're lucky, we'll make it past any enforcers to our ride. He's usually good at squaring things away like that."

"Is this the first time you've been caught?"

"No. Sorry to be so hard on you, but just because we might make it, doesn't mean you can ever be so careless."

"So the ruling parties and enforcers know you about teeth-eaters?"

"No. Deleon has the means of covering up our trail. I don't know how far his reach extends, but the government hasn't hunted us yet."

"Sorry. I'll be better next time."

I wanted to say that I believed him, but I didn't. I knew how it felt to be an impulsive kid at his age and felt that his confidence was even more pernicious based on his privileged upbringing.

I received a notification.

Deleon: Thanks for letting me know. I've alerted your driver. You should be fine, just hurry.

Petya: Planned on it.

"How much longer?"

I checked my map. "Grab your stuff. Hide behind the sides of the doors, away from the window.

The voice spoke over the intercom: "*Now arriving: Gibson - Indigo District East station. Please gather your belongings and prepare for your stop.*"

He tripped, throwing his duffle bag across the floor as he scrambled red-faced towards the cabin wall.

I peered through the window. The train hadn't slowed yet. "Is this close to where you lived?"

"No, I lived more north, near the–" his fearful gaze shot to the windows as hisses of air signaled the skytrack slowing.

"We'll talk another time. Follow me as fast as you can."

He nodded.

"Don't worry about getting shot. Unless you have a couple of direct shots to anything vital, your Bite will protect you from the initial light shots."

"Shot? Zeg, Petya, I–"

"I told you this would happen. If we make it out alive, I hope you will have learned your lesson." Zeg I sounded like a cliche parent.

"Okay."

"Like I said, I'll stay in front."

Is this how my poor excuse of a life would end?

No. I would have no problem burning my reserves to dash free of any light shot. Boyband was my problem. Even if Deleon understood, I failed to save the kid, I could never forgive myself. To be given such a responsibility and fail it so early on into the assignment was a damaging reflection of my character. Damaging, but true. What good had I done since my arrival in the Republic? Maybe my life would have been better off complying with the Medislavian tyranny.

No. The Republic had its problems—classes, poverty, gluttonous consumerism to name a few—but it granted me an opportunity to do something with my life. I hoped I could discover what that was once I left Deleon's service. I hoped I could discover something other than an illusion of what could have been a good life.

"Arrived: Gibson - Indigo District East station. Please mind the gap. Thank you for using Republic Skytrack."

I patted his shoulder and pushed him behind me.

The doors opened.

An Indigo streetburner revved its engine and flashed its headlights on the pavement. I would have thought it odd to find the car off of the street, but the dark red smear before us was more daunting.

I stepped from the car, looking both ways.

"What are you doing?" Boyband pushed me.

I swatted his hand away and moved aside for him to step forward.

"Zeg," he muttered.

The red smear had cracked pieces of enforcer armor scattered throughout with the bodies to match smashed to the sides of our path.

I looked to the driver's seat to see who had plowed over our would-be squad of assailants. A woman with short hair and an optical implant band like Tevon's waved us forward. The back door facing us retracted into the roof.

Boyband was breathing heavily as he basked in the massacre.

I hit him on the back with more urgency than politeness. We ran to enter the car.

The doors shut right as we entered and pushed our duffle bags under our feet.

The engine roared, and the car accelerated faster than any vehicle I had ever been in.

Boyband looked like he was going to shout a panic-fueled accusation. I shook my head and took the lead.

"How are you going to cover that up?" I held my tone back from bitter condemnation, rather holding to anxious curiosity.

The driver looked at me from the rear-view mirror, or at least it looked that way. One could never tell with optic implants.

The rider in the passenger seat turned back to face us. She wore the same Indigo tracksuit worn by the driver, but her blonde hair reached her shoulders. She had at least twenty years on me and had invested plenty into modifying her face to look like someone of my age. Even with prosthetic advancements, it was easy to recognize an unnatural face.

She smirked at us, not sharing the panic we felt as the streetburner accelerated. "After everything you've been through, you choose now to doubt Deleon? Sure, he's not the best but he's competent."

"I didn't know he–usually he doesn't send actual people to help us. Tools, bots, hacked access, sure, but this is excessive."

She shook her head and faced the front. "Just because they were law keepers doesn't mean they deserved to live any more than your victims. No need to act surprised, we know enough about Deleon's Blue Imps. Oh, and if you try to bite us, you'll be dead before you can touch us."

I nodded, though I doubted her claim. "And you're our Indigo counterparts?"

"We don't have the hypothalamic implants, thank the light."

I would thank it, too. "How long have you been working for him?" I hated to resort to small talk, but at least it was about something other than the weather and inflation. I couldn't let myself forget about the enforcer massacre, but she seemed unwilling to discuss it.

She sighed. "We don't work for him, just alongside him."

I checked on Boyband. He breathed with forced control and clenched his eyes shut.

"Did he hire you?"

"No point in hiring someone from the same organization." She laughed and elbowed the driver, who made no reaction.

"What do you mean?"

"We work for another Beacon. Deleon is going after the presidency, we are—"

"Enough." the driver said. Her voice was rough and dry.

"You're right," the passenger said. "Your worldview is about to change, but there are certain things you cannot know until you advance far enough. Who knows if you ever will? Deleon seems to like his Imps as servants." She muttered the next line under her breath, though I could hear it. "They don't last too long, anyway."

I moved around, trying to look through the windows for a sign of our destination. "Are we still on track for the Violet district?"

"Of course. Why wouldn't we be?"

The passenger continued to speak to the driver in a quieter tone. I had missed the substance of their conversation while adrift in my anxieties but figured they wouldn't have shared anything worthwhile with us in the backseats. They were transport and collateral coverage. They had no need to help their cargo beyond their assignment.

"How much longer?"

"To the Violet border? About an hour, but we are going north to the center. You ever been to Jinai?"

"Never been to the Indigo district, why would I have been to the Violet?"

"May the light help you fit in. You'll need the luck."

Trust Deleon. Even if I couldn't trust him as a person, I knew he would care for his tools.

The morning was in full glory as we left the densest part of the Indigo district. Gibson was a cluster of skyscrapers. The outer areas were just as populated but lacked the agricultural titans that did little more than flaunt their wealth.

I felt the warmth of the sunrise. It was clearer outside the continual smog of the Blue District and below. Even if the sky was artificial, as most things were, it was a comforting reflection of what had once been. I wondered how it would be to live in the distant west, far beyond the glowing Districts of the Republic. As far as we were told, no one lived out there except for nomads and exiled wanderers. Though I had little to appreciate in my life, at least I was not alone.

Despite that pleasant thought and the kid beside me, I felt empty within. I fell into my neurospace, turned on the playlist I had named *Romanticizing Melancholia* and listened.

I selected a socitab in my neurospace and let my mind succumb to the social drug. The love and appreciation I felt rushed through my dopamine crazed mind would expire before the end of the ride, but for now, it was enough to forget.

I never saw myself as an addict, for it was never something I wanted to quit. Socitabs were part of me.

CHAPTER EIGHT

Violet Heaven

R alia: You good? Deleon said you had a problem with the kid.

Petya: Yeah, I think we've got it covered.

Ralia: Sorry you got stuck with the pompous shac.

Petya: He's actually not that bad. Just needs to learn to control his hunger.

Ralia: Look at you warming up to him! I always thought you would be a good father.

Petya: Things well for you?

Ralia: So far. Think I'm on the cusp of discovering something that will get Deleon going, but I still need time.

Petya: You can explain it to me when this is over.

Ralia: Still using?

Petya: Just when we have downtime.

Ralia: Set the fixes aside. Give the kid your attention and you won't feel as empty as you like to think you are.

I didn't respond. The speedburner pulled away from traffic and turned down an alley. I would have assumed it to look like any other dark alley in the Blue district, but it was well lit and cleaner than any

Blue street. The perfect state of the Violet District was too ideal to trust. We came to a stop and the doors unlocked.

The woman in the passenger seat looked back. "Pleasure having you, but get out. Your place is just down the street. Take care."

I muttered a thank you. Boyband did likewise as we exited with our duffle bags.

I gave my neurospace a glance.

Ralia: Love ya, Pet. Don't go dark on me. If the kid is too much of a problem, I'm here to chat.

Petya: Thanks.

It was a dry response, but she knew how much I appreciated her. I had never been an affectionate person, at least since I arrived in the Republic. As the stereotypical agents often said in the mindshows, trust makes betrayal hurt even more. If I trusted anyone, it was Ralia.

Boyband shook his head and blinked with wide eyes.

"Sleep too long?"

"Just a little, but I think it helped. What kind of a night is three hours of sleep?"

"It's not too short for us. Your Bite will help with that. Just takes some getting used to."

He shrugged and slung his duffle bag around his shoulders, then frowned at it.

"What now?"

"Is this all I have to my name? A bag of clothes that aren't even mine and some other random things?"

"The clothes are yours now. Even if we are in the luxury district, you need to remember that we have been brought low by Deleon."

He scowled.

"Doesn't matter if you like it or not."

He shook his head and grunted. "Let's just go."

I nodded and led us out of the alley. Not that I could see Janai in its full glory, I felt dirtier than any rodent.

Everyone who passed by wore skin-tight clothing with pulsing violet. Dark, concentrated visible-ultraviolet glowed from all styles of jewelry, making the gems of the past seem like mere street rubble. Their hairstyles were just as extravagant as they were portrayed in the mindshows. Eccentric colors, mostly violet and indigo, with asymmetric lengths and patterns shaved in any short sides.

I was used to receiving glares, but not any so accusatory. I could only fathom how uncomfortable Boyband felt after a life of being on their side and so suddenly turned.

I looked down at him, seeing the nervous quiver I had expected. "Deleon sent me a fair amount of lumens to pay for a change of clothes. Would that help you feel better?"

"Yeah."

Maybe it wasn't wise to relieve him from discomfort so suddenly, but we would need it to go anywhere with Anton Jackson.

I pulled up Deleon's plans in my neurospace as we walked down the voguish street walled by skyscrapers that burned their violet light even in the daytime. I had to stop myself from thinking about the injustice shining in my eyes, but it was difficult to ignore that a single business's ultraviolet light could have powered a yellow block of houses for a week. The allure of power, though it was greed-inspiring, led me to see why Deleon had invested so much in rising to power. Wondering once again what that entailed and how he imagined accomplishing it, I turned to his files.

"Got Deleon's plans on your interface?" I asked.

"I thought–"

"We'll find an outlet on the way, don't worry. Pull it up. We need to stay on track. Ralia's already completed a fair share of her assignment."

"She has?"

"I think so. Something like that. You got the file or what?"

"Yeah, yeah, I've got it."

I read through the last part of Jackson's description again.

He believes you are coming to introduce a new cochlear implant that can improve the human reception for Finian music.

"Keep your focus on Jackson," I said. "I don't think we can get to Naoma without him."

Jackson is expecting you at 2:00 pm in Reef's studio.

Select here to input the target's address.

I did as the message prompted.

Reef Records: Janai center. Twentieth floor.

The location was about a seven-minute walk down the street. I added the location of our temporary apartment and found that it was a mere three minutes behind us.

"Let's go back and drop everything off after we get some clothes. We can head to Jackson's studio after."

Boyband nodded. He continued to stare up, continuing to read the report.

I placed the mock implant in Devóne's luggage. It has a mild hallucinogenic effect when applied, giving the illusion of amplified Finian technology with my own touch of alteration. Give him a chance to try it, then take it back. If he passes it on, he'll realize it's nothing more than a fix. All you need is access to his superiors.

Update! Ralia found the following potential Firstlight parent companies that might be tied to the Entertainment party: Better Tech, Techvax, Beut-AI.

Try these names out if you reach his superiors. If anyone is experimenting with Exos Sapiens, they are a danger to Osteolyte. If you find a connection, take out Jackson and work your way up the ladder. You did it with Firstlight, I trust you can repeat it.

I tapped out, but Boyband's eyes continued to flash.

"So he thinks he can take out an entire company with the two of us?" he asked.

I shook my head. "Not an entire company, just an appendage. Deleon can't stand competition. Have you heard of Gift-year?"

"No."

"They were another small company that tried to cure techbone like Haven Health."

"How?"

"Easing symptoms rather than curing the cause. Haven's Okre-pinate actually works, but you have to continually use it or the skin will start to degenerate. Great for the rich, worthless for those who can't afford continual treatment. Gift-year did very little to those suffering from techbone, but studies showed that it gave the afflicted another year of life." I shrugged. "Sounded like a con for the hopeful to me, but Deleon wanted us to take them out, so we did. Our team eliminated the owners and fed incriminating misinformation to their primary stockholders, while Ralia wiped their system of any data that could be used to rebuild the company. Their decline wasn't immediate, but they disappeared after a few weeks."

"Gotcha, so don't worry about it."

"I never said that. We thought Firstlight was like Gift-year, but it turned out to be larger than we had hoped. I thought Deleon was in over his head until those two picked us up in the speedburner."

"Why?"

"Because it shows that Deleon's organization is larger than I thought. Maybe that should make me more nervous. I have no idea what the 'Beacons' they mentioned were. Very few people admire

Haven Health's presidency, but I wouldn't trust Deleon, or anyone who gives him orders, to govern the Republic."

"I hate politics. It was always something I left my parents to care about."

"Neutrality is no longer a choice. The only problem is that neither side looks promising."

"Sides?"

"Deleon or whomever he opposes."

"Then why not turn against Deleon?"

"If I stop serving him, I can never make things right."

"Right? The zeg is that supposed to mean?"

"Right for people like me. Right for immigrants that thought life would be better in the Republic but receive a cold embrace from the streets."

Boyband complained that I restricted our shopping selection to the discount racks. He still held onto luxury, no matter how much he tried to seem like the lower District scum that I was. Even though they were discounted, the Violet discards were much more extravagant than the nicest one could find in Zingang.

We left our bags behind the doors of our twelfth level apartment, not taking time to look at the amenities.

As we left the apartment complex, I looked up at the projected violet clock a hundred feet above the street.

1:02

"You wanna go early?" Boyband asked.

I moved my shoulders around and flexed my arms. "I think I should have gone a size larger."

"The higher the district, the tighter the ware."

"Whatever."

"So you wanna go?"

I nodded and led the way towards the studio.

Perhaps I was just used to oversized wear, never having been given the chance to purchase my own. I chose a jacket without strips to burn the little light we had. Even if most people around us burned their light on fashion, we did not need to seem like the most elite, only background matter.

The more lumens we spent, the more I recognized how much Deleon kept from us. Our spending had not reached any capacity, nor had we received any warning. Perhaps he did have the resources to accomplish his absurd coup.

Boyband and I had chosen similar nylon amethyst jackets to at least blend into the violet allure of the city. They were slightly thicker than a windbreaker but allowed sufficient mobility despite the tightness. The hoodless collars rose two inches, as if we were trying to hide our necks. I left mine zipped up, but Boyband let his neon blue T-shirt show with the logo of some pop band that I had never heard of named *Nummersent.* He thought it would help us blend in with Jackson, but I doubted that the band was even a Finian headliner if we found the shirt on a discount rack. Our matching pants were tight, yet breathable, giving us the classic tracksuit look of the privileged teenagers back in Medislavia. I laughed at the comparison, rather than mourned the memory. Boyband understood what I meant when I explained it, having seen the Medislavian mob stereotypes in every recent cheap action mindshow.

I felt more comfortable attracting fewer glances in the busy metropolitan center. An agoraphobic would suffocate as a wrong step in any direction would cause us to stumble into a passing pedestrian.

I released the tension from my shoulders and tried to appreciate the city's allure rather than giving any thought to our deal with Jackson.

I looked up at the violet advertisements cast across the sky.

Speed and rage 14 - Family forever. Plug in now at the East Janai theater before general neurospace release.

Sex and lust - Stream the new Top$avage album. Start your free trial with Fin+ now.

Zeg, if entertainment wasn't propaganda, it was a cheap creation to pull in light from testosterone-fuelled car chases or blatant hedonism. Wanting something else reminded me of watching the obscure mindshows with Ali. I looked at Boyband, wondering what he liked, but all the same relieved that we did not have to resort too often to small talk.

I looked up to the ads, rather than watch the procession of heads before me.

Haven Health - the future of health in your bones.

The CEO of Haven Health, President Delighty Liu's face came into the advertisement. I turned away before I could hear any of her ghostwriter's words.

bAInk - The Rupublic's most trusted financial AI for 100 years.

Dentisure - light your teeth any color of the spectrum. 9/10 Dentists recommend for cavity prevention.

The thought of teeth made me salivate. I almost drooled at the thought of endless sets of perfect teeth for us to eat, but met a reciprocal disappointment, wondering how we could ever conceal our feeding.

"You good?" I asked Boyband.

I tapped my teeth as he looked at me.

He furrowed his brow, then gave me a reassuring nod. "Of course they sound good, but I don't need to eat now."

"We'll figure it out with Jackson." I said. "If things go red, we'll just take his."

"Fair enough."

"Regardless, I want something to eat after."

"You like sushi?"

"Never had it outside of a skytrack station."

"Zeg," he exaggerated a gag. "That's guk compared to what we have at home. We'll find something here for you to understand the taste. You plug?"

"Yeah." I patted him on the back. "Sounds pulse."

The ten minutes from our apartment to the skyscraper that hosted Reef Records Janai studio passed as if in seconds, despite the frequent stops in human traffic.

We entered the building, conscious of our wears as we saw everyone on the base level in violet or black suits. I held my head down as I walked to the elevator and pressed the button. I had assumed that a building with a pop music studio would be much more relaxed, but there was no relaxation in the Violet district. Falling behind the competitive capitalism would toss one free from their party's monopoly into the lower districts.

The elevator doors opened, and we entered. I noted the camera in the corner and another one above the touch screen pad. I hoped that Jackson liked his privacy.

The face of a violet haired woman smiled back at us from the screen.

"Which floor?" the AI asked.

I tapped on the list below rather than interacting with her.

"Twentieth floor," she said with a smile and waved goodbye as the screen faded to advertisements of various upcoming concerts.

"Why are you so happy?"

Boyband's smile grew even larger. He shrugged. "Come on. I don't care for Naoma, but this is her zegging producer! Even if I'm from a few Districts above you, meeting a celebrity is a special occasion."

"I guess. Naoma isn't the only one he produces. He does Thera Sween, Four Color, not to mention his own band, Seats, and he helped with New Arm's most recent album."

"Zegging New Arm. I get that they are all trying to sell something, but you would have thought the Tech Party would have chosen a more discreet name."

The AI woman walked onto the screen and waved. "Twentieth floor. Have a nice day, made better by Freeskin - sample noviderm today on the second floor."

"Which way?" he asked.

I pointed to the right. To a sign of a violet dolphin swimming around a record. "Seems apparent to me." Violet signs glowed to the left, but none of them suggested any correlation to music.

The floor was made of white tiles with marbled pulsing purple. A false sky shone on the ceiling with small drifting clouds surrounded by blue. I saw past the illusion, but the ceiling was still much higher than I had anticipated, reaching the height of three floors all together.

Before I pulled on the ultraviolet door with a smaller version of the logo, I sent Deleon a message.

Petya: Going into Jackson's studio now. I'll keep you updated.

I waited a minute before entering and shared my neurospace interface with Boyband so he could see the conversation. Deleon replied after a minute.

Deleon: If you are in there for more than an hour or two, let me know that everything's alright. I trust you.

"He sent me a message," said Boyband.

"What is it?"

"*Don't try to use your coercion mod on Jackson. We can't bypass the Finian system to make it effective.*" Focus returned to his eyes as he looked at me. "You ever met a Finian?"

The image of a cyborg dolphin came into my mind. "I've seen plenty of them in ads."

"That doesn't count."

"I know. You?"

"Seen some, never spoken with any. My parents would host conferences that I could occasionally attend. I think the Finians still look down on the Socstans as blue-collar workers like most of the other parties, but there were a few animal rights activists who came to support what we did on our farm."

"But you didn't do anything with the ocean, did you?"

"No, but I think they still recognize that they are more animal than human. Probably because we are too prideful to accept them."

I whispered as I reached for the door. "We both know that if the Finians never advanced music technology, they would be living in the slums of the Orange district."

I pulled it open and was hit by a wave of synth riffs, followed by a voice that robbed me of confidence.

We walked in and shut the soundproof door. A mechanical figure sat in a chair facing away from us. The performer beyond the window stopped singing beyond her floating microphone and the synth player behind her stopped after finishing his rift.

She looked exactly like she did in the hologram but wore the light to match the violet light of her home district.

Naoma.

Her teal hair was now pale violet, but it still had the multicolor holographic strands on the sides of her face. Her eyeliner, lips, and nails were all painted with the dark violet that glowed with the light of peak affluence. The way they shimmered with the artificial white light in the recording studio confirmed my suspicion that she wore *actual* light instead of mere color. I wondered if she changed her style with her concert locations, but figured the Districts adapted their holos to match the light they could afford.

"Excuse me?" The microphone passed her voice beyond the recording room.

I stared, saying nothing. "Anton?" She rolled her eyes and shook her head as she walked back to talk to the synth player.

Boyband giggled as he elbowed me. I wanted to kick him. I didn't care about the zegging Neon Idol. Even if a couple of her songs scratched a certain itch from time to time, I hated all that she stood for. Though she was living, as far as the Entertainment Party claimed, she was just as good as any other shac that tried to force their product upon the Republic. What I hated most is that besides the obvious themes of tech implants and governmental trust in certain songs, most of her lyrics suggested no product placement. Love wasn't linked to any specific product, nor was romanticized sadness. Subliminal messages, for I knew there had to be some, were the most dangerous form of advertisement.

The thing sitting before us finished tapping a large touchscreen control board with hands of different skin colors. The chair rose as it swiveled around, and the figure stood. "A bit early, by my count. Mind if we finish this set?"

"No problem." Boyband pointed at me. "He's a fan."

My gaze had pulled from the disgruntled Naoma and locked on the cyborg before me. Anton Jackson was a decorated Finian with a torso flashing multiple shades of violet as if he wore a sparkling chestplate. Tubes came up from the side of his dolphin head and formed a band around the top to keep it moisturized. His mouth remained open as he spoke and if it moved, it was not in sync with the words that came out. His left arm was pale white and bare up to the shoulder, while the other was darker and only reached just past the elbow before it joined his smooth robotic shoulder. He wore shorts that revealed most of his tan thighs, the legs matched but he wore no shoes. He looked young, though I had no idea how to age a dolphin, especially one with human body parts attached. I wondered if he was one of the few saved from the sea before complete pollution or if he was bred in the Republic in the last few decades.

"Is that pulse with you, du?" he asked.

I nodded. I tried to control my breathing and shaking hands.

His laugh was his natural dolphin call. "Settle, my du. She's just another person, like all of us." He whispered, "A bit pissy if you ask me." He laughed and sat back down, then turned to look at us. "It'll be better for all of us if we give her some time to finish. If you're still all wired up, I've got some puffers in the back to soothe the nerves. Take a seat and enjoy the little show."

I smiled and nodded, though I had no intention of getting high on his terms. A fix, on the other hand, sounded like a light-sent mercy, but I had to stay focused.

Naoma turned back and raised an eyebrow in her sneer. "You done?"

I nodded more than was needed and joined Boyband on the blocky blue leather couch on the left side of the door.

Anton tapped the control pad, then called, "Take seven: *So unlike me*. Let's hear it!"

The synth player wore headphones without a top strap, which I later realized were part of the new Finian-based tech implants that were able to amplify one's enjoyment of music to a "spiritual" level.

Regardless of what they did, he seemed to be enjoying himself as he bobbed his head along to his playing.

I didn't pay attention to Naoma's lyrics, averting my eyes whenever she looked at me. I couldn't see her as anything other than the product of the Entertainment Party that I believed her to be. To see her as human would complicate our assignment. I couldn't see Jackson as a person. Perhaps that was my hatred of tampering with living organisms. I had no problem adding implants to my body and tampering with my mind with any fix I could find, but to make an animal into a mock-human was a step too far.

"—to escape, oh, try to escape my hard-wired shell."

Her music was as enjoyable as any other pop, but I couldn't feel the cerebral sensations, almost hallucinations, that accompanied Finian music. Seeing how it was all done led me to figure that Finian technology was merely a part of the audio programming when streamed. Realizing that I still felt the music's full effect worried me. If they implanted their programming in a crowd while attending a concert, how powerful was their technology?

"Love it, Naoma!" Jackson shouted as the song ended. He pointed at the synth player. "Absolutely pulse! You too, Dawson. But you know that. Both of you, thank you so much. Feel free to hang around if you want while I speak to these dus."

Naoma sighed and placed her hands on the back of her head. "I need a touch-up."

"Got a date tonight?"

She scoffed. "You know the studio won't allow that, Anton. Lust-filled kids want to imagine themselves with me. Makes it harder if I have a partner."

"You've always got me by your side."

"Ew."

"No, no, not like that, you know what I mean."

"Whatever. You comin', Dawson?"

"Yah, I think I'm gonna hit a memtab while we have some time. Got some vacations I wanna revisit." He looked at Jackson. "Yah know, du?"

"Yeah, I know. Drop by when you're done. These dus have something you'll have to check out."

Jackson shut down his control pad and dimmed the lights in the studio as he turned around to us. Naoma's microphone floated towards the wall and docked itself. A green light signified it was charging. Even in the elite district, lower lights still had their use when higher lights would fry weaker circuits.

"So, you two from around here?"

"South of Janai." I said, pulling up Deleon's false history for us.

"Not bad, not bad." He rolled his chair towards us.

I leaned back and put my arm over the back of the couch. "Less foot traffic makes things easier."

"Yeah, that gets old fast, doesn't it? The twenty-fifth floor has a skytrack terminal. With an elite pass, I rarely have to walk the street." He pulled a small bottle of lotion from his pocket and applied it to his hands. "Well, let's see it. Is it meant for humans, or will it work on my people too?"

"Should work for both." I pulled the device from my pocket and handed it to him.

He held it up to his right eye, examining the silver shine on what looked like a flattened pill. "How do you use it?"

"You got light burning in your system?"

"Yup."

"Peel off the back and put it on your...temple. Burn some light towards it and put something on. Give us some of your stuff." I hit Boyband's knee with mine. "Leon here is a fan of the Seats."

"Nah, man, Naoma here is better, but I appreciate it, my du. So you're Leon. What's your name again? Can't remember if it was in the meeting request."

"Davor."

"Ah, that's right." Jackson swiveled his chair around and returned to the control pad. He peeled the back part of the cochlear tab off and stuck it to his gray flesh. He had to press hard and move it up and down, but it eventually stuck like any other electrode. "You two have one, too?"

"Nah, just came here to show it off. Boss doesn't want us taking too many around, though we've given em' a run. Play some music and you'll see. We'll just sit back and enjoy whatever you put on."

"Deal. You like Shokz?"

I looked at Boyband, who shrugged.

"Never heard of 'em," I said. "But I'm always looking for new stuff."

"They're not necessarily new, but they're worth discovering. Really foundational to my music. Check this one out. It's called *Heaven's Hit*. From their second album, but their third is the best, in my opinion."

Discordant electric chimes and beats sounded with high vocals. It was jarring at first, but gradually grew on me, like the kind of song that doesn't gain value until you gain the acquired taste for the band's style. Violet and indigo lights pulsed around the room with speakers spreading the sound evenly across the room. I didn't see any images pulse with the song and realized that the music likely predated the Finian revolution.

He leaned back in his chain and pressed his hands against the sides of his head and whistled through his blowhole. "Zeeeeg, du!" His eyes darted back and forth.

"You good?" I asked.

"Zeg yeah I am. This thing is full pulse! You boys don't mess around, do you?"

He laughed and made a variety of sounds as the song played. Despite the tensity, Boyband and I found ourselves laughing with him.

He nodded along with the beat as the song concluded and peeled the device from his head. "I think you've got yourself a buyer."

"Great!" I clapped.

"But as you know, I'm going to have to run it through the execs. I'm just a part of the system. Aren't we all?"

"How soon can you schedule a meeting with your superiors?"

"We'll get you in soon. Relax, du. You guys want something to eat or drink?"

"I think we're good."

"You want anything, lil' du?"

Boyband looked at me. I didn't need to ask if he was craving teeth. I remembered the visceral hunger that motivated my every move after I gained the bite. "I'm good, I think."

Jackson nodded and held up the device again. "So, is this the finished product?"

"Close, but that one will only last a few hours. The real devices will be placed subdermally for a permanent connection to the cochlea to burn your light for a continual charge. You can activate and deactivate them via your neurospace."

"Thank the light, the Tech Party started supplying even the Orange and Yellow Districts with neurospaces. Call it forced advertising like those anti-tech radicals if you want, but it sure makes it convenient to sell pulse tech like you've got here." He laughed and scratched his head. "I guess that only solidifies their fears, but hey, not our problem, right? Make money, ignore problems. Zeggin' luxury of the high districts."

Boyband's smile fell. Was he starting to see affluence as I did?

"Does it still have a few charges?"

I nodded.

"Pulse! Care if I give it another run?"

"Just one more. Don't want to damage the product at this stage, you know?"

"Yeah, yeah." Jackson whistled. "Hey, Daw, come here for a sec!" He shook his head and spoke with glee. "Oh, he is going to love this. "And bring some puffs too! Gotta treat these boys right!"

A voice called from the other room. "Yah, du, gimme a sec. My mem's about to finish. I ever tell you about the time when I was a kid an'—"

"Just finish it out!" Jackson shouted. "You boys in a hurry?"

"Depends on what you have planned."

"Sorry about Dawson. He's a bit of a memtab addict. You boys use? I can hook you up?"

"Nah." I said.

"I'll take a socitab," Boyband said.

Jackson clicked, and it sounded like tsks. "That's sad, du. Can't get all hung up on the socials already when you're so young. You're in the prime age to live the real stuff."

Boyband looked at me with an accusatory glare.

"He's right." I said, though I wanted one myself.

"Woo!" Dawson shouted as he walked in. His black dreads bounced as he walked. "Man, I gotta go back to the low islands soon." He held out his hands and held four blue spheres with rounded spikes, shaking them before us by holding the tail. Cartoon eyes looked around from the bottom as if they were dazed.

"You boys puffed before?" Dawson asked as he handed Boyband one. I was reluctant to grab it but did so as if it was taken from a toilet. I preferred cyberdrugs, not those that messed with the brain's chemicals rather than the implanted system.

Boyband shook his head.

"Not really my kind of thing," I said.

Jackson clicked.

"Yah don't want to refuse this, du," said Daw.

"Sorry," I said. "I don't want to offend your...culture...or anything. It's just that I–"

Jackson clicked again. "Settle, du. This isn't anything like the chemicals they sell on the Orange streets. I pay *good* money for fresh puffer fish extract. Completely natural and the toxin is distilled and processed here in Janai. It's better for you than any chemical tab they'll give you in a hospital."

Boyband shook it. "I thought only Finians could use puff?"

"Straight from the fish? Yeah, but that's why these have a filter. Don't worry, Davor. The filter is made from pure plant fibers as well. Humans like the artificial stuff in food and drugs, but we *animals* like to stay as natural as we can."

I almost laughed as I looked at the human arms and legs connected to his robotic torso. "Alright."

Jackson whistled. "Pulse! You'll zeggin' love it. I've even grown too soft to take it straight from the fish. I have em' shipped in ready to puff like this. Daw and I hit at least twice a day."

Dawson bounced his head. "If it wasn't for Naoma, you'd be beggin' in the Orange."

They laughed, and we forced ourselves to join in.

I held up the puffer to my eyes and looked into the rotating cartoon eyes. "Is it an upper? Downer? Hallucinogen?"

"Bit of everything." Jackson moved the tail to the edge of his mouth. "Suck it in as if it was a straw. Not too much, not too little. Just a taste and swallow."

Boyband and I looked at each other and did as told. He coughed and hissed. "Zeg!"

"Yeah, it's sour." Jackson took some from his own. "Take more. You'll get used to it."

I sucked more. I burned my tongue, but it was sweet. My vision clouded. I felt dizzy. The surrounding sounds meshed into a dull buzz. I looked at Dawson, who had dropped his puffer in his lap without taking a single hit.

Boyband's head fell onto my shoulder, and I lost consciousness.

CHAPTER NINE

Cracked humanity

"You wonder why I never want to give it a try."

I tried to open my eyes to the soft female voice. I was laying down and something held my body still.

I heard a dolphin click. "You know we can program tolerance into your mind so your body can handle it like mine."

I groaned. My stomach and throat burned. I was cold and stark naked, laying down on metal. A metallic smell tied to burnt wiring lurked in the air.

"Ope, here we go. You gonna stay, Naoma?"

"Why not? You've got me booked for the rest of the day. Might be more interesting than another recording."

"We'll get to that."

Blurred images of varying color under an encompassing blue light formed into clear figures. Violet glowing straps held each of my appendages down as well as my chest. I was in a room lit with poor artificial light and lined with metal walls. Large screens facing away from us hung from the wall to my right with floating light-cast control panels below.

I turned to look to my right. Boyband groaned as he joined me in a dazed consciousness.

"There we go!" Dolphin clicks and a voice I recognized. Anton Jackson.

Another dolphin clicked with him, then spoke in a deeper artificial voice. "How much did you dose them with, Anton?"

"Checked the puffs after. They both had only about ten concentrated micrograms each. Light-weight shacs."

"Petya?" Boyband asked. I turned and locked eyes with him. He looked just as much the terrified child I imagined him to be. His clothes had been stolen as well.

"That's one's Petya," said Jackson. "You ever get the other one's name? He called himself Leon."

"No." the other Finian said. "He wasn't a part of the raid."

"Wha–" I coughed, still trying to reach consciousness as my head spun and pulsed. "What is happening?" I thought about burning some of my Bite reserve to reach mental clarity but had enough somberness to recognize that I would rather be bound and dazed than bound and voracious.

"Did you read his space?" Jackson asked.

"I couldn't. The firewall is beyond anything I've seen."

"Do you think another Tech Party sent them? Maybe they don't want to get rid of all tech but just want to dominate the market."

"Doesn't everyone?"

I leaned my head up and looked past the two Finians at Naoma, who shot a small orb of violet light from her fingernail, watching it float around until it went into the light lines on her chest. She no longer wore the skin-tight performance exosuit to create holos, but a jacket and pants similar to the ones we had purchased. They were white with stripes and designs of violet light.

I sighed as I let my head rest.

"Are you going to have them talk now, Bank?" she asked and turned her bitter smirk on me. If I didn't hate the false god that she was to every fan, I did now.

"Give them a minute or so longer to wake up," the other Finian called Bank said.

Jackson clicked. "Now you see why Reef won't let you touch puffs."

"Or fixes," Naoma sighed. "Still sounds like a waste to me. Who needs to fix their mind when you have all the light you can get?"

Cocky. Condescending. Naoma was pure violet.

"How 'bout the little one?" Anton slapped Boyband with his pale hand. "You with us yet?"

"The zeg do you want?" he barked back. "Pet–Davor, what's going on?"

"You can lose the act, kid. Anton, sit 'em up."

I almost lost consciousness again as blackness clouded my vision for a moment. We sat up, still bound to the metallic beds, and faced the Finians' glare with Naoma toying with her light again.

"Yah with me?" Jackson said. He nodded and turned to Bank. "Yup, I think yah are."

Bank folded his arms and a neon centipede the size of my forearm crawled up his bulky shoulders. He had a matching set of dark-skinned arms that met a metallic torso at the shoulders, though the chestpiece was like that of a common android: human-shaped with a carbon fiber case. I couldn't see his legs. The base of his head was similar to Jackson's but had a metal plate on one cheek and three deep red scars on the other side. Scar repair was already an aged modification. The only reason people had them was to make a statement.

He spoke as Jackson did, no words syncing with the movement of his mouth. "You took out the Firstlight branch, now what do you want?"

I didn't know how to respond. Had Deleon led us into a trap? No, but whoever told him to pursue Reef Records and Anton Jackson must have. Who is manipulating you, Deleon?

"What do you mean?"

Jackson smacked Boyband and Naoma laughed.

"Please don't," I said, realizing that it would only incentivize them to continue.

The neon centipede crawled towards Bank's hand.

"What is that?" I shouted. "You gonna try and eat the data from my space? We–" I stopped speaking as I felt something already digging through my neurospace, but still unable to pass the firewall. "What are you doing?"

Bank tapped the back of his head.

I shook mine and felt what he was talking about. Something connected the back of my head to the table. I turned to look at Boyband, feeling the restriction of the cord as I did so. "Look away!"

He turned away from me. A black box connected to a woven rope of cords held his–and my–head to the table.

"Wired hacking still holds its value. Humans are too quick to dismiss physical matter. Perhaps that is why you found it so easy to neglect the ocean. Do the damage, pay the price now with us."

I scoffed. "Quit it with the environmentalism. You know as much as I do that I had nothing to do with any of that. It was before my time."

"But it's still happening today."

"Like I said, I don't have anything to do with that. Is that what this is about?"

"Nah," Jackson said. "Didn't you hear us? Firstlight. We've followed you since."

Followed who? An alias created by Deleon? The Osteolyte front, or what he was hiding beneath it? I didn't even know what that was. I was worried about our current predicament but not as much about them mining for my internal data. Sure, they could exploit us with the Bites , but I doubted they could uncover even that. Deleon had assigned Ralia to encrypt all of us after he modded her bite. X-rays, circuit sweeps, any form of detection would show that no one had ever tampered with our hypothalami. If that held true, blocking even the most efficient infiltrators, perhaps the Bite's held supernatural technology as Deleon had suggested.

"Even if the kid wasn't there," said Bank. "We know he's a part of the system."

I tapped into my neurospace to inform Deleon of what was happening.

COMMUNICATION DENIED

Zeg. I tried a multiplicity of ways to work around the cyberblock and was met with the same message.

Bank laughed. "Keep pressing and you'll only get more error messages. You are stuck here until you help us."

"Then what do you want?" Boyband asked.

My heart raced. The kid had a burning hunger and no need to serve Deleon. My loyalty was too conditional for a true alliance, but even I knew that I couldn't turn on my master. I had to keep the kid calm.

"What do *you* want?" Jackson asked. "You hit Firstlight and now you're climbing up to hit the next wire to the brain."

I was too dull to come up with a solution. Let the kid talk. What did he know beyond what they had accused us of?

Boyband shook his head. His bowl-cut hair was almost completely gray. "We're just servants to the guy who wants to be the next big thing. If you work for Firstlight, isn't that what you want? Haven Health down? Liu out of office?"

Jackson laughed, but Bank shook his head as he spoke. "Zeg, kid, you really don't have anything do you?" He looked at me. "New recruit, huh? Well then, what do you have to share with us?"

I stared at him with eyes as dead as I would be if we didn't find a solution. As the neon centipede hissed and pointed its frontmost legs in my direction, I let out the only words that could come to my mouth. "He's right. We're just working for some guy who wants Haven out so he can step in."

"I wouldn't put assassinations and corporate destruction past a politician, but the Republic is a lot more complex than that. No one wants the presidency just for the sake of it. Your boss must want something."

"Exactly. *Something*. Once he has the presidency, he is beyond my concern."

"What's his name, then?" asked Bank.

I stared at him.

"Company name? Organization?" Jackson slapped my exposed leg. "Come on now!"

I sucked in through clenched teeth and shook my leg. "Where are my zegging clothes?"

Jackson clicked. "We've got friends that will pay good lumens for some appendages like yours."

"Why don't they just buy their own?"

Bank scowled. "It's harder to find good body parts today. Do you know why?"

"Not as many junkies and 'beyond-redemption' sick people for you to harvest them from?"

He shook his head. "Come on, you know we're past that. Almost all of the appendages we use come from consensual agreements. People here in the Violet District decide they would rather have a cybernetic arm than the one they were born with, we offer a discount on the tech if they hand us over the dead flesh. The problem is that with Techbone and the associated propaganda behind Haven Health's focus on it, fewer people choose cybernetic replacements each day. If neurospaces weren't mandatory, I know plenty of people would avoid even that much technology."

"So," Jackson stepped forward. "You'll give us what we want, or we'll get to harvest something from you. We ran physiological scans on your bodies and both of you have taken exceedingly good care of your flesh."

I hadn't, but I knew that the Bite had compensated. "I've already told you everything we have! If we asked you two the same questions about your superiors, would you have any answers to give?"

Their dead stares left me wondering.

Jackson whistled. "Bank, give the 'pede a try before we take anything."

"What is that?" Naoma asked.

Bank raised his arm with the neon centipede. "We ran the physiological checks, but this thing will run the final cyber checks. If we take any appendages, we have to make sure their flesh isn't ridden with malware. If we give an arm to a Finian with undetected malware, their boss might be able to hack the host and—"

She waved him away. "Yeah, I got it."

The centipede rose on Bank's arm like a cobra. He smiled with malice. "Which one first?"

I looked at Boyband. His lips were quivering and tears ran down his cheeks.

I have to do it, don't I? "Not him."

"Big brother speakin' up!" Jackson folded his arms and leaned back against the wall by Naoma. Her head looked up and her mouth was slightly open. Her eyes flashed with the wonderment of a neurospace distraction.

If she couldn't bear to watch *it*, how would I survive whatever *it* was? I kept my mind on a track towards her, not relenting to quiver in fear of the centipede.

She seemed an automated product of theirs, part of me wondering if she was actually an AI creation. So called AI "art" was still looked down upon by most of society, but I wouldn't put it past these Finians who had made their derision of humans known. I would have settled upon this conclusion, until Naoma showed this sliver of humanity. What if she had a human heart beyond her produced personality? It was wishful thinking for a violet elite. But what was there for me to gain if she had a soft core?

My eyes turned from her and at the centipede as it used its pincers and front legs to pry my mouth open. Despite my jaw's Bite-enhanced clench, the centipede flattened and split itself between my teeth, working its way further into my mouth. It reconstituted and naturally opened my jaw with its fist-sized cylindrical body. Its legs opened my mouth as wide as it could go. The corners of my lips burned as if ready to tear.

"Petya!"

Boyband's shout was the last thing I heard until my mind was overtaken with a cascade of code. The few sensations I was spared were the centipede's razor legs tearing at the roof of my mouth and burrowing upward. It felt as if cankers covered my mouth and salt had been poured over every surface.

I didn't care if I failed Deleon.

End this.

Take my arms.

Take the kid.

Kill everyone I love.

Whatever you need.

Please end this.

Kill me. Kill me. Kill me.

I vomited red chunks, not knowing if they were pieces of my mouth, across my naked body. I contorted with shivers as the centipede returned to his owner. Moans escaped and I shook my head, eyes blurred with tears. How many hours had they kept me in that hell?

I looked up to see the centipede plug into Bank. "Zeg!" he shouted.

"What?" asked Jackson.

"He's zegging ridden with viruses encrypted beyond anything I've ever seen."

"Did you wipe it?"

"No, it was a zegging neuroblocked."

"Maybe you should have taken longer? What was that, thirty seconds?"

Bank grumbled. "Fifty two. I've never seen cybersecurity like that. We'll need a wipe mod."

"Need help grabbing it?"

Bank nodded and waved for him to follow.

I continued to cry, regretting every desperate thought that had passed through my mind. Still, I felt I would cry again if the centipede returned to purge my mind.

Boyband spoke my name. I turned to look at him but saw that Naoma hadn't left. My eyes were clear. So were hers.

She stood and walked over to us, standing in between our metal beds.

"Please," I whimpered. "Please just let us go. You're not one of them. You're as much a follower as we are."

She laughed. "You don't know anything about me. If anything, I own them. The poor dolphins wouldn't accomplish much without me."

They wouldn't, would they? I turned to Boyband. "It won't work on the Finians, but it might on her."

He furrowed his brow. "Huh?"

"Use your mod."

His eyes widened and he looked up at Naoma. His breaths quickened.

"They're coming back, you know," she said. "Trying something will only make it worse for you."

Her eyes shot back and forth between us.

I smiled. "Do it, Boyband."

His voice was mechanical and as direct as thunder. *"Unplug us."*

She whimpered and leaned over. Her eyebrows arched and she grabbed the sides of her head. Her cosmetic light flashed in a variety of shades. She faced Boyband, stepped towards him.

"Now!" he demanded.

Her inhibitions dissipated and she moved to the back of Boyband's head and pulled it free. Bloody wires came from his skull and the skin of his scalp regenerated to cover the plug's entry point. If his Bite hadn't healed his wound, she could have ended it all for us.

Shivers shook my being as she unplugged mine.

"*Now the light bindings.*"

She hesitated.

"Zeggin' shacs—shoulda–right?" Jackson spoke down the hall, but his voice fell away.

Naoma walked towards a control panel on the right wall, checking on us frantically. Her movements were shaky. Her face lacked the confidence that it had held before.

She tapped on the pad and the lights on Boyband vanished. He sat up. "Thank you. Thank you."

Her eyebrows were still arched. Her previous condescension was the antithesis of how she now appeared. "Please help me."

"*Let Petya go!*" Boyband demanded in a powerful whisper.

I moved from the bed immediately after the lights disappeared. "What did you say?" I asked her.

"Get me out of here." She ran to peek around the corner, then ran to grab my shoulders. "Please. I let him free. I helped you, you have to–" She stopped speaking as footsteps approached the room.

Her hands were warm, a comforting contrast to the frigid table.

"Remember what I said when they take me back. Don't forget to help me."

"What?" Boyband asked.

I grabbed her arm. "What do you mean?"

"You zegging shac!" Bank shouted as he ran to pick Naoma up.

"Hey, hey!" Jackson held Bank back until he lowered her down. "She's a lot more than an advertisement."

Bank nodded, then charged at me. He seized my throat and shoved me back down onto the metal table. "Anton, turn the light bindings back on."

Violet lights rebound me to the table. My head pulsed. The black shock from the slam dissipated just in time for me to see Bank do the same thing to Boyband.

Naoma shook in the corner. "Please, Bank! Anton!"

Bank launched his neon centipede at her and it burrowed into her mouth.

I cringed and turned away as she experienced the same torture I had mere moments ago. What had caused her to betray them? Why was he using the centipede on her? What data was there to force from her neurospace? She hadn't absorbed any of our data when she freed us, had she?

Naoma coughed and vomited as Bank retracted his centipede.

I strained my neck looking up at her.

She wiped her mouth and smiled, confidence pumped itself back into her. "Sorry, were you saying something?"

Bank sighed and looked at Jackson, who smiled. "Naoma, yah good?"

"Uh, yeah, why wouldn't I be?" She scowled at me. "What are you looking at? Anton, get that perv to look somewhere else. I don't like it."

"Naoma?" I uttered with desperation.

She scowled. "Got your eyes off of me." She pointed at Bank. "Why don't you use the centipede on him?"

"We already did," Jackson said. He looked at Bank. "Settle down."

"I did what we had to. I don't care how much you value her. If we didn't do something quick, it could happen again."

Naoma smiled.

Bank walked over and twisted Boyband's head, dug through his hair, then dropped the kid's head with enough force to leave a pounding headache.

"Look at this, Anton!" he said. "She unplugged them and corrupted all the data."

"Then just plug them back in!"

"I can't. They're... healed or something, I don't know."

Jackson stepped up, turned my head, then let go. "Naoma, come on girl, what did you do?"

She shrugged and shook her head. "I have no idea what you are talking about."

"We'll take them to the Red," Bank said.

I stopped breathing. He couldn't have said what I think he did. I turned to Boyband, finding that he looked as astounded as I was.

"Why?" Jackson asked.

Rather than scream my futile refusal, I listened in paralysis.

"They should have been bleeding after she unplugged them." Bank turned Boyband's head to show the back to Jackson.

"Do you think their owner jacked in a derm-web?"

"No chance. This penetrated further than the skin. I wouldn't go as far to say that they are invincible, but I think these shacs can help us with extractions in the Red. Techvax will pay a lot for them."

Techvax. Was that one of the companies Ralia mentioned? Zeg. I can handle not messaging Deleon, but I needed her.

"Are you giving up on extracting the data from their neuros?"

Bank shrugged. "Seeing this, I think we can get more from them in the Red. Moles are always in abundance, but these things are something else."

"If you think so."

Bank nodded. "Give me a minute." He walked towards the wall and leaned on it with folded arms. His eyes flashed as he tapped into his neurospace.

I looked at Boyband again, knowing that a conversation would be unwise, but defied my inhibitions. He stared up at the ceiling with eyes wide. I laid my need to speak to rest and did the same.

"Naoma, what was that?" Jackson said in a hush.

"I'm sorry, did I do something?"

"Ah, my girl, I either want to kiss you or hit you. I'm sorry for Bank. You're still with me, right?"

"Of course."

"Did you do anything to help these shacs?"

"Pfft, those zegging junkies? No chance. I couldn't stand their filth on me. Those lower Districts are ridden with viruses. I don't want to risk anything touching my neuro."

"You are compliant?"

"I am compliant."

"Just a glitch then, I guess."

"If you think I missed something while you and Bank stepped out of the room, then yes. I guess my neurospace glitched."

Bank clapped as he stood, his eyes refocusing. "The execs want them in the Red for an extraction. They need Reef's street team as well, film crew included."

"Why? What do they want, a music video?"

Bank shook his head and looked at Naoma, then back to Jackson. "An ad. I told them about your girl's unstable system and they want to utilize her before she goes haywire permanently."

"You want what now?" Naoma asked.

Bank gestured toward her but looked at Jackson. "See what I mean?"

"Nah, man. She's under control. That's how she always is. You don't make the calls, I do."

"Don't ignore what happened just a minute ago. I don't care if you can rewire her. She's a risk. You want to argue with the execs?"

"Zeg, no."

"Then you'll get her and her film team. Techvax wants her face on their product."

"But the Red, du, really? I ain't goin' there, especially with this prize of an artist."

"She'll be fine. Any risks will be left to these two. They'll keep us on the edge and well protected."

Jackson looked at Naoma. "You good to come with us?"

"I am compliant."

Jackson clicked. "Zeg, du, this'll be a wild ride."

Bank clicked. "I'll grab some other light bands to help us keep these two secured. I'll meet you and Naoma on the first floor. Our ride should be here in fifteen minutes."

"You–"

"I knew you would agree, Anton. But when it comes down to it, neither of us has a choice."

"I guess you're right."

Bank left first. Jackson did something on the wall's control panel, then waved for Naoma to follow him from the room.

She gave me a passing glare as she turned the corner to leave. Her eyes were bitter and her sneer condemning. The girl who had freed us was no longer present in the face of the Neon Idol.

Chapter Ten

Red Glow

Boyband and I sat in the back of the Techvax sky shuttle. Bank's goons who had taken us from the interrogation chamber were also Finians, but of a much less impressive build. They say across from us, neither had human legs and each only had one human arm.

I could barely turn my head to look at Boyband with my neck held by my rigid collar. They had clothed us in black jumpsuits with violet light patterns throughout for some advertisement with Naoma. Though we would look impressive in the recording, the violet lines served to constrict us with less mobility than we had in the metal tables. Our individual fingers were held stiff. Only our heads moved.

I looked as far as I could to the right and saw Naoma sitting with Jackson and Bank through the dark partition. Bank had said that two more skyshuttles followed in tow with the film crew and Techvax representatives with plenty of additional armed guards. The guards would hold tight to the crew the entire time, while Boyband and I would be fully exposed to the fiends and hellish elements of the Red District.

I couldn't fathom what that entailed. All I had heard about the Red District seemed the equivalent of horrifying myths used to terrify children into obedience. Even when I first arrived in the Republic, I only had to resort to dwelling in the Orange—with plenty of threats to be cast down to the Red. Orange was a wasteland with Yellow being a light-forsaken slum for society's most hated outcasts.

The Red District contained fiends no longer worthy of being called humans. I suppose it was fitting for Deleon's "Imps."

Boyband remained mute since our departure. His view of the Blue had likely been my equivalent of the Orange. Half of me had wanted him to be humbled by the lowest district, but my other had matured. The kid did not deserve punishment for his affluent bias. His prejudice for the lower class had been bred into him, yet it was still mild compared to the vast majority of higher District heirs. I wanted to meet his parents to see how they compared. Living as SocStans, the former lower-class blue-collar workers, perhaps their views would be more tolerant than most privileged aristocrats. I would have made sure to meet them if we survived the Red District endeavors, but I never could. They had died alongside their son's innocence.

Boyband was aging quicker than any kid his age. I experienced the degradation of his late teenage years alongside him. Perhaps he deserved to learn of my journey to becoming Deleon's servant. I wanted to begin the extensive tale but would not in the presence of vindictive Finians who would mock my chain of unfortunate events.

Even if I shared my past, I would be alone in my experiences. Thoughts of distant family and friends-turned-enemies made me miss my light-forsaken home country. Even if I were to return, I would be shunned for what I had become and what I had done to reach this point.

I tapped into my neurospace, readying a socitab to dissolve my desecrated self-worth. If my neurospace had been blocked, at least I had the mercy of my addiction to turn to. It made me ever more distant from my current companion, but I needed the relief. The only thing that stopped me was a voice over the intercom.

"Destination approaching: Red District - Eastern drop station." A sinking feeling in my stomach indicated the descent. It was smooth and controlled, but my heart was the opposite. My feelings of isolation dissipated as I heard Boyband's heavy breathing at my side. Even though the kid was conceited and a narrow-minded braggart, none of my negativity towards him mattered anymore. He would make it out of this. I wouldn't allow the opposite. There was no reason for him to suffer. He never made the choice to join Deleon. That was forced into his hypothalamus.

The partition lowered just a crack. Bank's voice was still slightly muffled, but we could hear him well enough. "Fins, grab the handles on their backs when you exit. Don't hesitate to squeeze the lightburner if they struggle to cooperate."

"You got it," one of them said.

The other nodded, then shook his head, realizing that Bank couldn't see him. "On it."

I could hear something moving below us as the intercom spoke again. *"Please hold for landing. The doors will open automatically when safe."*

I barely noticed us touching the ground. I tried to stand upon instinct, but the light lines on the jumpsuit held me still.

The guards stood and approached us, both of their eyes remained on the back door of the skyshuttle.

My suit loosened around the neck in time for me to see the back door retract up like a garage door.

Beyond the steel frame of the skyshuttle, I saw an expansive darkness with faint red lights rising vertically. They appeared to be the rims of buildings, but my vision was dampened by the artificial white lights in the shuttle.

Bank approached from the side with Naoma and Jackson in tow.

The guards reached behind to grab the handles between our shoulder blades. I regained my mobility, but dared not risk much movement.

My hunger grew. Boyband's could only be worse and it would grow more insidious by the minute.

As we stepped outside the vehicle, the other two skyshuttles landed to the left of ours. A group of six emptied out of one, five out of the other, many of them carrying a vast array of equipment. As they approached us I could see full-capture cameras and recording equipment ready to shoot whatever they had planned.

"Hold the excitement," Bank said. "We still need our *guests* to find some fiends for us to use."

The implications of his statement pressed dread into me, regardless of the definition. By no means would I be pleased to search the Red wasteland for jelly fiends, but if he referred to any other fiends, I could only fathom what hellspawn lurked in the crimson darkness.

The guards pressed us forward and the back of the skyshuttle shut, leaving us in the darkness of all but the few lamps of white light held by the film crew.

Bank walked over to speak with them, leaving the rest who had come in our shuttle to stare into the abyss.

Having often worked at night with only the blue lights of the Blue District to provide meager light, I was no stranger to the dark. Despite the red lights of the Red District being even weaker, I found that my night vision had improved drastically. Everything was still dark with a faint outline, as if I looked out under the light of a full moon, though it did not shine above us.

Deleon's upgrade.

What it had meant to advance from violet to indigo in the anti-spectrum still left me with a vast array of unanswered questions. My vision had improved, my reflexes sharper, and my physique fortified were mere guesses as to what it all meant. My mind remained the same except for a haunting detail that visited me in dreams and the ghost of my peripheral vision.

A presence lurked with me. If I was not so skeptical, I would call it a ghost attached to my Bite. Even to a delusional junkie, it made no sense that a spirit was connected to my embedded technology.

Regardless, a humanoid swine lurked in the depths of my mind.

The horror of my self-perceived insanity was easy to forget as I saw the Red District more clearly.

I wondered what had caused this city's fall, for it was an abandoned wasteland of dilapidated buildings and crumbling skyscrapers. Red light burst from broken fixtures, sparking like electric blood and shining upon the lurking horrors.

Humanoid figures patrolled the streets, though I feared to learn what they looked like up close. The Red District was not meant for humans. The poorest of the Republic's citizens had the Orange District to call their own, even most of the criminal exiles. Only the cruelest criminals and monsters in the truest definition were said to occupy the Red. Glowing skeletons wandered in the distance. Lumps of flesh moved beneath the red light like slugs in pursuit.

Bank returned with two members of the Techvax film crew. I tried to send Ralia a message and received the error that I expected.

The man and woman at Bank's side were humans, at least in their appearance. As they came to sell, there was a fair chance that they were shacs or a similar android model. I had no need to trust them, so it didn't matter to me either way. They wore dark clothing of your typical bureaucratic type with small lines of indigo light. Even though Techvax worked with Reef Records, they still had a ladder to climb.

"Boys," Bank whispered and waved us closer.

Our captors pushed us forward without any time to act of our own accord.

"Are you listening?"

I nodded, then looked at Boyband. His gaze was stuck in the dark allure of the distance. Red light reflected in his dilated pupils. He bit his lip and quivered.

"Devóne!" I said in a forceful whisper.

He turned to me, but it did not feel like he was focused yet.

Hunger is a distracting shac.

"Look at him."

He turned back to Bank, and I followed.

"Thank you. Now, we need to be delicate. If you two step out of line, you will be punished and forced to comply. Death is not an option for you. We cannot waste materials."

"Agreed," the woman at his side said.

"Agreed," the man repeated.

Bank gestured to his companions. "These are the operative directors and marketing representatives from Techvax." He looked at Jackson. "Anton, bring your girl over here."

Jackson made sure his apprehension was visible in his sigh and walked over to our party with Naoma close by him.

"Show em' the product," Bank said.

The female rep removed a capped syringe from the messenger bag at her side and showed it to the group. "This is Techvax's current Techbone vaccination, trial model 2.6."

"You already have a vaccine?" Jackson blurted. "Why didn't we know about this yet?""Shh!" Bank put his human finger before his dolphin mouth, then checked over his shoulder towards the city and sighed.

"Almost available for market use," the woman said as she handed the syringe to Jackson to observe. "It's been in development for years, and frankly, it needed more time. After the Firstlight attack, we made sure to expedite research and agreed upon this advertisement with Bank to ensure that we are prepared to distribute as soon as it is available."

The man nodded. "Bank's discovery of these boys' supposed invulnerability worked perfectly with our plan for an advertisement."

The woman continued, "To be prepared for public release, we agreed upon this marketing promotion for campaigning as soon as it is available."

"We're shooting a commercial," the man said. "The execs plan to broadcast it to anyone whose neurospace data does not include support for Haven Health and anyone else who shows an interest in Naoma, tech upgrades, and the general public if they cannot afford premium ad blocks."

Jackson handed the syringe back to the female rep. "So once this is market-ready, how can we be sure that it will actually *cure* techbone and not just produce more glowbones like Okrepine? Eliminate that and you'll demolish Haven."

Everyone looked towards the city at the mention of glowbones. The neon skeletons continued to wander from a safe distance.

"Simple," the man said. "It doesn't strengthen the bones, rather it attacks the viral component that causes the degradation of bones once combined with certain tech implants."

"Viral?" Jackson asked.

The woman shook her head, scowling at the man. "As far as our research can tell, no, Techbone is not a virus, but it is easier to think of it that way.

The man nodded and forced a laugh. "Yeah, that's what I meant."

She glared at him and continued as his smile diminished. "A latent force resides within those whom techbone affects that begins to wear away bones once it interacts with the light injected with tech implants. This latent factor awakens with certain light frequencies, causing it to become parasitic as it feasts upon the host's bones. The parasite continues to live on in many people even after the body's degradation, this what survives as Exos Sapiens or 'jelly fiends.' Many of the parasites die with their host, but jelly fiends are the occasional continuation."

She held up the syringe. "If we can eliminate the parasite before it has a chance to interact with light from tech implants, we have no reason to worry about techbone developing."

The man stepped forward, checking her for reassurance. "While we have come with the purpose of filming an advertisement, this will also be the first out-of-lab test on an Exos Sapien of the current vaccine model. Firstlight had the last one on the market. Regulation makes it almost impossible to obtain a fiend without coming all the way here. Now that we have you two, we can risk capturing them."

The woman nodded. "Eliminate the parasite, eliminate the risk."

Bank and Jackson seemed pleased at the solution, but I felt sick to my stomach and the nausea spread outward. I thought it was a voracious hunger, but it was more unsettling. The back of my head pulsed with an insidious headache. I clenched my teeth to hold back a moan. I would have collapsed and clenched my stomach if the light-laced jumpsuit did not hold me in place.

"Agh!" I shouted and clenched my eyes closed.

"Did you pull the handle?" Bank asked the Finian who held me.

"Must have," he replied, but I know he had no part in it. No light had touched the back of my head, where it felt like a demon was ready to erupt.

The pain diminished, and a voice emitted from that portion of my skull. It made no sense, but I knew it was true. If I hadn't been so focused on the sensation, I would have dismissed it for a sleep calling my deprived mind to slumber. The voice was rough and quiet, originating from the back of my skull–*my Bite*–and speaking to the rest of my very being.

"*Lies. Not parasites.*"

I could finally breathe without a vice around my mind and heard Boyband as I came to my senses.

I looked at him. His face was red with exhaustion, darker than the lights around us.

"Not parasites," he whispered.

My core trembled.

"What'd you say, kid?" Jackson said. He pushed the Finian behind Boyband away and grabbed the handle. "You doubting these reps? I'll pull it you zeggin'--"

"Enough, Anton," Bank said.

Jackson looked at him and shrugged.

"Give back control?"

"Pfft, whatever."

The Finian guard grabbed Boyband's handle again.

I couldn't spare time to ponder upon the surreal coincidence encountered by Boyband and me. My focus returned to Bank and the reps as I felt the lights on my jumpsuit compress slightly. Still, the unease from Boyband's words remained.

"Thank you, Anton. Now, you two boys are going to head out into the District and fetch some jellies for us. The reps have very specific standards for the advertisement and will send over the details for size, girth, et. cetera."

"What the zeg am I doing here?" Naoma pushed past Boyband and would have knocked him over if light bindings hadn't held him up.

"Eye candy," the male rep chuckled.

Naoma opened her mouth and raised her fist but calmed herself as the female rep held up her hand. "He's not wrong, but there's a better way to say that. This is not about sex-appeal, though I assume most of your audience of a certain age follows you for that very reason. We need your face because—well, why else do we have an agreement with Reef Records? You're nothing more than an advertisement agency. I've spoken to Anton about your history. You've advertised clothing, cosmetics, alterations. Your music is enough of an advertisement itself, and now you are going to sell pharmaceuticals."

"But—ugh, why would I—"

"Are you compliant?" Jackson asked.

She straightened her posture and smiled at the female rep. "I am compliant."

I checked for Boyband's reaction, but his dismal stare had been replaced by a feral glare. I restrained a pitiful laugh. Even if Techvax, Reef Records, or whoever owned them all knew that we eliminated the Firstlight operation, they gave no sign that they knew *how* we had accomplished it. Their ignorance of our curse would be their demise if we ever allotted a degree of freedom.

"Are you listening, then?" Bank asked.

"Sure," said Naoma, keeping Jackson in her peripheral vision. "Thank you Anton. Well then, miss *Neon Idol*. Once we have the jellies, we'll have you inject a few of them with the vaccine on camera. This'll prove its worth. We'll cast your script onto your neurospace interface. Don't worry, the boys will grab a few trial jellies for you to get comfortable with the script and such. We don't expect perfection the first time, even from people like you."

Bank pointed at the guard holding onto Boyband. "Keep a better hold on the kid."

Boyband straightened. His face turned to a stone glare. Anything that robbed the kid of his humanity pained me like a worried parent. Still, no one could go further than Deleon in robbing the kid of his purity.

Naoma brushed her lilac hair behind her ear and looked down. "So, I can just... stay here while they go into the city?" She looked up at him and tucked her hair behind her other ear.

The male Techvax rep grinned too widely for comfort.

Bank shook his head. "You're not charming anyone. Anyone who matters, at least. You have nothing to worry about. You've got all of us here to protect you. The only threats to our plan are well under our control." He glared at me. "Anton, is his messaging open to my neurospace?"

"Should be, give it a try."

Bank nodded. "Check it now, skunk."

The bleached line must have been wearing out, but it was still enough to grasp attention. It was a small hold I had on a distant childhood and a charisma lost to forced solemnity.

New message from user: Porpoise_0002787. Accept? Appeared across my interface. I felt bad that he was still seen as a number in society, but only for a second. All he had done to me had exhausted any pity I could offer. I figured Jackson would at least have a name for himself. While most Finians could be seen as lower beings, the most affluent and influential were exalted with Naoma and any other entertainment star. Where did Bank fall into this? He didn't seem to be owned by Reef and it wasn't typical for a Finian to be a part of a pharmaceutical company. Their value was in the Entertainment party, or high in their own society within ours.

I tapped to accept the message.

Bank nodded. "Now forward it to the kid when he calms down. If he compromises this, we won't hesitate to eliminate him. We only need one of you here. *Make* us need both of you. Got it?"

"Yes." My guard released the handle. The other group of Techvax members trained light rifles on us. "Give me his handle for a bit. I'll keep him under control until he calms down a bit. Criminal or not, teenagers are difficult."

Bank let out a genuine, airy laugh. "Let me do it."

Boyband's guard moved him and the handle towards me and I took it.

"Gotcha kid," I whispered. "Just hold on for a bit longer." We earned a few stares, but it wasn't something I was not already accustomed to.

Boyband managed to speak, but he sounded like a junkie unable to concentrate as he limped through withdrawals. "What about weapons?"

"What about them?" Bank said with arms folded.

"If we're going to walk out there, shouldn't we have some protection? What if something comes after us?"

"That's why you're here. If you can heal from the cerebral plugs, you won't have a problem out there. If you worry about anything, it should be radiation."

"Glowbones aren't radioactive," I said.

He shrugged. "Whatever, I don't care. Enough complaining. If you took out Firstlight, grabbing a few jellies shouldn't be a problem. We don't want you to kill them, anyway. If we gave you weapons, you would just be more of a risk to us."

I smirked. "And we're not already? You just said we were enough for Firstlight."

"Shut the zeg up," Jackson said from behind us.

"*You* 'shut the zeg up,' Anton!" Bank said. "Just go. The sooner you bring them back, the sooner we can leave."

He walked up to us and secured a band around our right wrists. Each had a faint white ring around it with a small cylinder across. "These light rings will help you see a little better. Use the rod on top if you need to shine some more light on a particular spot."

Boyband tried to look closer at his band, but his suit restricted the movement as I held onto the handle on his back. "Are the... things out there going to be bothered by the light? Isn't it always dark here?"

Bank shrugged. "The pollution keeps it dark, so I figure they won't be too keen to have harsh artificial light shine on them, but you'll have to find out for yourself. I sent you the size requirements, now go. Take multiple trips if you need to. We didn't bring anything for you to haul them back with."

I checked the message on my interface. The measurements and weight requirements meant nothing to me, but he provided a link to download an optical measurement software. I queued it and skimmed further down the message. He wanted six fiends, which would be a cumbersome load for anyone without a Bite. I was strong enough at the base anti-violet level and figured it would only be easier in anti-indigo.

"We're waitin' on you." Jackson kicked my shin, then grunted as it hurt him without phasing me.

I stepped forward, relieved to have control again, all the while terrified that I had to proceed into the unknown cityscape.

"Let me go," Boyband said through clenched teeth. His breathing was louder than his harsh whisper.

"Prove that you can control yourself and I will. Just keep going a couple more feet."

"I need to eat."

"Yeah, I figured. I'm not that oblivious. Don't worry, we'll find you something."

"Like what?"

I checked back over my shoulder. Everyone was still watching us from under their artificial light.

"Petya?"

"Jelly fiends don't have any teeth and you sure as hell aren't going to try to eat from glowbones. Find something else and it should be fine. Even animals can hold you over, but it's like eating flour instead of a meal."

"Why not glowbones? They have teeth."

"Do you know what they are?"

"Radioactive skeletons that glow. Rejects of experimentation."

"Nah, you've got it all wrong."

"Who says? Deleon? Why should I trust him?"

"No, Cut told me."

"The doctor?"

I nodded. Checking back to see them watch us as we walked into the red abyss. "He's one of the good ones." As far as I could tell, though, I held back my reservations for the sake of the argument. "Do you know how Haven Health made its way to the presidency?"

"Okrepinate."

I nodded. "But why is everyone researching alternative solutions if we already have a cure?"

"It just helps with the symptoms, right? Or is it too expensive?"

"A little of both. Have you ever seen what happens if someone with techbone stops taking Okrepinate?"

"No."

I pointed to a glowing skeleton in the distance. "You have now."

"You're zeggin kidding me."

I shook my head. "Most cities have enough sense to deny a patient an Okrepinate prescription if their income is below a certain level, but that doesn't stop greedy healthcare companies who would rather have all the light they could hope for while ignoring the consequences."

"But how do they become glowbones?"

"Okrepinate is great if you stay on a consistent schedule. Miss a couple of doses, and your skin starts to rot. If you're too poor to afford frequent treatments, it will fall off and a few of the organs will remain suspended in the skeleton. When people are on course for complete skin rot, District regulators will ship the sorry shacs here to become glowbones."

"But why do they glow?"

"Cut told me that Okrepinate is *close* to the cure. Apparently the treatment involves doses of physical light, but not how Cut says it needs to be used for an elimination of techbone. The drug invests light into the bones and if the treatments do not keep them steady, they'll try to generate their own light and corrupt the body. Seeing how they can still move as skeletons with very little connective tissue leads me to believe that the light is actually a living thing."

I gradually let go of Boyband's handle, and he continued to walk beside me. We proceeded onward, but I said nothing of it.

He watched the passing ground and shook his head. "So if Cut gets that, does that mean he is close to a cure?"

I shrugged, but he didn't see it. "We'll see, I guess. I would say as close as Techvax. We'll see how theirs works."

"Maybe it can cure us."

"I think we have a more complex illness than techbone."

"What are we then?"

"Parasites."

"Please don't say that." His voice shook.

I opened my mouth to ask him why but stopped myself. I knew. "You heard the voice too?"

He nodded, then looked up. "I would rather look at the beasts of this city than think about that. Maybe later, but not now."

We both looked at the city. We had entered from the outskirts but now made our way onto central streets. My eyes were almost completely adjusted to the light. I looked back, seeing only a white square from the Techvax crew.

Broken glass littered the ground as well as burnt papers, and reddish viscous blobs that reminded me of the jellyfish I would see washed ashore back when I was a kid. Back before the ocean went black. I figured they had to be remnants of jelly fiends. Some even looked like flattened arms and legs, but were too small for our requirements, even though they moved.

The physiology of the jellies was a mystery. Even though Techvax claimed to have a cure for them, it didn't make sense. They couldn't restore lost bones. The medical field had become a battlefield of misunderstandings and ignorance as companies toppled one another to climb the research ladder to obtain power through market control.

Empty skyscrapers rose on each side of us, though the tallest had fallen, destroying others in their wake or leaving heaps and chunks of rubble in the street. Despite the evident collapses, the road had been paved enough for vehicles to drive through uninhibited. Why it had been that way or why anyone would need to was another question that I had to abandon.

Rocks moved and waste rustled to Boyband's right. We stopped and moved closer. There was nothing large enough to hide any glowbones. They wandered the streets ahead. We were drawing close enough to see the dark sockets of their eyes.

The sound came from behind a broken metal fixture with colored wires sticking out. Wet gnawing and sharp scrapes.

I took a step closer. Boyband darted ahead, plunging my hand into the open orifice before I could reprimand his lack of caution. He pulled out a writhing rodent, bigger than a rat, but it did not look quite like a racoon. Before I could have a proper look at it, Boyband bit off the entirety of its muzzle. Two beady eyes stared out and the remnant of a bitten tongue flopped out. Boyband tossed it onto the cracked sidewalk before the running blood reached the cuff of his sleeve.

I grimaced as he chewed with moist crunches.

He wiped blood and fur from his mouth. "Do jaw bones do anything for the hunger?"

"Not that I've noticed. I get the occasional chunk of jaw when I'm as hungry as you are. I think other bones aren't bad if you get a bit, but it's like eating cartilage in chicken. The Bites need teeth and nothing else will work in their place."

Boyband nodded. "These teeth are small and sharp, but I think they'll do for a bit. I see what you meant earlier about human teeth. Animals are nothing in comparison."

"Like drinking a jug of water to stave off hunger pains."

"Let's finish the job before it gets too bad. I'll find something better when we're done."

I doubted they would give us any freedom, but kept my mouth shut. I waved for him to follow me back onto the main street.

He spat out bits of hair and wiped them from his mouth, then onto his pants.

"Is the aftertaste kicking in?"

He chuckled. "I was so blinded by hunger that I think I might puke if I went back and had a proper taste of those teeth now. It was like charcoal. The light only knows what it was eating."

I offered a pitiful chuckle, mocking our circumstances. Charcoal was a perfect description for what we saw. The whole city looked as if it was coated in a black veil. Only the occasional shiny machinery or flickering, cracked screens broke away from the darkness.

"Have you tasted charcoal?" I asked. "I can't say that I've ever touched it, but I've seen plenty of camping scenes in mindshows."

"Never tasted it, but I've touched and smelt it. My dad and I went camping a couple of times."

"Where? Did he fly you out to the west? Real humble."

"He did, but–it's not like that."

"Like what? If I never had the luxury to do anything like that. Ever since I came here, I haven't been able to escape the interconnected cities."

"Was it like that back... in your old home?"

"Everything's been modernized. Medislavia is no exception, but it's not quite as bad as the Republic. If you want anything here resembling nature in its true form, you have to have the money to travel." I kicked a broken piece of asphalt, regretting it as it left my foot. "Come on, let's keep moving."

We left the curb and continued on the main street. The signs of old businesses had been blackened out along with everything else. The only color besides the red lights was that of protruding tubes and wires from recently busted screens and fixtures. Even though everything looked the same, small differences in aged structural wounds told stories of more recent destruction. I ignored the damage, not wanting to entertain the idea of what kind of behemoth could cause so much damage.

We passed by some jelly fiends, but many of them were too small or damaged for Tachvax's purposes. The highest remaining buildings were still ahead, along with the most intense red light that almost covered entire skyscrapers. We kept our distance from the surrounding alleys as we spotted a few lurking glowbones. I had no intention of learning if their walking corpses retained any humanity. The rumors opposing such an argument were enough for me not to risk our chances.

"Why did you come here?"

I raised my eyebrow. "What do you mean? I had no choice, just like you."

"No. To the Republic. Why'd you leave Medislavia."

"Politics beyond your care. Anyone that you knew who stood for one side or the other is an attention whore who doesn't know the smallest thing about what is happening overseas."

"I've heard plenty, but I don't see why I should pretend to understand foreign politics when I don't even understand our own."

"You're a smart kid. Let's leave it there."

"Try me."

"Huh?"

"I won't try to understand, but I want to hear about your side of the argument."

"I told you before. I don't want to talk about the past."

"Come on, you'll hear more about mine when we head back to investigate the SocStans."

You still think we will? Deleon will be impressed with how we did here, diving into the Entertainment party. Right, kid? We are the peak of human performance and made it a whole few hours without getting captured. If only Deleon could see us now!

Zeg, I hated my increasing cynicism.

I looked around as if making it so no one else could hear. For years, I had grown so used to keeping up my shell of a recluse, only opening slightly for Ralia, that I had forgotten that I *could* talk about it. I held back a snide remark of denial and risked a chance on the kid.

"The Medislavians are every bit as greedy as people say we–they are. They are corrupt and manipulate the public with every bit of media and technology into thinking that the Arabasians are greedy and that if they associate with other powerful countries, that it is a threat to the existence of said countries. Pride. Manipulation. Corruption in its most vile form. If you are fine believing their lies, life is good. Question your authority and you're a traitor."

"And that's what you did? Question their authority?"

"Question it, oppose it, protest it. All the above and I became more radical the more they threatened me."

"Were you a politician?"

I held my hand close to Boyband's back, ready to pull him away from any danger. He was slower to react to anything with his hunger draining his Bite. My reflexes were diminishing but would last for a few more hours unless we had to burn our reserves. I had to stay ever more cautious as the glowbones on the sidewalks turned to watch us as we passed.

"Yes? No?"

"Sorry. I guess I was as close as you can get to one without an official position, maybe even more influential for the general public. I was a social media influencer. Ran campaigns against the Medislavian war effort, continually posted, recruited. I even had a team that sabotaged the campaigns run by Medislavian radicals."

I was waiting for him to ask, *"Is that why you are so addicted to socitabs? Do you crave the adoration you once had? The attention from countless supporters? The constant online interactions?*" His question never came, for I knew all along that the accusation was my own.

"Then you left?" He stopped and pointed to a body jelly fiend that moved through the gutter like a slug. Its eyelids hung open, but the eyeballs had since shriveled up. Limp hands stretched out and slowly pulled it forward. The arms bent in full arcs, no bones to restrict their movement.

I scanned it with the application. It was just a bit larger than their requirements. "First one of the day...night. I'll take it. You can grab the next."

He leaned over. "Let me help you pick it up."

"Move!" I pushed him aside as a glowbones ran at us, only visible to me now that he had bent over.

He caught himself with a hand on the ground, but I continued past, ready to stop our neon green assailant. I had expected that I would hear any approaching, but the little tissue that remained on the glowing corpse helped muffle the creaking of bones and padded its feet. It ran with outstretched hands and looked easy enough to knock over. I had no idea what it wanted, for it surely could not eat us, but that didn't stop it from attacking.

Neither of us had a weapon. Rather than risk touching it with my hands, I swung my leg up in an arch right before it reached me, catching its hunched neck with my heel, and slamming it to the ground.

With the accuracy and acceleration of my attack, I expected its bones to shatter against the concrete, but it was the ground that ended up cracked. It looked up in a slow daze and lifted its crooked smile to glare at me. The glowing bones remained intact, but the impact had jolted the jaw enough to tear the tissue holding one side of its jaw onto the skull. A violet pupil floating in its eye socket stared back with a feral anger that needed no eyebrows to convey its hunger for revenge.

Boyband stomped its rib cage against the ground but lost his balance as the intensity of his attack rebounded through the unbreakable bones.

It pushed itself up and stood with a hunched back. I was frozen in thought, trying to figure out how to end its horrid existence, for it no longer deserved to be called living.

Boyband tossed a chunk of twisted metal debris at its side. It rocked slightly but continued to quicken its pace towards me as I peddled back.

"What are you doing?" Boyband shouted. The glowbones fastened its hellish eyes on me.

"Trying to figure out how to stop it! I'm not running–I just–"I stopped speaking as it mumbled and hissed at me. Without lips and a tongue, none of it made any sense.

Straightened to perfection and shining without blemish, except for the obvious neon glow, its gnashing teeth almost broke my enhungered will.

Boyband approached it from behind while I kept it held in front of me.

I swung my leg into its crotch out of instinct, thankfully never having faced such a creature. Its hands of bones and pale remnants of flesh held onto my shoulders with vice grips as it fell forward with my kick. I continued to press back on the shoulders as it relentlessly pulled its face towards mine to bite.

Boyband grabbed its legs from behind and tried to pull it off of me, but its grip was relentless. I leaned back and we both stretched it out wide.

"Keep pulling!" I shouted. Both of us shouted and grunted, only stopping as pops became tears and the skeleton split in two. I pried its hands free, hearing some of the bone crunch, and it fell on the ground, but continued to crawl towards me with mangled fingers.

"Zeg you, you zeggin' skele-whore!" Boyband shouted and he jumped on the glowbone's ribcage. He continued up and down, still no crack evident in the bones, but some of the tissue tore and the spine fell into pieces. His hunger fueled rage increased with each hateful stomp. If I couldn't feed him soon, he'd go just as feral towards any human we met.

Part of me wanted to allow him to lose control with the Techvax crew.

He grabbed the few vertebrae still connected to the skull and drop-kicked it down an alley and stared at it as it rolled. His back was hunched, ready to prowl for his next prey. My heart felt like it was vibrating, but it slowed as his breathing calmed.

He turned back with a vile smile, one that told of violent cravings.

I looked around. A few glowbones had noticed, but none of them had started towards us. My back aches as I crouched and threw the jelly fiend over my shoulders. It was dead weight, but I could feel my Bite burning my reserves to lighten the load.

While we had to venture further into the city, the apparition within me warned of more malicious dangers ahead. I couldn't see the swine's face anywhere, nor did it speak, but I understood that we had to remain away from the city's core. Staring at the incense red center with writhing shadowy tentacles. At least that is what I felt I saw. If I were to venture onward, I knew my descent to madness would only quicken. I killed my curiosity, recognizing that I was never meant to learn the secrets of the Red District.

Boyband was lost in a similar state. Our apparitions had acted together once again. I would ask him if he saw the humanoid swine but now was not the time. Our captors had an assignment for us to finish.

I patted him on the back and pointed ahead. "Five more."

Chapter Eleven

Deception Sells

Years of slouching had strained my back even in my early adulthood. The consequences of a lazy posture would have caused my back to pulse as I carried the jelly fiends, but the strength of my Bite eliminated it. It didn't bother me much that I had burned through my reserve. What ate me from within was much more of a moral conundrum. My past choices no longer affected me because of a tech implant. If too many people sided with such an ideal, our society would collapse into carelessness. As I thought, I realized we were too late. Without a cure for techbone, most people still risked getting implants all for the sake of convenience and pleasure.

Boyband dropped his two fiends on the ground. I was glad to see that they didn't splatter upon impact. We laid them out evenly, as the rest of the film crew joined us.

"Will these do?" Bank asked the female rep.

She walked down the line, pausing for a moment to scan each of them. "The second and fourth are too small for my liking, but they'll suffice for the initial testing."

My mental fortitude wavered. What use was there in compliance if we could never escape? Tortuous memories of the neon centipede returned as I looked at Bank whisper to the Techvax reps as they removed their filming equipment. If the centipede had been only for a system assessment, I couldn't fathom the horrors of what he might do to ensure my cooperation.

Boyband's shaking had stopped as he cast his stare down to the jelly fiends, probably having the same mental crisis that I was. I wanted to help him, but how could I ever find the motivation if I lost it for myself?

The need for a socitab burned, but I cast it aside, letting the addiction be clouded out by a need to give Boyband the life he deserved. He was a privileged shac, but no one should live their days out as a pawn of some corporation.

"You." The male rep pointed at me.

"What?"

"Grab the one next to the kid."

"Why not have him grab it?" I looked at Boyband. His eyes remained on the fiend. "And why do you need six?"

"Shut the zeg up and do as they say!" Bank shouted.

I walked over, grabbed it, and hauled it towards the crew.

One of their crew members set up a tripod with a violet cube on top. He tapped it and the vicinity the size of a room, changed to look like a Violet penthouse, complete with white-violet chandeliers, a window with top-of-the-city outlook, and countless other amenities worth more than I had ever owned.

"Right here." The man tapped his foot on an altar in the center of the room. I laid the writhing fiend down on it and latched it in with a grav-switch on the back. Any limits to hologram technology I had previously believed in were cast off.

"Alright now." The female rep removed a syringe from her suitcase and handed it to Naoma. "This'll just be a trial run. Follow the script and we'll correct as needed."

Naoma nodded and rolled the syringe between her thin fingers. "Just me, the fiend, and the boys?"

"Zeg no!" The male rep laughed. "Just you, the fiend, and the cure." He waved me away.

She uncapped the needle and flicked it with a violet fingernail.

"Careful, girl," said Jackson.

She glared at him. "They said this is just a trial run."

"But the vax is the real thing," the male rep said.

"He's right," the female attested. "I wouldn't use it on yourself yet."

Naoma scoffed. "So it's not ready, and you're shooting an ad?"

The female rep sighed and turned to Bank. "Is she going to do it or not?"

"Jackson?"

"Hihow, Bank."

"Get your star to cooperate."

"Naoma. Are you compliant?"

Her snark dissipated with her prideful reluctance. "I will comply."

Regardless of my derision for her, her subjugation was horrific to witness.

Everyone ceased their chatter as she took her place next to the fiend, sparing it a single disgusted glance.

"Ready?" a Techvax member said from behind an array of multi-lensed cameras. He wore a headset too aged for what the company flaunted. It looked like a virtual reality headset from twenty years ago, but the quality of the video would prove it's worth. Regardless, I had no intention of watching it.

"Ready?"

Naoma nodded.

Boyband turned to watch the crowd with a trembling stare.

I fell from my pensive observation and lost all other concerns in the wake of his needs.

The director with the vintage virtual reality helmet raised his hands. As he did so, the cameras focused on Namoa and the altar. "Rolling in three, two." He pointed at her and nodded.

How much did everyone else know what would happen? Had she had any rehearsal while we fetched their fiends?

Instrumental pop played through surrounding speakers. The octaves were much higher than her usual background music and too spunky for her often melancholic style. It was loud enough to set the scene and mood, but I knew they would have to add it in later edits.

She looked into the frontmost camera and its multiple lenses, but I could see the faint flashing in her eyes as she read from her neurospace. With the abundance of edits they would have to do, it would have almost been easier to cast an AI Naoma in the advertisement. Even though these people treated us like slaves, they still held to some ethics. Whether the decision came from ethics or a hatred for artificial minds didn't matter. The outcome was the same.

"Our world needs saving," she began with perfect posture and a confident smile. "We all know someone who has been affected by techbone. We've all felt its sting. While other leading medications help to alleviate symptoms, I choose Techvax."

She removed the cap from the syringe and stepped towards the jelly fiend. "A cure is no longer a fantasy."

The fiend writhed as she leaned over to administer the vaccination. Its boneless appendages flopped like tentacles, though it could not escape.

She pressed the syringe into the torso, right where the sternum would have been. The fiend let out a screeching hiss that caused many of the crew members to cover their ears. After a few seconds, its arms stopped moving, and it went still.

"With Techvax, techbone will die with–" She shook her head and laughed. Her eyes regained their focus.

"Agh, cut!" the director groaned.

"Hey, Naoma, what's up?" Jackson stepped forward cautiously to remain behind the cameras.

"Who wrote this zegging script?"

Her remark was her usual condescending sting, but it was a step out of her expected compliance. She was on the border.

We could break her again.

I looked at Boyband but held the plan back for a moment. We could break her now, but I was sure there would be a more opportune moment to do so undetected. Boyband would relish in a grand feast of teeth, but our survival was much more likely if we could slip away undetected. Drifting into the Red sounded just as abhorrent as working with Techvax, but I was willing to test our chances.

"The marketing team," the director said. "Back into position, let's try again."

Naoma let out another mocking chuckle. "I think the script needs touching up."

"Ah, come on," the male rep said. "It's not like your lyrics are any better."

It's not like she writes them, anyway. I tamed my grin. I lost it after noticing Boyband's shaking hands. He was getting worse, but we still had time. We needed it. Zeg, by the light please give it just a few more minutes, kid.

"Am I the only one who sees the problem?" She picked up the jelly fiend's arm and dropped it. It slapped against the altar, dead with the rest of the body. "'*With Techvax, Techbone will die*'. You really want me to shoot a commercial where I kill a jelly fiend with a lethal injection? Is this really your solution? Aren't there better ways to kill these things? Come on, Anton. Reef is actually going to tie its name to this guk?"

The male rep raised his hands and shook his head. "Nah, you've got it all wrong. Have you ever tried to kill a jelly fiend? No, I didn't think so. There's a reason we ship the damn things here. Smash them, cut them into pieces, and they'll still crawl around. *That*. That *death* that you caused is actually a cure. The injection wiped out the parasite within, leaving only the corpse to remain. *That* is what the cure is. These jellies are no longer people, only a grotesque husk for the parasites to use. If we use that injection on one of us, it will kill the parasite within, preventing the volatile reaction between the parasite and light-powered implants that cause techbone."

Naoma shook her head and looked back at the jelly fiend. "I still think it is a touch too–wait." She crouched down to look at it with her eyes only a foot away from its face. "It's moving! Your *cure* doesn't even work!"

"We clearly stated that it is still in its trial stage," the female rep said.

"So you are going to sell a product that might not even work?" Naoma said. "The entire Republic is going to invest all of its hope into a cure. You can't deceive people like that."

"Naoma!" Jackson shouted.

She raised a finger, her glare still on the female rep as she stepped away from the altar.

Jackson stepped forward, his mouth open and ready to reprimand.

Boyband's hands were in pale fists that shook with his down-turned glare.

We had to do it now.

I moved close enough for the sides of our feet to touch and whispered. "*Coerce* her. Now."

His breaths were just as unsteady as his heads. His enslaving appetite ate at him like the parasite they spoke of.

"Devóne." I pointed at Naoma, as Jackson drew closer to her. His call for compliance had to be on the edge of his tongue. "Tell her to come here and free us now."

My confidence in Boyband had undeservedly dwindled.

"Naoma," he called. She turned with the film crew to look at us. The control in his voice frightened me. He had become a true predator, equipped to deceive his prey into walking onto his mouth. He kicked the jelly fiend beside his feet. "Why don't you take this one?"

She looked at Jackson. He shrugged.

"*Come take this one,*" Boyband demanded.

Jackson stepped forward. She put her hand on his shoulder and proceeded toward Boyband without her producer.

"Might want to keep a hold of his handle," I said.

"*Let me help you,*" Boyband demanded.

She nodded.

"*Do you know how to take this suit off?*" he whispered.

She scowled at him, relaxed into her typical demeaning smile, and nodded.

"*Set us free.*"

As she reached for the back of his suit, I knew that a mere breath lasted until hell was set loose in the form of two Imps.

I prayed that she actually knew how to free us from the suits but knew that it would be much easier if we remained compliant.

Life would have been easier if I had stayed in Medislavia, ignorant and passive. I had chosen otherwise and would have to again.

"Wait until we're both good." I whispered to him.

He nodded.

Everyone watched us except for a few members of the film crew as they adjusted the equipment. I could only see two light rifles on the backs of two guards but was sure that someone had to have hidden personal protection. Even if they hadn't perceived us as threats, no well-minded group would ever enter the Red Districts unarmed. Having faced a glowbones, I now knew that their weapons would be ineffective, but it was the thought that counted.

The light in Boyband's jumpsuit dissipated, leaving him in pure black clothing.

"Hey!"

"What are you doing?"

"Bank?"

"Anton, make her stop?"

"Stop that!"

She moved and deprogrammed mine before they could make sense of their shouts.

I swung my arms, feeling freedom once again, and looked at Boyband.

He felt the release of light and sprinted with a feral prowl.

I dashed after him, passing him as I burned the rest of my Bite reserve, utilizing the speed modification.

Despite the rush of the situation, I saw him go for the closest Techvax rep, not worrying about the guards whom I pursued before anyone else. I reached them both as they were raising their light rifles.

I jumped with inhuman acrobatic precision, landing on their raised hands with my feet at the same time. I slammed the rifles down onto their legs, flipped to maintain my balance, and pounced again as they stumbled and dropped their weapons.

Utilizing my Bite felt so good, knowing that I could satisfy my appetite immediately.

I jabbed two straight hands into their throats before they could stand straight. The tips of my fingers protruded out of the other side. My strikes broke through their spines as if they had been mere pebbles in the way of a plowing truck.

Having forgotten caution, a shot in the shoulder quickly reawakened me to our circumstances. It felt no harder than an opportunistic punch but had torn a hole through the jumpsuit. Beneath the fabric, my pale skin was without blemish. I wouldn't have been surprised except I saw the light hit me in my wide periphery. Someone had shot me with pure violet light, yet it meant nothing.

Zeg me, Deleon. Your upgrade might have saved my life. Is that what it was? The last blue light shot I had taken before the upgrade had torn through flesh and blackened my rib. What *is* the anti-spectrum?

Boyband screamed as he bit the mouth out of the female Techvax rep. Only the top of the male's head remained as blood spilt from the neck like a spilt water bottle.

Worry about everything else later.

I looked for the person who had shot me and hunched over to prepare for an evasion. Almost everyone was running back to the sky shuttles. If my attacker remained, they were smart enough to invest their hope in a stealthy shot. Regardless, it would do them no good.

I made a quick check back to see what Naoma was doing.

Zegging idiot. She was sprinting towards the center of the Red District. I could understand that our tactics were intimidating, but at least we had some human morality left inside of us, no matter how little. The Red District was absent of such hope. The demons within only wanted to satisfy their–zeg. Sometimes I can be such a hypocrite.

I wanted to run back and steer her away, offering solace in my bloody hands, but Boyband was my priority. We would finish the rest of Reef and Techvax, *then* I could chase after Naoma and—

I felt another shot hit my thigh. It stung, but left no mark.

The zegging girl was killing my focus.

It wasn't the first time.

I slapped my leg, amplifying the pain from the shot to center my focus.

"Come out, you zegging coward!" I shouted as I walked towards the debris along the way to the shuttles. They were close but still had time before they reached them. Time. Mere *seconds.* If the poor marksman hit me, so be it.

"Boyband!" I shouted without even looking at him and pointed towards the escapees. "Take 'em all out or Deleon will have our balls!"

I heard his chuckle and an exhilarated shout. It was a relief to hear him leave his feast, all the while disheartening to hear his joy over an oncoming massacre.

Two shots hit my back. I heard the clicks synonymous with a crime against nature.

"Give me back my zeggin' girl you shac!"

I spared a glance back. I had expected Bank to be the one with enough bravery to remain back, but it was Anton Jackson who walked towards me with a light pistol pointed right at me.

"Zeg em' all! They used us anyway! Just give me back Naoma!"

I chuckled and continued to run.

"Zeg you and your–"

I barely felt the shots hit my back as I continued. Many flew past, with a few taking down some of the Techvax team. Rage blinds almost as much as hunger.

Boyband ran towards Bank.

I burned through the last bit of speed I had in my bite to meet him there, but Bank beat me to it. The Finian freak seized Boyband by the throat, lifted him up in the air, and shook violently. The kid clawed at Bank's arms, but to no avail. Whatever unholy strength had been implanted in us was a match for his hybrid body.

Bank barely turned his head in time to see my fist slam into his face. The impact was intense, but I felt like my fist slid right off of his dolphin skin.

Boyband kicked his feet up at Bank's arm, causing the Finian to drop in a second of distraction.

As the kid stood back up, I went for another punch into Bank's cybernetic core but barely dented the metal casing.

He chuckled and kicked me with a foot that felt like it was charged with a violet-powered piston. He stole my breath and launched me back several feet.

"You freaks really did single hand Firstlight, didn't you?"

I felt like the ground shook beneath me as he walked closer. Deleon's bites had taken us to a level above typical human existence, even when pitted against those with top-of-the-line strength implants.

I was terrified. I couldn't run away, but I had a kid to keep alive. *And a girl to stop from killing herself.* The rest of the company pounded on the skyshuttles to open their doors. Their lights turned on.

"Zeg you!" Boyband shouted as Bank was three feet away from me as I moved back like a cowering crab.

Bank shook his head and whistled through his blowhole. Bloody mucous flew out and dripped down the side of his head. My effort was not fruitless. Still, it required more.

He pointed at Boyband with his snout, but his left eye continued to stare at me. "The kid wants to take the fight into his own hands. Should we let him? How stupid are you two to turn on all of us?"

"*Come kill Bank!*" Boyband shouted. I felt the power in his voice, though it had no sway on me.

Bank laughed out loud. Even if he felt the power in Boyband's tone, I doubted he believed it would work.

Two, three, then four people from the Techvax crew left the shuttles just as the doors were opening.

"*All of you! Now!*"

Those who had entered spilled out from the doors and ran towards Bank with the ferocity of the glowbones that had assaulted us.

His inhuman smile lost its glee as the sound of pounding feet neared him from behind.

I stood as he looked away from me but held back my attack.

Boyband jumped after the first approaching members of the horde and ripped their jaw free to satiate his immediate need to feed. Coercing one person burned enough of his reserve. I was lucky he wasn't stuck in a feral mind after such a bold move.

Bank punched and kicked the first few crew members that reached him, but even the greatest system disintegrates under an accumulation of seemingly harmless viruses.

Without any weapons on them, they took stones, pieces of forgotten debris, even camera equipment and used them to pulverize Bank. His hands reached up for mercy. The tide overcame him and his stretching arms fell down with the blood that pooled below the pile of thrashing bodies.

One of them kept trying to climb to the top but continued to slip and fall. Each landing left a gash in exposed skin as he fell like a drunkard.

I pulled him back from the pile on Bank and ate his teeth.

Boyband approached me with a mouth covered in red. He looked at the others, then at me.

"He has to be dead by now," I said.

"*Enough.*" He spoke with a voice that stilled them to the quietness of his calm voice.

They climbed down and filed into a perfect square formation like an army of unprogrammed shacs.

"You good?" I asked him.

"Yeah, a little lightheaded, but eating right after that call helped."

I smiled and shook my head. "By the light, you could have killed yourself right there. I appreciate what you did, I mean... we needed it, but don't deplete yourself that much."

He nodded.

I'd never done it, but Deleon had demanded that we remain away from such an extreme. Perhaps that was another lie, but I was not willing to risk it with him.

He nodded towards the others. "What do we do with them now?"

I checked back for Naoma, not seeing her violet glow anywhere. We would still make it to her. We had to. She was as much a prisoner as we were. I did not forget Naoma. We'll make it out of here.

"Eat as many as we can."

He looked back at the rest of them. "I–"

"I don't care if you think or say you are full. You can't have anything left after that mass-coercion. We'll eat as many as we can and kill the rest. We can worry about the bodies later."

"Why worry about the bodies? What freaks would care about a bunch of dumped bodies in the Red District? Like they said, this is where they dump jelly fiends."

"Even if some people dump bodies, it will be pretty easy to figure out that these are all from Techvax."

"And? Techvax isn't primitive. Their people will know this crew is missing and there is only one place to find them. Maybe they'll blame it on Reef. If they blame it on us, who the zeg cares? That's Deleon's problem, right?"

I looked back for Naoma. Another futile attempt.

"You don't plan to go back to him after this, do you? We've escaped. Might as well continue."

"I have a deal with Deleon."

"Then we'll find a way around it. My parents may be dead, but they have resources. What was the deal?"

Not enough resources to change the Republic. Still, maybe there is another way. "I'll tell you later."

"Something to do with your past life?"

"Something like that."

"You think we can take one of these skyshuttles to my old place? Fulfill Deleon's mission or go against it, we need to head there."

"Maybe, but I want to find someone first."

He followed my gaze back to the abyssal center. "Really? She's got you zegged up like every other desperate shac."

"You remember what happened when she freed us the first time? I want to explore what that was."

"Then let's set that aside and eat these shacs before they come to."

I looked back for a different target and saw a scarred fin poking up behind some debris. He would die a coward.

"What is it?" Boyband asked as he walked towards the others.

"Hold off a moment longer. Jackson is still alive back there. He shouldn't be as strong as Bank."

Boyband called to the human husks. "*Six of you, go finish him off.*"

Jackson poked up his head and ran. I would have chased after to help slow him down, but he limped and hopped. The poor Finian had probably tripped in haste while trying to shoot me. I hadn't even touched him.

The six crew members reached him in seconds.

I slapped Boyband on the back and smiled. "Now we can eat."

Chapter Twelve
Remnants of an old society

With all the fuel I had in my reserve to power my speed mod, I had to taper back to stay with Boyband. It had been months since I had been so well fed.

We left three corpses with their teeth, even after taking two full sets for Boyband to try if we grew desperate later. Just because I could only eat fresh teeth did not mean he was programmed the same way.

"You good?" I checked over my shoulder.

"Trying. Do you see anything?"

"Not yet."

"Are you sure we should keep running? What if we go past her?"

"Unless she had implants, she couldn't have made it too far. Keep looking. We'll turn back and go another way if we need to."

I had to watch my feet to make sure I didn't trip over any jelly fiends. The few glowbones that chased us gave up after a few seconds of pursuit.

What else had the elites tossed in this light-forsaken wasteland? We passed by the occasional body part that was not flattened by bone deprivation, but I figured it was much more likely that they had been pieces of shacs rather than human remnants. After seeing the lengths people like Deleon would go to in order to achieve their goals, it wouldn't surprise me to see actual corpses rather than the ones we had left.

"Naoma!" Boyband shouted.

I glared back at him. "You're just going to frighten her further away from us."

"Can't be worse than what we see here. How long have we been running? We would have passed her by now."

"Twenty minutes maybe? You're probably right." I slowed and roasted my hands on the back of my head with my arms spread wide.

"What should we be looking for?"

"Violet light? I don't know."

"Should we go back and try another street? How big do you think this city is?"

"No idea. Any luck with your neurospace connection?

He shook his head.

I wanted Ralia more than ever. She would be able to crack through the neuroblock and find Naoma. She would–no. She was brilliant, but I was not incapable of everything she could do. I had to think like her. Without a charge, the neurospace would shut down, leaving me as simple as a techless human. Our neurospaces lacked the connection for most of their online functions, but the bare system still had its basic programs.

Please, Naoma. Please show me that you have left your light on.

"What are you thinking about?"

"Huh?" I turned to him.

"You're quiet and staring. Did you figure something out?"

"What is your neurospace charge at?"

"Sixty-five percent. Why?"

"Mine's at twenty-three. We'll have to rely on mine."

"What?"

"I need to burn through the charge so it will search for a light source to charge it. All the red here wouldn't even give it half a percent. Violet, though, that could give it a good charge. If Naoma is still burning her cosmetic light, I think I can locate her."

"Why would she still use it? Any glowbones would go right after her."

"Yeah, but she doesn't have the evolved night sight that our Bites give us. It's a risk, but I bet she is still using it to see her surroundings. Even with the red, you're pretty much blind out here."

"You're zegging lucky. It might work."

I nodded and turned on every signal-searching program alongside every mind-capture camera and recording tool I had in my system. I lost a percent after five minutes.

Ten more minutes passed. I received a notification.

Warning: system entering low-power mode. Certain functions may be restricted. Please insert charge soon. Would you like to search for light?

Please select: Yes or no.

I tapped yes.

Searching.

Searching.

Searching.

Low light sources detected nearby. Red light will not produce a sufficient charge. Expand search for higher light?

Please select: Yes or no.

Yes.

Searching.

Searching.

Searching.

Violet light source detected. Small source - inserted charge would increase current charge by eighty percent.

Small source, my ass. Zeg, if a strip of light from her jacket or from her light paint could complete a system charge, how different was the technology in their District that ran solely on violet?

Would you like this source added to your personal map?

Yes! Yes! Yes! Just do it already!

Please select: Yes or no.

Yes.

Please wait.

If we survived this, maybe I could use saving Naoma as a way of coaxing her into buying me an upgraded system. It grew slower by the day. Such an expense for her would be petty lumens.

Coordinates added.

"Got it."

"Send it over!"

"Sorry, I can't even do that. We're lucky they didn't block this."

"She better help us remove the blocks then if we are going to waste so much time saving her."

I doubt she'll see it as that. Maybe she had encountered enough glowbones by now to know that running into the center of the red wasn't the wisest decision. Light above, please let her still be alive. Even if she was a poor resource, she still had to have a working neurosystem. That much would be enough. I held this belief, knowing that if it proved false, we would have no other solution.

I waved for him to follow and ran back to where we had come.

"Hey!" he shouted. "Slow down or I'm going to have to eat her teeth!"

The kid's appetite had almost doomed us before. If he couldn't graduate from his infantile need to feed every minute, he would be more of an obstacle than an asset.

We slowed down as we ran into an alley as wide as my outstretched arms. The coordinates had led us two blocks to the west and back a few streets, but we hadn't been too far off before.

"Is she here?" Boyband's feet stomped as he came to a stop.

"The coordinates say so, but she could still be a street over. Do you see any light?"

"Only the same red dread."

I pushed aside empty trash cans and other remnants of a destroyed society. Black hid under black.

"Zeg."

I turned back to see if Boyband had whispered the curse, but he just scowled at me.

My attention shot back in front of us as a piece of blackened rubble broke as it hit the asphalt.

We both looked up. Naoma's violet eyeliner still glowed as she looked at me from the rooftop.

She moved back from the corner and I climbed up the fire escape like an adrenaline-fueled ape.

She had moved to the other side of the roof as I reached the top. Her eyes checked the ground below too many times for me to trust her.

"We're not going to hurt you." Zeg, even that makes me cringe. "Please, Naoma. You helped us, I want to help–"

"You zegging freaks! Get away from me!" She stepped atop the edge of the roof.

She wouldn't believe anything sappy, even though I actually wanted to reward her kindness. Forced kindness. It didn't matter. She saved us.

"Why would we hurt you if you're our only way out of here?"

She stepped down but still held close to the roof.

"There we go. I'm going to step closer to you. If you try to move back, I will reach you before you can jump."

She moved back, defying all logic.

Zeg me, girl. I kept quiet, praying that Boyband didn't hear my next words. I needed to win her with something other than intimidation, so I tried something antithetical to my personality.

"I'm a huge fan. I think I would die if you stopped making your music."

"Ew, I mean–"

I wanted to jump off the edge myself. I was an awkward person by nature, but my conversations rarely went this poorly. There was a reason Ralia did most of the talking on assignments.

"I'm sorry. Just–just please." I checked back, but Boyband hadn't reached the roof yet. "Help us out of here and we'll leave you alone."

She brushed her ruffled hair behind her ears. Only a few of her fingernails still glowed.

I stepped forward. "Remember the room with your boss and Bank? You told us not to forget."

"And you haven't."

"Right! We're here to follow through on... whatever that was."

She sat with her back against the short wall on the edge of the building.

I took a step forward.

"Stop and sit. I hear your friend coming up, too. Keep him down there and keep your distance. If you want to talk, we'll talk, but it's going to be under my demands."

I put my palms out to her in surrender, nodding as I sat.

"Tell you friend to back down."

"He won't hurt you either."

"Don't care."

"Boyband, wait down there."

"Okay." He grunted and mumbled as he climbed down.

"What kind of a name is Boyband?"

"Maybe I'll tell you later."

She scowled. "If I get close to him, I don't want him to make me do anything. I can feel when he uses that modded voice. I don't care how it works, but you don't need it anymore. Anton doesn't control me anymore."

"Thank you?"

"What?"

"You can thank us for breaking the control."

"Piss off."

I chuckled. Warmth filled my chest as she smiled. "So he was controlling you?"

"What tipped you off?"

"You were curt, condescending, ignorant of our suffering–"

"All the attributes of a celebrated idol? Yeah, I hated it."

"But you reached out in humility after the kid spoke to you. You were... I don't know if vulnerable is the right word."

"It is. If you were forced by a neurovirus to act with the diva attitude of *'the Neon Idol,'* you would also reach out in vulnerability if someone had given you a glImpse of your true self again. Zeg, it's like I was a spectator to some pompous slut. All I could do was watch her crude behavior as she acted on Anton's every whim. If it means anything, I'm sorry I acted like a jerk of a shac."

"I know how it feels."

"Really? Is that your excuse for killing everyone down there? Yeah, let's talk about that. I saw the kid do something and have reason to believe you would do the same. Why would that bowl-cut freak *eat* the Techvax reps? Sure, they were being dicks, not to mention the Finians, but why in the good light would he, you, *eat* your captors?"

"You can't make me hate myself more than I already do."

"Is that an excuse?"

"No, just a statement. Your people use you for what, propaganda?"

"Propaganda, advertising, it's all the same today, isn't it? They controlled me with a virus while my inner self watched it all. My songs, talent, all programmed. Dress me up nice and hide controlling messages on my chart topping music. I'm better than the best shacs or billboards out there. Sorry to ruin your love for me, 'number one fan,' but I'm just Reef's product and property of their countless clients."

"I knew you were fake already."

"I can see that smirk. You're still disappointed. Still, don't think that your admiration hides what happened back there."

"Rather than being programmed for propaganda like you were, we were forced to complete assignments for another medical company. Seems that everyone is in the race for power these days."

"Political small talk is almost as bad as talking about the weather."

I chuckled. "So you want a meaningful conversation?"

Her smile dropped. "I want to know why you eat people. I don't care if you're paid or programmed assassins."

"Give me a moment while I repeat myself, but everyone is in the race for power. What is power in a world where tech implants turn your bones to dust? Medicine. Treatment. We work for someone who created a "cure" that he forced into us. It's an implant that heals the bones, but requires continual nourishment of pure, human-derived calcium. Why not gallons of milk or supplements? I don't know."

"So you eat the bones?"

"Teeth."

"You're like zegging vampires."

"If we needed iron instead of calcium, I suppose we would be."

She looked away, lips quivering with nausea.

"I told you, I hate it. Whatever your owner did to you was worse because it was his choice."

"That doesn't mean I liked him."

"But you worked with him."

"I had no choice."

"Now you do."

"You want me to help you?"

"We'll get out the Red. Help us out of our ownership and we'll help you out of yours. We both have a start. We're off the grid and we killed your owner."

"But that's just one piece of the Conglomerate."

"Like I said, a start."

"I have no reason to trust you."

"We broke you out of your trance the first time. Coming from similar circumstances–"

"I don't think they're that similar."

"Coming from similar circumstances, we both know what it would mean to have freedom."

"Who says I don't want to return to the Violet heights? I had everything I could ever want."

"Under a simple *proprietorship*, right? Don't you want to be *a real girl*?"

"Zeg off." She swatted her hand and chuckled. She looked at their dimming nails and sighed. "I'll follow you out of here. We'll see what happens next."

She started to stand.

I did so as well. "So you trust me?"

She stepped back. "Are you saying I shouldn't? I don't even know your name."

"It's Petya, but no. By all means I want to give everything so that you *will* trust me, but–"

"Tone down the obsession."

"Sorry, I don't mean that. I just–we just need your help if we are going to change anything."

"Change? An 'ask later' kind of thing, right?"

"Exactly."

"I am never quick to trust and would not say that I 'trust' you, but you are my most likely way out of here. A few glowbones on the way here almost took me out."

"I could have warned you about them."

"But you didn't. You weren't here, were you? You were too busy killing the rest of Techvax and the Finians."

I stared at her and shrugged. "I already told you why we did everything."

She sighed and started towards me. "Just keep the kid in check."

His appetite control isn't well developed. I held that back. "I'm his superior. He'll do what I say."

"Take out the Neon Idol and you'll have the whole world after you."

She stopped a foot in front of me. Even with messy hair and clothes torn by the sharp boney fingers of the glowbones, she represented beauty perfected. Even with the purple glow paint that had gone dull and worn off of her lips, they were real. If she had any beauty augmentations done to her skin, I couldn't see them. Raw, natural beauty, with only fashionable additions such as her violet eyes that bit me with the temptation of Eden's viper.

"What if I take her away from the world and give her her own life?"

"We'll see what our future holds."

I smiled. It felt like the first hopeful one I had shown in months. Even years.

Boyband and I kept her between us as we ran from the center of the Red District. Now that we had to wait for her, he saw how painful it was to slow your pace in the grave of a once-great city.

Kicking aside the glowbones that came close enough for contact was as easy as swatting a fly after a proper feast of teeth. We slowed ahead of Naoma as we reached the skyshuttles. I wanted to clear away the bodies, but there was no use in blinding her from the truth. If she remained with us for a few days, she would see the feeding repeated.

"I'm surprised you kept up with us for so long." Boyband winked at Naoma. "I mean, even if we were holding back."

Her queasy state diverted from the scattered bodies as she looked at him. "Check your ego, kid. I might not have whatever you do, but Reef kept me in peak shape. Running beside anyone else, I wouldn't have a problem."

"Okay, wait, 'kid'? I'm nineteen."

"Making me a decade older than you. Keep that winking to yourself."

"I–you–gah! Just because you're famous for being beautiful, because your music is corporate hypnotic trash, doesn't mean a bit of kindness means that I'm in love with you. Petya, now. He's only a year younger than you now that's what I call perfect–"

"Where's the third?" I said without a hint of our distracting playfulness.

"Huh?"

"The skyshuttles?" Naoma asked.

I nodded. "There were three before, right?"

"So you didn't kill them all?"

I couldn't tell if she spoke with ridicule or relief. Only two shuttles remained, each without lights turned on. The bodies lied undisturbed.

I ran my hand through my hair, scratching my scalp with an intensity to distract me with pain rather than worry. I looked at Boyband. "Did you check the skyshuttles?"

He shook his head. "You?"

"Well, I thought I did, but just the back. I must've missed the driver's seat."

"What does that mean?" Childlike worry had returned to his voice.

"A Techvax employee knows what we are."

"But Reef captured and used us, right? Maybe Techvax has no idea that you did the Firstlight job. Maybe it's someone dumb enough to think that we are property of Reef or whoever owns them."

"Techvax does."

He looked at Naoma. "Does Techvax own Reef?"

"They're investors. No one really *owns* Reef. Anton lent our resources out to the highest player who wanted to run their propaganda. Wait... I guess the Finians technically own Reef."

Boyband shook his head with a furrowed brow, his mouth opened so that his front teeth stuck out. "But the Finians are a race, not a political party."

Naoma chuckled, not with playful humor, but in a polite mocking.

"You disagree?"

"Even if they aren't a Party, they all want the same thing."

Boyband looked even more idiotic with his front teeth hanging out in confusion.

She sighed. "Light and human body parts. Not everyone is as wealthy as Jackson. Even if you are a wealthy Finian, it doesn't mean you'll have access to appendages."

Boyband grimaced.

"And what you two do is better? They just want a body."

"Then why not just use the cybernetic appendages humans do?"

"Nature seeks nature. Call the transplants unnatural, but even if they require tech implants to work, they like real flesh more than metal."

Boyband shook his head and waved off the lost argument. "Do you think they'll connect us to Deleon somehow, Petya?"

"Not sure. Regardless, he'll find out."

"Is that your boss?"

"Yes."

"Then why isn't he monitoring you–right, the neuroblock."

"Yes, but his blindness is better for us now."

"So we *are* going rogue?" Boyband asked.

"You *did* say you would help me escape," Naoma said.

I wiped my face to ensure they knew how tired I was. Zeg, I needed a socitab. I needed the false reassurance that someone was caring for me, holding me up rather than the opposite.

"You will, right?"

Her violet eyes grasped me again, forcing me to lie just to see her smile. She gave it to me. That was enough. I set the thoughts of using a socitab aside and returned her smile. "Yes."

"Then let's do it. Where are we going?"

I looked at Boyband. "Deleon will expect us to be dead or still working with the Entertainment Party. Regardless, there is a chance he will find us."

"Why?"

"We have to go to your place, among the SocStans.""So exactly where he wanted us to go?"

"Yes. If he finds us, I want it to be set up under our conditions."

"You want to trap him?"

"No, I just want to make sure we have the support we need."

"You think my people, my parents' people, are going to be *that* willing to help us?"

"If we solve your parents' murder."

Boyband scowled.

"Who else would kill them? Isn't it obvious that Deleon did it? He must have wanted you for some reason. We'll enter the Indigo District, gain the SocStan support so when we *let* Deleon learn where we are, we'll have the support we need to eliminate him."

"You really think he did it? If he did, why would he send us to them?"

"Are you compliant?"

"What?"

"A trigger phrase for control. The neuroblocks have separated us from his control. If we tried to rebel while in the district, he could manipulate our neurospaces into seeing the SocStans as our enemies."

"Sounds convoluted."

"I know, I mean, I *don't* know everything, but I am sure that we have to go there."

Naoma stared with confusion.

"I'm sorry. Zeg, I'm a mess. I–we just want to get out of here."

We turned to look at the skyshuttles.

"Someone will know what happened here," I said. "We just need to move things along before the consequences of our feedings follow. We'll figure the rest out later."

Naoma started towards the skyshuttles. We followed and moved in close behind her as she opened the door.

"Do you know how to drive it?" I asked.

She leaned in, tapped on the control interface. "Whoever drove it left the control key in here somewhere.""But can you drive it?" Boyband asked.

"I had my musical talent downloaded. Set aside all the controversy with skill downloading, but I *can* download the driving skill set. The connection here is pretty terrible, but it should work. It's a simple enough skill that shouldn't invite any other problems."

"Do it," I said. And walked around to enter through the door on the other side. Boyband followed. Naoma sat in the driver's seat. Her eyes flashed with the lights of the neurospace.

"Any luck?" Boyband asked.

She continued to stare without a response.

"Naoma?" he asked.

I leaned over to look at her. "Skill downloading must require the entire mind."

"You ever tried?" Boyband asked.

"No. I was never wealthy enough to bypass the laws to do so and wasn't willing to risk my neurospace system on it. It's kind of funny, isn't it? How we still care–at least I do–about laws and morality after all that we...you know..." I sat back in my seat and looked up, leaning my head on the inflexible headrest. "You holding up?"

"Despite all the guk we're going through, I'm feeling pretty decent. I haven't felt well-fed since I gained the Bite, and I'm heading home."

I rolled my head over to look at him.

"No, no," he said. "I mean–I get that nothing will be the same. We're going there, but I'm not *really* returning. Still, it doesn't mean I have to be so down, right? You said we're going to prove that Deleon killed my parents. That's our way out! Sure, anyone associated with him will hate us, and the Finians if we can get her out of their grasp, but I am *sure* we can have the SocStans on our side."

The plan was a perfect work of fiction. That did not stop me from giving it my all, but it was still a fallacy that I couldn't count on. I had not fed Boyband and Naoma lies to trick them into compliance. I had lied to them as much as I did to myself. My deception would come at the price of friendship and any remnants of self-respect that I retained. If all else failed as I assumed, perhaps the plan would succeed enough for them to escape. Naoma was sure to have supporters elsewhere to help her find freedom. If Boyband found support in his parents' allies, I could give myself as a scapegoat for Deleon's rage.

I opened my files for a socitab. Boyband averted my addiction once again.

"You're quiet again. Zeg, you really *do* need Naoma. The music was enough, but now she's going to make everything worse when she leaves us."

"What?" Before scowling at him, I made sure that Naoma was still occupied. She failed to react to Boyband's comment and her eyes continued to flash.

"I might have been out of sight, but I listened to the conversation you had with her on the roof. You were happy. Alive. Not the melodramatic 'uh, my life sucks, give me my depressing synths,' guy."

I chuckled and elbowed him.

Boyband leaned forward to look at her, then rested back against his seat. "You two would go well together."

"Anyone would look good with Naoma. We don't even know each other. We've had one actual conversation outside of her controlled mindset."

"Then change that."

"You're holding up though?"

"I said I was. Let's keep it that way."

Naoma grabbed the steering wheel, then revved the engine. "Where to?"

"How well do you know the Indigo District?" Boyband asked.

"I've toured around it plenty but never drove there myself. Do you have an address?"

"Saved into my neurospace, but I can't send it over. Just look up Eclaine D&A. Our farm isn't far from the distribution center."

"Found it." The skyshuttle balanced as it rose into the air.

"How far away is it?" I asked.

"Four hours. Think you can handle that?"

"Yeah."

"We should arrive just before sundown."

Boyband chuckled. "Zeg this smog really throws things off."

"It doesn't help being drugged and awakened by captors," I added.

Boyband tapped the entertainment panel and groaned.

"What now?" Naoma asked, her eyes now fixed on the holographic course cast before her.

"Can we use your music library? Zegging neuroblock won't allow me to connect to it."

"Sure thing." She tapped her temple. A second later, an array of music appeared on the panel. Chart-toppers rotated through the top of the screen, mood-based playlists rotated below, and Naoma's personal playlists were listed on the right side of the screen.

Boyband spoke with a nasal mocking. "Don't miss the Neon Idol's new single! Stream *Let's Eat* by Naoma now!"

"Try it and we're sitting in silence," she said.

Boyband held his hands up to defend himself. Her attention remained on the course.

"Let's check out the playlists, then. Maybe your taste in music is better than Petya's."

She cracked a smile.

Boyband scrolled through her playlists. "*Girl power*, typical, *sad*, I bet Petya would like that one, *cute*, he'd like that one even more, *classical, pop inspo, Anton's recs, sabbath*, I didn't take you for the religious type."

"Wow, isn't that weird? There is more to me than neon fashion and catchy lyrics."

Boyband continued to read. "*Mood, Reef–*"

"Do that one. It's got some good crowd pleasers."

"So not Petya's type."

"Are you as pretentious as he says you are, Petya?"

"If the band has more than five listeners, I'm out." We both laughed. "No. I like a lot of Reef's stuff, but I guess I might see their stuff differently now. Is that what is on that playlist?"

"Yup. Anything Anton has produced. I added most of my colleagues' discography, but you won't find a single song of mine."

"Do you get along with them?" Boyband asked. "Did you?"

"Anton's Naoma did."

"What does Naoma's Naoma like?" I asked.

"We've got a long ride. Plenty of time to tell stories. Why don't we start with you, *Boyband.* Tell me how you got that name?"

"The first day I met Petya. I was instantly bothered by his skunk hair."

I couldn't ignore the clock. I enjoyed the ride, but struggled to do so, knowing that we would be thrown back at the mercy of the world when we landed in the Indigo District. The world had been cruel, and I had no hope in its kindness.

An hour had passed since we told Naoma how we had come to meet her. The story itself was straightforward, but we got caught on a tangent trying to explain what we were even doing for Deleon.

"So your boss wants to reach the presidency by destroying Techvax and the associated competitors?" she asked.

"Something like that," I said. "He sent us out to weaken certain pillars of society, but he seemed most interested in eliminating anyone who wanted to use jelly fiends. When we told him what we found at Firstlight, he kind of freaked out and sent everything to eliminate them. He's obsessive and impulsive, but I had never seen him so concerned. I assume he knew what we would find and that we were just sent to confirm his suspicions."

"He's confusing like that," said Boyband.

"More like illogical," said Naoma. "I don't see what jelly fiends have to do with the presidency."

I shrugged. "Maybe they are the key to the cure. If someone is on the same course as he is, he's set on eliminating them."

"And why did he want to send you to the SocStans?"

"He needed every connection to Firstlight out of the way," I said, "even if only some of the parties have connections. We'll see if we can find anything. Even if we are not complaining about his assignment, it might be good to know what he is thinking."

She looked at Boyband. "But solving your parents' murder is our main goal, right?"

"I hope so."

"Yes," I said. "Everything we deal with seems to be connected somehow, but I want to set Deleon aside for some time *if* we can. He's always manipulating us, so maybe we'll discover that he didn't actually kill the Eclaines and that their deaths are connected to jelly fiend research. I don't know. I don't know how big his company actually is. Maybe they are just a piece in a larger puzzle like Reef or Firstlight."

"What about his promise, Petya?"

"What promise?" Naoma asked.

"Petya is loyal to him because Deleon made him a promise."

"I thought you said you just needed money after losing everything?" she asked.

"Yeah, I did, but..."

"He always avoids talking about his past. He was some celebrity or politician, something like that, but will never tell me about what *really* motivates him."

"Then why don't we talk about your past, Boyband?" she grinned.

"You will soon enough. We're *literally* flying to my family farm."

"Fair enough." She looked at me, eyebrows slightly raised to compliment her pitying smile.

"Oh, come on," I said.

"Only if you want to." She faced ahead.

"I only avoid talking about it because it pains me. It sounds stupid, I know. I like the Republic, despite what I've experienced. It's corrupted and imperfect, but better than Medislavia. Aside from the feral consumerism, I appreciate the values that formed the Republic. I mean—just don't take what I see as hate speech. People complain about inequality, the economy, sure there are plenty of problems with the Republic, but the immigration system is atrocious. The Republic used to be a sanctuary for freedom and—zeg—'living out your dreams,' but it's gone against all of that. Deleon promised me to help change that, but to see what I mean, I'll have to tell you the rest of how I came here."

Boyband looked down to hide his grin.

I recounted everything I had told Boyband about my political motives and social ascendancy. While Naoma and I were both known by most in our respective countries, the politics she campaigned for in her lyrics were more accepted than my anti-Medislavian proclamations.

"Medislavian control assassinated one of my close friends—a once mentor—and passed it off as an ignominious suicide in prison. I had no choice but to flee the country of my birth."

"So you did?" Boyband asked.

I stared at him.

"Sorry, just trying to stay engaged."

"Are you involved in politics, Naoma? I mean, of course you are, but are you familiar with the intricacies of the Arabasia war?"

"No, and don't overestimate my political involvement. Most of who or what I was, was a construct of Reef Record's purposes."

"I'd like to get to know your *true* stance on matters."

"Now is the time for your story, not mine."

"Right. Well, suffice it to say that the Arabasians are victims, any Medislavian motive other than control or greed is a lie, and so forth. I left my country and found refuge in South America, just beyond the Republic's border. "Knowing that illegal immigration is still a politically charged topic, I made sure to do my research before hoping to walk across the border. I was given a date to cross the border and had the next few years planned out. Plenty of Arabasians had done this process, and I figured we were both refugees from my country's regime. Why not follow their path? I crossed the border, spent a year in 'detainment,' i.e. a prison, and was left to fend on my own in the Republic. When I left my country, I had a year's worth of salary, plenty of valuables to trade for necessities upon arrival, and a whole backpack of sentimental possessions. When I left the detainment center, I had an out-of-date neurospace that had been deactivated upon crossing the border, a pair of worn sandals, and my tattered jumpsuit. They confiscated everything else, though I am sure the guards never reported finding them as they left their job with months of stolen lumens in their neurospace bank."

"Petya," Naoma began, "I'm—I don't know what to say."

"Sure, everyone praises the refuge and freedom the Republic offers, but it conveniently forgets those with similar circumstances as mine. I've met plenty of other Medislavian refugees along the way. The Republic Immigration Control System, RICS, had no problem separating couples, families. I saw them take everyone who spoke sign language away from a deaf refugee. How the zeg is that just?"

"Zeg, man," Boyband muttered.

"They woke us up at four in the morning to feed us, then didn't give us anything until sundown. I have always been slim, but I lost thirty pounds within my first few weeks. You'll find this funny, Naoma, based on our particular 'diet'." I tapped my teeth. "I used to be a vegetarian. A real health nut, but they would only feed us hyper-processed garbage that even the worst eaters in the Republic would refuse. I'm not talking about the living meat logs they created to generate quick cuts, I mean rats, organ sausages, and printed meat, if we were lucky. I don't think I saw anything green on my plate the whole time. Sure, I get it, we were never living in luxury, but they couldn't even bother with printing produce or giving us cheap replications of what one would consider a plant. They gave us plenty of printed bread, though. Cheap and filling, even though cardboard would have been better on the stomach." I chuckled. "I was so constipated that by the time I left and had my first *real* meal, I think I shat out another ten pounds."

They laughed, but they were reserved.

"Look, I could complain for hours. Time has passed and I've learned to move on, but that doesn't mean I forgot. What did Deleon promise me? Change. Zeg me if I was too naïve to believe him, but I think he would actually do something for me if I helped him reach the presidency."

Naoma chuckled.

I remained stern. "I get it. It *is* laughable. Zeg, everyone wants to be the next Haven Health, but Deleon is the only one who has *actually* cured techbone."

"What do you mean?" she asked.

"That's what we are. We joined, or at least I did, for medical testing with a high payout. I was too desperate, starving, and zegged up on socitabs to even think he might *give* me techbone. What else would anyone worry about curing? Cancer was cured decades ago and Alzheimer's is a distant memory." I would have laughed, but no one seemed to get the joke. I couldn't blame them. I was in the middle of a rage-fueled rant.

"We joined, he gave us the virus, or whatever it is, and then stopped it with our hypothalamic implants." I tapped the base of my neck. "Our 'Bites' as we call them, keep the bones continually growing beyond techbone's disintegration, but of course, we have to feed them.

"Deleon would never use this technology on the public, but if he can make something close enough to a cure, I think he might be the one that can actually do it. Techvax's vaccine didn't prove flawless. If Deleon wants to wipe them out and anyone else using the fiends, I think he might pull it off. If he does, and if I'm loyal, then he can help refugees avoid the mistreatment I faced. A corrupt side of me tells me that all the killing I do is worth it if I can change the Republic in just one way for the better."

"So, do you want to help him?" Naoma asked.

"Zeg, I don't know. Either I stay a prisoner, or he does when we expose him. Maybe I was too naïve to think he could do anything."

"I'll keep his promise," Boyband said.

"You? How?" I asked.

"The SocStan Party may not be the current president, but they still have plenty of power from the last two terms. Zeg Deleon. Let's prove that he killed my parents and I can guarantee the rest of the SocStan Party will side with us in the name of justice for the Eclaines."

"It's a nice thought, kid, but–"

"Shut the zeg up. And don't 'kid' me. We are going to do this, just like you said. This was *your* idea. Now, let's follow through with it. I get it if you doubted yourself and if you still do, but I want more than revenge. I want freedom and I can't have that with Deleon breathing down my back."

I smirked and nodded. "We'll see what your people have to offer."

"It'll be tough, but just because I was the only survivor, does not mean I don't have any connections."

He pointed at Naoma. "And what about her?"

"What *about* me?"

"How in the light are we going to hide the biggest pop idol in the Republic? Farmland isn't what it was in the old mindshows set in the twenty-first century. It will look rural, but it is just as connected to the world as everything else."

Naoma tapped her temple. The violet glowpaint on her eyelids and nails disappeared. Her hair was the same length, but of a dark brown shade with small light streaks. She no longer looked like she was of Asian descent but was a pale white like me.

"This won't be the first time I have to blend in," she said and tapped her temple, returning to her former fashion. "I figure we'll all want a change of clothes after the Red District, anyway."

"That will work for a bit," said Boyband, "but the whole world will know you are missing."

"Then let's take care of everything so I can make a reappearance."

"Take care of what?" I asked.

"Gain the SocStan support and eliminate the zeg outta Reef Records, Techvax, and anyone else who wants to enslave me again."

Chapter Thirteen
Better Beef

Boyband shook me awake as we descended. I awoke to orange sunlight cast across fields of yellow and green grain.

Multistoried barns stood close to each other like rustic skyscrapers. Switchback conveyor belts moved to shuttle crates up through multiple doors that had the outward appearance of red wood, though I knew it was just an imitation.

"Is that it?" Naoma pointed to the holomap on the dashboard.

"Yup. My parents' farm is just north, just past the distribution center and outlets. You'll see plenty of blue barns in a line with a field on one side and a lake on the other."

"Got it."

"Park to the right of the third one."

She did as she was told, landing on a concrete pad before large glass doors. The Eclaine farm looked more like a village with a row of buildings to complement the description. While most of them still held the visage of farmhouses, the square structure and modern build of the one in front of us told that it was the office building.

Boyband led us to the doors. Naoma walked with eyes straight ahead. I couldn't help but marvel at the backs of grazing animals hidden amongst tall grass. Bubbles and occasional jumping fish filled the lake. Could these be *living* animals? They were bound to have some. While I knew they had plenty of estate, this much could be only purchased by moguls of *true* animal products. I wondered what actual milk tasted like. Did real cheese *actually* grow mold?

My knowledge of how the SocStan party worked was limited to rumors and Deleon's ramblings. He, like many who invested in an ever expensive secondary education, hated that the once-poor jobs now thrived. Any excuse to validate his elite education found ground in complaining. When the world saw construction work, farming, and other trade positions as secondary, society broke at its seams. A new generation pursued those undesirable jobs, making the world realize how essential they had become, and turned it for a profit as one of the leading political parties. Androids and AI dominating positions in the tech industry only helped to prove the worth of the SocStan plight.

The doors opened automatically. A man in an indigo suit sat on a swiveling chair in the middle of a circular desk with multiple floating security panels showing movement around the farm campus.

"Devóne?" He dropped a tablet onto the desk as he stood. He had a dark complexion and was bald with a vision implant like Tevon's, except the silver band on his curled around the circumference of his head.

Boyband chuckled. "Thought you'd never see this face again, did you, Lorren?"

Lorren shook his head and stepped out through the hole in the desk's circle. "But–but–your parents. We thought you–"

"I'm not."

Lorren scowled and looked up at Naoma and me. "Were you with them the whole time?" His voice switched between humble confusion and a stern tone to match his security guard composure.

"Does it matter?"

"Of course, sir. Sorry sir."

"Have any of the other families been asking about me?"

"No, why–"

"Who owns the estate now?"

"Your father's sister is currently in a legal battle over that matter. It began days after you...left."

"Battle between what people?"

"The surrounding farms have all appointed their legal representatives to turn the land over for a public auction. They believe that such a crucial part of the republic's agriculture cannot fall into inexperienced hands. Your aunt wants it to stay with the family. No one has found a will. That remains yet another tenant of controversy."

"Has anyone said anything about who murdered them?"

Lorren shrugged. "With the drama following the event, one finds it hard to believe that this was a natural disaster, but there is little known."

"How much of the farm burnt down?"

"Only a few buildings on the western side. Your home remains standing."

"Which buildings did we lose?"

"Two warehouses and your parent's office"

"Hmm."

"Do you think that office had anything to do with the murder?" Naoma asked. I was relieved she remembered to adopt her disguise.

Boyband shrugged. "We'll talk about that later." He looked back at Lorren. "Send a few members of the tech team to the mansion. I have a neurospace issue that needs fixing."

"Of course, sir, but–where in the name of the light have you been?"

Boyband scowled. "Away." He turned back and waved for us to follow. He spared Lorren one last glance. "I'll send you a message when my neurospace is back online. I want you to send me everything you have on my parent's death investigation, the legal battles, anything a *curious little boy* like me would want to know."

"Of course, Master Eclaine."

"Don't worry, Lorren," he said as we walked through the doors. "The legal complications will pass on as soon as they know an heir to the Eclaine empire has survived."

"Zeg, look who's in power now," I chuckled.

"Where are we going, Devóne?"

"Stick with Boyband. We're going back to my home. I'm going to find out who zegging killed my parents."

"Hey," I put my hand on his shoulder.

He glared at me, then relaxed as he remembered that I wasn't one of his parents' servants.

"Let's get some sleep."

"Piss off."

"I would like that," Naoma said.

"My piss?"

She rolled her eyes at Boyband. "I don't care what implants or mods you have. My body needs rest."

"But we don't, right Petya?"

"You *especially* need it. The Bite will let you stay awake perpetually with proper feeding, but the mind can't handle it. Life demands order. Zeg it up and you zeg yourself. Regardless, I want to lie low for at least the rest of the day. I need some time to make sure we aren't being followed and to cover our trails. Our minds need to be refreshed for what is coming. Get us back on the neurospace network with those tech assistants and I'll get an update from Ralia. Is your place safe?"

"We got all we zeggin' need. Might not have all the violet powered defense that *Miss Neon Idol* had her whole life, but we have plenty of sentries, automatons, automatic turrets, you name it. We'll kill any shac that tries to touch our cattle, or us in this circumstance."

Naoma opened her mouth with a furrowed brow but let her frustration puff away with a sigh. Was her past so simple? Had Reef taken her as a talented singer or did they *make* her into one? She was human, wasn't she? I felt sick even considering that she could be a shac. She could be transmitting everything we say. Maybe we didn't break her free from her shell but only disabled a program. I dug my fingernail into my pointer finger until it hurt. I had to think about something else.

"Are your cows real?" My voice came off forced and awkward, but they seemed to not think anything of it.

Boyband smirked. "Oh, you poor boy. Have you ever had non-printed beef?"

I shook my head.

"Zeg the farm. It's mine anyway. I'll give you a look and I'll have one of my parent's chefs make something for us. They have to be here still feeding the remaining workers. See the farm, eat, then we'll call it a night while we figure out the bugs with our neurosystems."

My tongue flooded with curiosity and hunger.

I couldn't fathom what it would taste like without the bitter sting of chemicals and the inherent burnt plastic aftertaste. I stopped before asking about trying some of his produce, if they had any fresh crops to spare. The cocky kid would be sure to share some if he had it, but I couldn't spoil my palette. Food was enjoyable, but more of a distraction when compared to the necessity of teeth. How long could the kid keep us here before he ate one of his family's servants?

"We'll have to keep moving," I said. "At least until we've settled matters with Techvax and whoever is with them."

"How do you hope this will end?"

We turned to Naoma. Real beef no longer occupied my mind.

"I want to come back here," Boyband said. "Get the zeg out of Deleon's cult and remove the Bite."

"And if they can't remove it?" she asked.

"Pfft, I'll find another way."

"You, Petya? Where do you see yourself? You can't keep running."

From what? Where? What about you? If I ran away from the grasp of society, would you run with me? "Boyband said the SocStans will help fulfill Deleon's promise. That is enough for me to think about. There never is an end until we join with the light, right? What about you?"

She smirked. I couldn't find sincere joy in her face.

"Back to music?"

"The world needs its Naoma," Boyband said.

She looked at the ground. "I'm sure I'll figure it out."

Boyband spoke after a moment of silence without eye contact. "Follow me. I'll show you around. It's about a quarter-mile walk to my place. My parents like being close to everything, but far enough to leave the business behind if needed."

"Your dad's office was here though, right?" I asked.

"With the other business buildings? Yes. Maybe we'll see what's left of it, unless they've already removed the damaged property. I doubt it. It sounds like a mess here. At least we've got plenty of ands on staff."

"Was Lorren an android?" I asked. Part of me hoped he was with how demeaning Boyband had been with him.

"No. He's one of the few humans. The personal chefs are human and a few others that require an artist's touch."

"Glad to hear your parents don't endorse algorithms as art," Naoma said.

"And-made food is always the same. The chefs here always surprise me. I get that you're not an AI-art supporter, but isn't your music based on corporate algorithms?"

"Why do you think I hate it so much? That's Anton's Music, Reef's music. Funny enough, the other artists he produces are all true talent, as far as I know. I guess I'm the only one of his that is owned by an outside company."

"Keep AI where it belongs," Boyband said, "in medical accuracy, bureaucratic functionalities, you know the rest. I do have to thank some AI for taking over certain of jobs. Without them, the blue collar labor of the SocStan founders never would have found worth in our modern society."

"You sound a lot more mature," I said.

"Zeg you."

I chortled. "There he is."

He waved for us to follow and walked a few feet ahead, flipping off any ands in the field as they did the menial gathering of a variety of crops that I had only seen in advertisements for restaurants that could only be found in the high end Blue District and above. Indigo light shone above the crops in a lattice of light rods.

"I'm sorry to hear how poorly you were treated as a refugee," Naoma said.

Boyband walked with his head held high, not caring to listen to us.

"Thanks."

We let the silence sit for a few moments.

"You didn't have similar experiences, did you?" I asked.

"My life before Reef is a blur."

I smirked. "I get that. It's hard to believe that I had anything before working for Deleon. It feels like a dream, too."

"No, you misunderstood. It is a *literal* blur. Knowledge, general human competence, it's all there, but the experiences are gone. You might have broken down one of Anton's walls, but some still remain. Will I pursue music when I'm out of this? Sure, I'd love to, but I don't know if I am capable of it without his programming. Even if I can sing, you can't *download* creativity like I downloaded the skyshuttle flight proficiency. You would think I was paid well, being the top selling artist for two years in a row, but Anton has no need to pay his products. The version of me he controlled didn't care about pay when everything was provided for me. Without Reef, I'm nothing."

"So you want to go back?"

"Zeg, no. I want to break down Anton's last wall to discover my past." She sniffed and looked away from me. "I want to be sure that I am human."

Her existential crisis burned what soul remained within me. I was sure she was human. She had to be. "We can test that by other means, you know?"

"I've done it before. I am human, but I mean–I need a past. I need purpose. If I have nothing but a memory of being a glorified advertisement for the Finians and their associates, I'm worse off than any and who go back to an artificial family at the end of the day."

"Belonging."

"What?"

"You want to belong."

"Sure, put it that way. I–I just don't know. I'm zegging lost, Petya. What I mean to say is that if we survive this, If you help me and Boyband live *actual* lives once again, you're better than any sin of eating teeth could ruin you. You can be–you *are* a good person. I don't care about what you have done. You ran out into the Red. Zeg me if you're some manipulative freak that gets off on this all being a cruel trick, but I doubt that. I can tell you're tormented by what you have to do."

She adopted her natural look. Her violet hair and makeup looked Indigo under the field's lights. "Don't give up on this."

Any boyish fantasy had been banished for the sake of reality. I could kiss her. I wanted to, only having known each other for a few days. She was beyond any dream imagined while listening to her music. She was not the Neon Idol, but a real person. Confused, terrified, and in search of purpose in an increasingly artificial world. Her eyes were magnets. She stepped closer. Our hands brushed.

She might have thought that I was a good person. I did not. I hoped to prove myself wrong, but knew the atrocities I would have to commit to ensure the future that she envisioned.

I grabbed my hands behind my back and walked up to pace with Boyband. Zeg, it was painfully awkward, but I was glad she came along.

"Here," Boyband stopped at the opening of a waist-high gate. He let us in first, then sped ahead after he closed the gate. A path stretched ahead, dividing two fields. The field to the left was dry and yellow with few patches of green and an abundance of floating indigo light rods. Beyond the field to the right I could see what I assumed was the Eclaine mansion. This field had no light but seemed much more cared for than the other. The lawn was green and cut to perfection. The few dead patches I could see regenerated after the cattle finished feeding.

I rushed to the fence on our right to stare at them as one moved towards me.

I laughed like a child and reached out to touch one.

"Careful, kid," Boyband said.

I looked at Naoma as she leaned on the fence to my right. "Have you ever seen them?"

She shook her head. "Just pictures, but I've had beef." She paused and cringed. "And milk... and cheese."

I chuckled. "Are you worried I'll be offended? Of course you've had some. You're from the zegging Violet District. I'm just—wow—it's surreal." I shook my head. "What kind of sad life do I have to almost cry over *real* cows?"

"And you'll taste them soon enough," Boyband said.

I looked over the field. "No indigo light for them?"

"Just like you said, we want them all natural. It requires a lot more care, but the sell value makes it all worth it."

"How many do you have?"

"Thirty."

"So you distribute locally?"

"We're the second most successful cattle farmers in the Republic. We provide at least a third of it."

My face was grim as I turned away from them. "No, you can't waste one on me. I'm fine without it."

"Zeg the Republic, Pet. It's zegged us all up, you most of all. Who cares? Parts of my parents' company are destined to fall when I own it anyway."

"So you intend to *own* it?" Asked Naoma. "With all the responsibility it requires?"

"I'll be the figurehead, the inheritance child that I've always been—I don't know. I'm just learning that I have a chance at continuing my parents' company. Don't expect me to know everything. I get it. I'm impulsive and a bit cocky—shut up, Petya—but I'm trying to do my best."

"I'm sure you'll figure it out." she said. "Right, Petya?"

I mirrored her scowl. "What did I say?"

Naoma laughed and Boyband joined in.

"Now," Boyband turned to the other field, "time to show you what you've been eating whenever you buy 'beef.' The milk makers are in a warehouse."

I squinted, trying to see what I was looking at in the dying field. The indigo light was dim, making it difficult to see the creatures as the setting sun fell beyond the horizon.

Naoma gagged. "Sorry." She turned away from whatever she saw in the field and shook her head. "What in the name of the light was that?"

I gasped and jumped back as I looked at one of them squirming near the base of the fence.

"Beef2. It's a stupid name, but the things are barely alive. Pure meat with a thin trail of organs. If you've never had *real* meat, this'll satisfy you."

A brown log moved like a worm towards us. Its sweaty skin shined under the light. It looked like one of the rotisserie meat pillars I would see back at home in shawarma restaurants. They were identical except for a thin outer skin, a mouth like that of a sucker-fish, and a single bloodshot eye.

I crouched to look at it closer.

"You like it, Pet?" Boyband crouched next to me. "You can touch it if you want. Those lips look awfully kissable!"

"Piss off." I stood. "The zeg is that, Boyband?"

Naoma still hadn't brought herself to face the left field.

Boyband stood and stepped away with me. "Beef2, just like I said."

"And how many of those do you have?"

"Countless. They asexually reproduce and ninety-five percent of their body can be eaten."

"How long has this been a thing?"

"As long as we've been living. When the environment took most of the animals, we had to look for edible alternatives that are better than printed meat. I don't know all the history or science behind it, but someone bred these things for meat. They have all that they need to survive. They did the same thing with milk. The same people replicated the necessary organs for milk, put them in a machine, and now we have milk and cheese that is pretty close to the real thing."

"You're making me into a snob like you." I shook my head and smiled. "I'd be happy to have the real stuff."

"Come on, then." He waved for us to follow him back to the back road to his house.

I smiled at Naoma, but she still hung her head. I spared the left field one more glance and struggled to breathe.

Out in the dark, among the rolling meat logs, I saw the humanoid swine once again. It glared at me. Huge tusks poked out from its mouth as it took heavy breaths. As if ready to harvest, it held what looked like a massive garden rake in its right hand. It was dressed in dark fabric too ancient for any living person.

It dispersed like mist after a second.

Zeg, I needed to eat and sleep. Telling myself that these excuses were the cause of this hallucination was the only way I could maintain sanity.

Stability was fleeting, and the swine would return.

Chapter Fourteen

The Enigma that is the Human Female

The chefs arrived to prepare our food in the Eclaine mansion only a few minutes after Boyband made the demand. Soon after their arrival, the tech assistants entered without an invitation. I should have expected them to be ands, but at least their appearance was not a human-like deception like most ands.

"Sir Devóne, how may we be of assistance?" The two silver ands said in unison.

"He's up here," I said from over the second-floor balcony. He wanted to look through his old belongings, but I was much more captivated by the hypnotizing scent of cooked beef. While the main chef was a human, he had two and assistants. The servants prepared the ingredients while the master created his art.

The ands passed behind me, their metal feet clinking on the marble stairs whenever they stepped off the carpet. I pried my gaze away from the kitchen, accepting that staring at them would only make the wait feel longer, and followed the ands.

Though the Eclaines were Indigo District residents, they did not shy away from violet decorations. Violet light shined through chandeliers, in glass sculptures, and wherever else they could impress guests.

"Just can't stay away from it?" Naoma asked. She sat on a king sized bed. Boyband sat nearby at a desk. His eyes were already flashing with an array of images and lights as the tech assistants connected to the base of his skull with a thin cable.

I shrugged and sat beside her. "This is all so... above me."

"Not anymore," Boyband said. "You've helped me. Now it's time for me to treat you to a better life. And don't worry about these ands configuring my neurospace. I told them to block any location service requests so we'll be out of Deleon's view."

"But we'll still be able to send messages, right?"

"Yup. Are you almost ready? They shouldn't be too much longer."

"One minute and thirty-three seconds remaining," one of them said.

"I think so," I replied.

"What's the first step?" Naoma asked.

"Investigate the remains of my father's office and have Lorren give me any security readings relevant to the 'accident.' "

"I need to reach out to Ralia," I said.

"That other girl from your group?" Naoma asked. "I thought you were done with them?"

"She's as much a prisoner as any of us. Besides, her hacking prowess outranks Boyband's ands."

They made no reaction to my comment.

"Do you think one of the surrounding or rival farms is responsible for the destruction?" Naoma asked.

"No. Even though my parents had competition, not to mention that all of them want the property now, none of them would be so direct with their attacks. It was politically charged and I'm sure of that."

"What do you mean?" she asked.

"You'll see. My father's office was not for farm research. Petya knows what I'm talking about."

"The war? Is that what this all goes back to? I nodded.

"Ejecting," the and said.

The flashing lights in Boyband's eyes diminished as they unplugged the cord from his head.

He stood and gestured to the swiveling chair. "Your turn, sir."

I smiled and raised my eyebrows. Tremors shook my mind as they plugged in, but I grew used to it after a few moments.

"I know I'm not as involved in this as you are," Naoma said, "but if you need any higher information or connections, I would be happy to help. Might as well use anything that I have before I burn too many bridges."

"Don't worry," Boyband said. "You'll be plenty involved. We'll make you the advertisement for *our* cause."

"Piss off," she said. We all laughed.

"Thirty seconds remaining," the and said.

"Do you have access to everything?" I asked Boyband.

"Pretty much. The messaging system is up. Deleon turned to me after you never responded."

"Ejecting." A barrage of notifications filled my neurospace. It surprised me to see how few messages Deleon had sent me. He knew I was reliable. Missing too many messages had to lead him to an obvious conclusion.

I read the last message.

Deleon: I'm heading to the Red District. Word has spread about the massacre. Respond to this message if you see it

I read the message to them.

"Zeg," Boyband said under his breath. "Have either of you seen anything in the news about the disaster we left behind?"

I shook my head.

"I've been watching the net," Naoma said. "Techvax hasn't made any public statements yet, but they have a press conference set for tomorrow morning."

"Zeg." I clenched my jaw.

Naoma put her hand on my shoulder but was quick to take it off. "We've got the night to prepare."

"What exactly?" I asked.

"Make sure that you and Boyband are safe, first of all, at least for a while. Even if they expose you as the guilty party, you'll have some time before they track us down."

"Unless they have tracking systems in their skyshuttles," Boyband said.

I held my breath but released it as Naoma spoke.

"No, they used a third party. Reef and Techvax planned to edit out the Red District from their footage to preserve the confidentiality of their operation. They only needed the jelly fiends. They don't want the world to know that they went to society's trash heap for an advertisement."

"Are you sure?" Boyband asked.

"Pretty sure, even if I'm wrong, what other choices do we have?"

"You better be right, then," he said.

"We'll sleep for a few hours, then–" Boyband cut me off.

"Why not take some stim shots?"

"Because we haven't really slept in days and like I said"—the image of the swine returned to my mind—"our minds need it more than our body."

"I did things like this in high school all the time."

"But you didn't have a Bite. Have you...seen things yet?"

"A monkey."

"It's happening."

"What is?"

"No zegging idea, but I don't like it. Even if it isn't tied to sleep, we need the rest to prepare for the hell that tomorrow will bring."

"Fine, but only a few hours."

"What is it, nine right now? We'll head to your parents' office at one in the morning."

"Alright."

"Naoma, you can sleep as long as you need."

"I'm coming with you."

We shared worried smiles.

"Did Lorren send you the files on the investigation yet?" I asked.

"Yeah. They're downloading right now."

"Perfect, I–" I stopped, once again unable to breathe. A message appeared on my neurospace interface.

Got your location. I'm coming your way.

I laughed in relief as I looked closer at the message. Ralia. Ralia was coming.

Petya: When will you be here?

Ralia: Half hour past midnight.

A zegging miracle.

Petya: See you then.

I relayed the message.

"How did she get our location?" Boyband scowled. He had only met Ralia a few times. I was sure they would get along well. Her hatred for Deleon burned brighter than mine.

"Who's she?" Naoma asked.

"A friend," I said. "One we can trust. She's a tech savant. I suppose her tech mod helped her work past the location firewall. Looks like you need better ands, Boyband. She might actually be the only one of us able to pin the Elcaine murders on Deleon."

"That's perfect! We'll prove he killed my parents and work out a way to pin his name to the Red District disaster when the whole Republic finds out about it!"

It all sounded so good. For once in my life, I saw hope in the cessation to my perpetual torture, ever since I raised havoc in Medislavia. I wanted to trust that we could achieve it, but I knew that our vision was all too small. We had to be missing something. If we weren't careful enough, it would be our demise.

"What if he isn't responsible for their deaths?" Naoma. "I know you hate Deleon, but what if this really is unrelated? Maybe he just took advantage of their deaths. Maybe he heard they were going to take a hit and he wanted to benefit from the remains?"

"Nah," Boyband said.

He wanted quick justice with no questions asked. I, however, understood her skepticism. "We'll see. Regardless, I think there is something here for us."

"Why?" she asked.

I looked at Boyband. Closure. "Boyband deserves to know what happened. If they aren't connected to Deleon, I'm sure Ralia can help us alter the evidence to make it look like he is responsible. It'll fit Techvax's narrative once we show that he is responsible for the mess in the Red District."

"You have a lot of hope in framing him for your actions."

"Ralia has all the data we need to prove that he used us."

"Then why didn't she go to the law before?"

I went silent for a moment, then spoke. "They don't have anything on Boyband, as far as I know."

"Zeg you, Pet. You don't mean you're going to take the fall for this?"

"I can have the evidence altered to make it look like I kidnapped you and dragged you along."

"No," Naoma said.

Boyband grunted. "You're not–"

I raised my hands. "We'll figure it all out. All we need to guarantee is that Deleon takes the fall."

"Impulse rather than a solid plan?" Naoma asked.

I shrugged. "Deleon usually did the same thing. He claimed to have this all planned out. Unless he held back most of it, I think he had the same idea. We'll discuss this all when we wake up. I think we have a fair start."

"My parents' office right when we wake up?"

I nodded.

A cowbell rang in the hallway.

"Gotta stick to tradition," Boyband said. "Time to eat."

Even though I wasn't tired, I looked forward to the rest just as I had as a child after being fed a late home-cooked meal by my mother. She tended to stick to pre-made and printed meals but always added her personal touch with a favorite selection of spices. I wondered what real oregano tasted like but was satisfied setting it aside. The steak was more than I could ever ask for. It was tender, juicy, and flavorful to the core. I considered asking one of the tech assistants to wipe that memory by tapping into my neurospace but decided otherwise. Even though life's climaxes never repeat, it is best to hold on to the memory. Remembering the highlights of life is often the key to surviving the darkest moments.

"How do you expect to sleep with this pressure?" Naoma guffawed.

"The Bites *need* rest, just like I said. Sleep is a choice. Don't look for a button on your neurospace interface, Boyband. It's more instinctual, just like choosing to burn your abilities."

Before I could ask him if it made sense, he was fast asleep on his bed.

Naoma and I were slow to stand, even though I doubted smacking him would startle a reaction.

"I know it will be hard for you, but you should try to sleep as well."

"I'll try." She stared at me, not taking a step away.

A familiar warmth filled my body. Her violet eyes stung with something I knew I should avoid. She had the faintest smile, but it was sweeter than anything one could taste. Something whispered that she wanted me, but I knew it was a lie. No one did. I was an imp.

"Goodnight." I opened the door. We both stood there. Any intimacy had been infected with an awkward tension.

She pointed at her chest. "So am I–"

"I'll just stay with him, in case anything happens. The kid is skinny enough and his bed is big enough for three."

Her eyes hunted at fear. Not of me, but of what was coming for us beyond the Eclaine mansion's walls. "Can I stay? I know he has guards and drones, but…"

"Of course. We–you–" I looked at the floor and kicked piles of clothes aside. I moved to pick Boyband up and set him on the ground.

Like a limp doll, he made no notion of being alive except for a slow and steady breath. "I'll keep watch on him. The floor is fine for us. We don't need the comfort of a bed to rest."

"Are you sure?"

"Of course. You're the priority."

"You don't need to–"

"Please, Naoma."

She smiled. Familiar. True. Comfortable.

I hope I didn't betray her wishes by turning away. Nevertheless, I did. I laid down a few feet away from Boyband and formed a pillow out of his scattered clothes.

"Goodnight, Naoma."

"Goodnight, *Pet.*"

I turned away, unable to hide my grin, and fell into a deep sleep.

A message woke me.

Ralia: I'm outside. Let me in plz.

Petya: Coming.

Naoma pushed up from her bed as I stood. "Is it time?"

I nodded. "Don't worry about waking him up."

"Don't want me to risk waking a moody teenager?"

I smirked. "Something like that. I'll be back in a minute. Might as well let him have it to sleep."

I descended the stairwell. The scent of cooked steak still hung in the air, but the ands had retreated elsewhere to their charging ports.

Ralia jumped onto me with a suffocating embrace right after I opened the door.

Her embrace returned me to the home I thought I had lost forever. In a world of superficiality and digital connections, she was one of the few who kept me tethered to reality. Ralia made me want to give up socitabs and pursue a life in which I uplifted others as much as she did. I struggled to do so. Nevertheless, I would try.

I almost wept as I looked at her. It had been but a few days, yet my world had fallen apart. Her eyes were safety. It was not the warmth and want I felt when looking at Naoma, but a familial bond.

"You hacked my location?" I asked.

"Sure did. I've had tabs on you since you went off the grid. I got a weak signal notification when you went back online, and that was enough for me to hunt yah down." She looked up at the faint light in Boyband's room. "Is the kid still holdin' up?"

"Yeah."

"I read something funny."

"And what is that?"

"The Neon Idol missed a show in Gibson yesterday. Someone also noted that her producers were last seen with Techvax reps. It just so happens that I know what the Techvax reporters are going to say tomorrow. Babe, I've got eyes everywhere, except, I guess, for up in that room."

She leaned forward and whispered. "Is zeggin' Naoma up there?"

I nodded.

She tried to suppress a grin but hadn't the will. "Are you with her yet? You know, *with–*"

"No, of course not."

She winked. "I've seen your top played songs, baby. I know what's cookin'."

She ran past me up the stairs. "Naoma! Queen! We hafta talk girl!"

I ran up with her and stopped behind her in the doorway.

"Are you the other member of their group?" Naoma asked.

"Oh ho ho." Ralia ran to hug Naoma. "Sure am! Ralia is–" She let go and looked at Boyband on the floor and kicked him. "Is he good?"

I sent him a message marked as urgent, praying that he hadn't blocked them. I had long ago, hating the distraction of any spam messages marked as such.

"Gah!" He sat up, kicking.

"Are you with us?" I said.

He scowled and swung a leg at me. I stepped back and dodged the futile gesture with ease.

Boyband looked up at Ralia. "Oh, you're here."

She crouched and kicked his forehead, dodging a weak kick as well. "Well, that's no way to greet your sister."

"Zeg you. I barely even know you."

"Don't care, we're all family, hun."

She turned to me. She was always stalwart and had an unrelenting optimism, but I saw the faintest quivering of her smile. Her eyebrows raised after a small dip.

"What's wrong?" I asked.

"We all just got back together, Pet. Do you want to dampen the mood already?"

"What's wrong?"

His face was tight. "Tevon is missing. Rather, I've lost contact with him and his signal is blocked beyond my compatibility of tracking."

"Where did you last see him?"

"I never *saw* him, but the last reading I had of his location was *leaving* the Memoryrunner hub."

"So he succeeded? Maybe Deleon pulled his location after he finished the job there."

"I don't think so. I have Ali's reading and he's with Deleon."

"Did you try contacting Ali?"

"No answer."

"And what about Deleon?"

"After hearing about you going off the grid, I wanted to hold on to myself before running to Deleon like a lost coward. If the whole team fell, I felt it would be better for me to run away rather than face his wrath for failure."

I looked at Boyband, then at Naoma, both of which looked at me with somber faces.

"What now?" Ralia asked.

"Boyband has his parents' empire to inherit. I know it sounds like a lot, but it is a lot more realistic than taking over the presidency. Naoma was a slave for advertisement and cannot return to her former procedures. I no longer need Deleon to fulfill his promise. The SocStans might not be the current presidents, but they have sway in politics. I'm investing everything in *this* now and... well–"

"Leaving Deleon?" Ralia asked.

I nodded.

She chuckled. "I would have hoped so after seeing this guk show. The man might have a company, but to lose so much of his investments–us–on random assignments with little to no explanations? Techvax and their associates will see Osteolyte reduced to dust."

"So you're with us?"

She shrugged. "I'm not really tryna put a label on it just yet. I *do* want out before I am swept up in the debris of Deleon's and Osteolyte's collapse."

"What the zeg was he thinking? I mean, he must have expected some difficulty. Deleon's a *smart* man. I'll give that much to him, but just like you said, this is an absolute guk show of a job."

"Oh, I don't think this is him zeggin' everything up. I bet he planned for you to get captured, but not to be left alone when that happened. He has means to work beyond neuroblocks, which is why Tevon shouldn't be missing. Someone has taken advantage of his endeavor and let the worst happen when he felt ambitious. Deleon is ambitious but controlled. They took that control away and sent us in blind. I bet you we had much more information sent to us for each assignment that was lost in the neuronet when someone interfered."

"Do you think it was internal?" I sat down. "What if it was Tevon?"

"I considered it but doubt it. I think it is as simple as a rival turning against him at an opportune moment."

"Any idea who it is?"

"Techvax's higher ups. Who is that? Now that is the part that I need to find out. To figure that out, I think we need to continue our investigations to see what Deleon was after besides control." She looked at Boyband.

"The zeg do you think I know?"

"Nothing, that's obvious enough. Don't feel bad. I don't know anything either, which is why we are here to learn."

"What?" he asked.

"*Why* Deleon did your parents in. There is something that they are involved in–maybe politics, maybe more–that we need to know. The Socstans still have some power, but his power focus was more centered on the Pharma party. I'm just here to join in the investigation." I chuckled. "Is it that perfect?"

"Nah, I don't think it is a coincidence. I think Deleon's adversary has zegged everything up and has pulled the strings to land us here to figure out how to truly incriminate Deleon. Techvax will make their announcement regarding the Red District attack. To make that truly incriminating, we need to prove his motive in killing the Eclaines."

"So we are supposed to just play along?"

She shrugged. "Okay, to be fair, a lot of this is just guesswork. What I *do* know is that we have to follow through with this little mystery before Techvax hunts all of us down. Someone is taking the fall, us or Deleon, and our success with this will determine who that is. If his opponent's goal is to solidify our hatred for Deleon by uncovering his deeper desires here, I think they might get their wish."

She sat beside Boyband and pulled him into a tight hug. Boyband lifted a hand to push her away, but she slapped it and left a bright red mark. "Now, loves, we are going to do what this little baby of ours wants to figure out who did his mom and daddy in. Sound good?"

Chapter Fifteen

The Light of the Eclaine Empire

"**Y**ou good?"

Boyband scowled at me. "Of course I am. I hated that zegging place. Call me a baby, but my parents spent too much zegging time in that office, especially my dad. Maybe if they weren't so obsessed with it, they wouldn't have died in a fire."

"They would have died anyway, hun," Ralia said. "Now, let's hope there's still an elevator. Which floor was the office on?"

"The whole zegging thing is an office."

"Do you know where they spent most of their time?

"They never let me in."

"Great, well, I would guess that they died on the upper floor." She pointed to the black husk that was the top third of the tower."

"Do you think we'll find anything?" he asked.

"Were your parents paper people?"

"Pfft, no."

She kissed his forehead and he squirmed. "Then we'll find a way."

The office building was not as tall as most of the other towers, but it still towered above anything one would expect to see on a typical farm. My rough assumption was based on what I had seen in the old mindshows. They still held to the rustic wood paneling on the outer walls, but the indigo lights betrayed any aspect of rural life. Even the Eclaine mansion was as modern as anything I had seen in the Violet District.

Boyband led us forward, tearing past the caution tape. He pulled a glass door open, even though he could have walked through the shattered remains of the other.

He moved his hands across the wall, smacking it every few feet. "Hopefully the lights still work."

"Is your night sight still undeveloped?" Ralia asked.

"No—I just—you know, I was thinking about Naoma."

"Do you sense a network?" I asked Ralia.

Her eyes flashed. "Nothing really. I'll have to plug in somewhere if we can find the center."

"Just don't burn through your whole reserve," I said.

Ralia looked at Naoma, then back to me.

"Of course she knows by now."

"Just checkin', babe. I made sure to feed before landing here, though I had to pay almost half of the lumens I had for a ride here. Have you two had your fill?"

I nodded.

Boyband took a moment to think, then nodded.

I furrowed my brow. "I don't like that hesitancy."

"I'll be fine. I know how to watch my reserve."

I checked to make sure Naoma was fine, but doing so only made her shrink away. "You're safe, Naoma. If he needs to feed, you'll be far away."

"Come on, Petya," Boyband whined. "You think I'm that weak? I'll keep you safe, Naoma."

"Oh, now she feels good," Ralia laughed.

Naoma sighed and stepped closer to me. "Can we move along?"

The lights flickered. They remained lit after a few moments of struggle. Boyband clapped "There we go!"

I put a finger to my mouth. "Careful. Even if you're sure we're alone, I don't want to risk anything."

Black footprints covered the ground with small piles of ash. I couldn't see any sign of the fire. It looked like a typical office building with a front desk, humble decor, and a directory on the wall.

"Floor by floor, then?" Ralia asked.

Boyband walked toward the directory. "Light - 203, Discussion - 304, Conference Room 4 - 506, none of this—wait, Executive Study - 701, I like how that sounds." He turned and pointed to the elevator doors. Black smeared around the cracks as if something had exploded from within. "But not how that looks. I'll try not to burn my reserve too much. You all can suck it up. We're taking the stairs."

I looked at Naoma.

"What? Just because I'm not one of you freaks, you think I can't make it?" She bumped my shoulder as she followed Boyband to the stairwell. "You know I'm kidding, right?"

"Of course, I didn't think you had it in you to make it up there, anyway."

"Not kidding about that—I mean—"

I smirked. "Of course I know what you mean."

"Zeg you."

Ralia rolled her eyes and ran past us.

The stairwell spiraled up and was walled with concrete, clearly only used for emergencies that hadn't happened until now.

I held the door open for Naoma. The other two had already walked through. She smiled. No remark from her was enough to speak of her exhaustion.

"Ugh!" Boyband grunted. He flipped his mask up. Ralia and I did likewise.

If the smell wasn't enough evidence of the fire, the collapsed roof and holes to the sky spoke of how much damage had befallen the seventh floor. One of the walls was covered in screens, half of which were burnt black husks, and the others cracked. A line of desks faces a similar fate, all except for two either burnt or crushed by fallen chunks of the ceiling. A puddle of dark liquid pooled near the far right corner, but it appeared too viscous to have spread further than a few feet. No lights shined, but the indigo illumination of advertisements in the sky above was enough to see dark outlines of where two bodies had been.

Boyband approached the closest one and crouched beside it. Naoma and I followed him while Ralia looked around the room for any surviving electronics.

"Do you think this was where they were?" Naoma asked.

Boyband shrugged. He touched the ashes and rubbed it between his fingers. "They had to have been taken, right, Petya? Please tell me I'm not rubbing my dead parents between my fingers."

"Someone else must have cleared this out before we arrived. Either their murderers took the bodies or whoever cleaned everything up. Did Lorren have a report on it?"

"Nah. Everything he sent me is a bunch of legal garbage. I get it. I'll have to sort through it all later with a lawyer to secure the business, but there was nothing to help out with the immediate predicament."

"Ah ha, yes!"

We all turned to look at Ralia, who was plugging a cord into the base of her skull.

She moaned as if tapping into the best fix one could buy.

Boyband abandoned the astonishment and grief, adorning a disgust so vile that we couldn't help but laugh.

"The zeg do you all want?" He pointed at Ralia. "That's zeggin' wrong–I–I don't want any of that."

She moaned and giggled.

"Ah, *zeg* cut it out already?"

She sighed. "If you could appreciate technology–mind you, not in a sexual way like you probably think you, sick freak–you would tremble before the system your parents have here, just like me."

"So it's good then?"

One of her eyes stopped flashing and looked at Boyband. "Babe, this is better than any Violet District guk. Damn, it's beautiful. Mind you, I am yet to surpass the firewall."

"Then how do you know it's good?"

"Because it's a shac to crack. Anything this encrypted is sure to be rich in taste. Give me a few minutes."

"Please be careful of exhausting yourself, Ral."

"I'm guessing we only have a few more hours until Techvax sends a squad after us. I can hold off feeding until then, even if I become hungry."

"Please don't worry," I whispered to Naoma. "Really, none of us will touch you."

She nodded and didn't smile. She doubted me as much as I doubted myself.

"Were your parents in a cult?" Ralia asked.

"The zeg's that supposed to mean?" Boyband asked.

She shrugged, her eyes still flashing. "A secret office that they forbade you from entering, extensive cybersecurity, targeted and killed by some random freak. Deleon has to have a reason to hate them and I wouldn't put being in a rival cult past him. That is... if he was the one who did it."

"Not that I know of. Zeg, you're making me question everything."

"Not the brightest, is he?" she said, facing me.

"Zeg you! What was I supposed to do, wander my way up here when they weren't looking?"

She nodded. "I would have. What kind of teenager were you? One with too much to distract him from his parents' secrets, I guess."

"Ease up on him, Ral. Where's our loving companion?"

"Bashing her head against this firewall. Maybe I would be more inclined to like the Eclaines if they were as naïve as most of the Republic. That's a compliment, Boyband. Your parents were smart and well prepared for a gal like me to come in and knock down firewalls. Doesn't matter though, I'm better than their precautions."

I could see his opinion of Ralia souring. She was most pleasant when confident in her ability.

"See anything noteworthy?" I asked him.

He kicked around at the silhouettes of bodies. "Not really. I mean... what should I be looking for?""What did your parents say this building was for?"

"Managing the farm. Logistics."

"And you were just fine with them not allowing you to enter? Zeg, and I thought I was naïve."

"I grew up never being allowed to enter and was used to it. Of course I got curious, but whenever I asked, they just said that they signed a contract with their distributors and other clients stating that they could not allow personal information to be viewed by those outside of the farm bureau and SocStan executives. They said I could have clearance when I was eventually let into the bureau, but no one can be elected to the position until they reach twenty one."

"What about the people who maintain the facility?"

"All written into the agreement. They were members as well."

"Okay, enough of that. Zeg, no wonder you stopped asking questions."

"Yup, plenty of exceptions and a long, boring trail of files and agreements."

"What I meant to say was, look around now that you can. We're in. See if there is anything you can find that *might* be a secret worth hiding, and I'm not talking about bank account numbers, even money laundering or debauchery. Just look for something, I dunno, interesting?"

He nodded. We started to wander around the room together.

Naoma followed. "The security was so tight, but now that a few floors have been abandoned, they think some caution tape will stop people from entering?"

"Some people have been inside," said Ralia. "I can see plenty of other failed hack attempts. I'm guessing a couple of rivals broke in, knowing what the building was for, but never able to find the valuable data. They just paved the way for us to walk in before anyone could put up some new doors."

"Lucky coincidence," Naoma said.

"Nah, babe, I just think we entered before they came back with a better crew. So, maybe, yeah, lucky coincidence. Everything is only going to get worse now as the legal disputes over the property increase. If someone loses out of the battle for ownership, you bet they'll storm this with everything they have left. That is to say, if this place is as good as Boyband makes it out to be."

"I never said–"

I interrupted him before he committed to hating Ralia because of one difficult hack on her part. "Ral, enough rambling, keep working."

"Babe, I'm–"

"If you're good, then let us focus until you find something of worth."

Boyband stopped and stared at a portion of wall near the edge of where the black reached.

"Arab–wait, you told me your parents…" I stopped talking as I followed a trail of thoughts.

Maps of Arabasia color coded like the Republic–even though they did not follow the color District system–spanned the wall. Some focused on cities, others in portions of the continent, and others on villages. Aside from the typical color spectrum, black squares mapped out portions of the map. I looked for a legend. I struggled to speak as I saw what they indicated. *Black = Medislavian outposts.* Military.

I shoved Boyband but pulled him right back after feeling bad. My mind raced. "You said–the war–your parents are anti-Medislavia, right?"

"Yeah, but–"

"What was that guk called?" I snapped my fingers. "Light essence?"

"Neon Essence?"

"Yes! Zeg yes! That's gotta be what this all is about. I thought your parents never talked about what they did here? Are you so empty-headed as to not make the connection?"

"Nah, I would've known that. This is farming, agricultural–"

Ralia spoke up. "They said enough for him never to grow too curious. Sure, they mentioned Neon Essence but never divulged the greatest depths. You're right, this is farming, because that is what they are doing in *Arabasia.*"

"I've had it with you, lady! You have no zegging idea what you're even talking about!"

"Lady? I'm a few years older than you, not some old–"

"You're in, aren't you?" I asked. "You *do* know what you're talking about."

She grinned with unflashing eyes.

"I've been in for a few minutes. It's taken me a bit to process it, but I think I know what is happening."

She sneered at Boyband.

"Aw come on."

"So *now* you want to be nice?"

"You're the one who–ugh."

She tapped on her cheek.

"The zeg do you want now?"

"A kiss from my lil' baby."

"Piss off."

"Ralia, please," I said.

"Kid's gotta learn his place. Now,' she tapped her cheek again.

He looked at me with eyes that pleaded for justice.

"Just give her what she wants."

He grunted, waddled towards her, and stuck out his lips to her turned cheek. Ralia turned to face him just before he kissed her cheek. His lips landed on hers. She grabbed his head, pushed her tongue in between his lips, and moved away with a smack to his cheek. "Ready to listen now."

"You zeggin–"

"Are you ready... to listen?"

"Yes." He massaged his cheek and scowled away from her.

She waved for Naoma and me to move in closer. "Your parents were smart to give you hints at the truth just to divert you from the real juice of it. This is probably related to what the SocStans did while they had the presidency, but I didn't look too deep. It seems like your parents had some relations with former President Anson. Yeah, the Eclaine farm helped provide for the Republic, but they, among other SocStan executives, farmed Neon Essence in Arabasia. From what I can find, Neon Essence is the pure form of the physical light that we use today."

Boyband let go of his cheek, but it was still red. "Like I told you, Pet, they were involved in this war for light. That's what your homeland wants, pure light in Arabasia."

"Not quite," Ralia said.

"What do you mean?" he asked.

"If they are farming this pure light," Naoma said, "then where is it? Are they using it for their farms?"

"It's in Arabasia, but traces of it are in the Republic, as far as I can tell."

"So my parents were benefiting from the war? Zeg, I thought they were just merciful to the Arabasians after relentless Medislav attacks."

"Oh, they're not greedy. The Medislavs want it for power, but it's sacred to the Arabasians."

"Then why do my parents care? I mean, sure they're nice people, but I never thought they would care so much about–no."

"So your parents are a part of some cult!" I would have laughed if the moment had not been so tense.

"But–but I–I feel I would have known about that."

Naoma shrugged. "It sounds like you did. You said they were always coming here. They told you it was a political leaning, but it turns out that the secret here must have been their culty commitment."

"Who asked you?" he bit back. "You're a celebrity. Everyone knows that the cult of fame is the biggest one out there. If you're famous, you've sold your soul to the devil for the sake of lumens. Am I right or am I right?"

"Chill, babyband." Ralia held up her hand to hold off any retribution. "It's not a cult, it's a religion."

"What's the difference?" he asked.

"I'll be the humble one now and say that your parents had good intentions. Unfortunately, there is very little to say about the religion itself. We can focus on that later, but what you need to recognize is that, like you said, this war is not about power. It is about lucre versus spirituality. Neon essence is the equivalent of nuclear energy compared to our light, even violet light, which would be the equivalent of a pre-light battery. Now, I've thrown out plenty of information that might sound interesting, but inapplicable. How does it factor in?"

"Deleon killed my parents to have access to Neon Essence?"

"I think so, but we still have some gaps to fill in. This Arabasian religious faction refers to themselves as Luxists or members of Luxism. I can see plenty of references in the database identifying Osteolyte, among other companies, as potential threats. These companies have contacted the Medislavian government, but their proposed alliances are worthless without sufficient influence in the Republic."

"So that is why Deleon wanted the presidency?" I asked.

"It checks out." She squinted her eyes, grunted, and clenched her stomach.

"You good, Ral?"

"Yeah, just a cramp." She sighed and shook her head. "Anyway, back to Osteolyte. Haven Health opposed the war, making such a deal with the Medislavain government impossible. From here on out, everything is based on assumptions and inference. The Luxists have been working with Neon Essence for some time. I think Osteolyte, or some partner company, raided an 'office' years back. Maybe Osteolyte has some, but

I think that is why they eliminated the Eclaines. They–Deleon–wanted more of it before their pro-Medislavian alignment was revealed to the Republic, which would have crushed their campaign. It is hard to find any open pro-Medislavian politicians after Medislavia declared so many raids on innocent Arabasian cities."

"And they are right to do so," I said. "My people were–are monsters."

"So that's what we have to do?" Boyband asked. "Use the evidence you have to incriminate Osteolyte and Deleon as a pro-war faction before they can do anything? It should be easy. You've got the evidence, right? Now we just need to pin the Techvax raid on him and we're free!"

"Sounds simple enough. Anything about the Ten Beacons?" I asked.

Ralia paused to search for a moment, then shook her head. "Is there something I'm missing?"

I shrugged. "Some people mentioned Deleon being one of them."

She sighed. "Frankly, I think we should keep things simple until we are in the clear. Once we have Deleon away from us, we can look into his and Osetolyte's ties."

"Agreed," I said as I looked at Naoma. Where will she fit in when this ends? Should she stay here to avoid the violence that is bound to occur when we face our once-captor? Even if she wanted to come, should we give her the choice?

She opened her mouth to speak but was cut off as our eyes flashed with an emergency neurospace broadcast.

To broadcast *any* message at three in the morning could only warrant the most disturbing news.

A violet-rimmed box appeared in my vision. A female news reporter sat at a desk with red, teary eyes. The image of President Liu was projected over her right shoulder.

The reporter's voice trembled as she spoke. *"Dear Republic citizens, we regret to inform you that President Liu has been assassinated."* The image changed to project an all too familiar face. *"The assassin has been apprehended and will be executed following his interrogation.*

Tevon. *Zegging* Tevon had murdered the president of Haven Health and the Republic of Capital.

Chapter Sixteen

I Really Want to Stay at Your House

"*We will broadcast details following the interrogation this evening. Those who wish to follow the story can do so on the Republic Central Broadcast Station.*"

The image changed to a red flag with the Republic's blue insignia in its center. The image changed before we could exit from the broadcast.

Videos of happy Indigo District families played with a break-neck change in mood. The father of a family took a glowing pill and continued on with them down the center of the indigo-lit street.

"*Letting light live,*" a soft woman's voice said.

Haven Health's logo appeared above the city as the image panned out.

The broadcast closed.

"And they couldn't end it without a commercial," Boyband scoffed. "A nice tribute to the president, right? '*She served the Republic well by selling her product. Never has the Republic seen a better sales-woman. May she sell ever more in the life beyond.'"*

Nobody laughed. I started to pace and pulled at my hair.

"No no no no..." Ralia rocked back and forth, hugging her knees.

"What in the light are you doing?" Naoma grabbed me by the shoulders and lifted my chin. Her eyes held my head up. I couldn't turn away from them. "Petya. Since when did you care about the President? Is she important to this?"

"You zeggin' who—"

"Shut up Ralia!" I sighed, my eyes still fixed on Naoma. "The assassin was another member of our group."

"Zeg." She gasped.

"Yeah. I know. They'll use their best to raid his neurospace and reveal a connection to all of us. We're done for."

"What kind of attitude is that? You were going to prove that Deleon is using you all, right? Get off your sorry asses before you're *actually* done for. We still have a chance." She let go and walked towards Ralia. "Where's that charm? The optimism?"

Ralia grunted. Her eyes were beyond the optimism her personality could foster.

"Back away," I said to Naoma.

"What?"

I ran towards her. "Get away from–" I stopped as I pushed her aside to grab Ralia, mid-prowl.

Ralia's pupils dilated. Her teeth were twice as long.

I held her with all the tenacity I could manage as we fell down. I laid atop her, but she continued to claw towards Naoma.

"Ral! Stop!"

"Give me the zegging violet whore!" she hissed.

Boyband shook, eyes looking back and forth between Naoma and I.

I grunted, squeezing Ralia as she crawled and pulled us towards Naoma.

"Help me hold her, Boyband!"

He jumped on top of us, squeezing me, but stopping any movement towards Naoma.

"The zeg is wrong with her?"

She continued to gnash her teeth and swing her hands at Naoma. She wore sharpened glowing blue nails that would be sure to cut into Naoma's flesh if she got any closer.

"She burned her reserve using her back mode. She would've–ugh, stop it Ral! Ugh–she would've been fine, but the jarring emotion after the news report must have drained her beyond her limit."

"Emotions can do that?"

"They can break the strongest."

Naoma crawled backwards, unable to stand on steady legs. She stopped as we made eye contact. "Please don't let this happen."

Zeg you, Ralia.

I reached my hand inside my mouth and ripped out the last tooth on the top and bottom of my left side. I shoved the bloody teeth into Ralia's mouth and pulled out a bloody hand with her bite marks in the meat of my palm.

She moaned as she chewed. Her eyes rolled back in quenched bliss as the teeth became dust.

"Are they going to grow back?" Boyband asked.

I shook my head and looked at Naoma. "Bites don't work like that."

We let go as Ralia stopped struggling. Humanity returned to her eyes as she swallowed. She looked at Naoma, whose chest rose and fell with quick, shallow breaths. "Oh, hun, I'm—I'm so sorry, I didn't mean to—" she ran towards Naoma with arms outstretched for a hug.

I grabbed her and pulled her back towards the ground.

Naoma's eyes were wide. She had peddled back a few steps.

"Ah, guys I—zeg, I didn't mean to—"

I looked at Naoma while I spoke. I hated the fear I saw on her face. She could never be like that because of me. I promised and committed with any honesty that remained within me. As long as I would know her, whether that be a day or years to come, I couldn't allow myself to break like Ralia. "Well, you did, Ral."

"I'm good now, I swear!"

"Yeah, but for how long?" I looked at Boyband. "Does your family have something better than the sky shuttle to get us back to Zingang?"

"We're really going back to Deleon?"

I nodded. "We're ending this."

"But what about Tevon and the president's assassination? They'll be after us, won't they?"

I sighed, loosening my grip on Ralia, but still holding her. She had ceased struggling, but I did not want to make Naoma any more flustered. "Yes, I get that, but the thing is, Techvax is going to have the world out for us after their announcement, anyway. Your 'friends' here will turn on you because I can guarantee the whistleblower who escaped has some way to pin the mess on us down there."

I looked at Ralia. "Do you have the files needed to pin the Eclaine murders on Deleon?"

"Not exactly on *him* but I have what I need to pin it on Osteolyte as a company. His name was never attached to it, but I'm almost sure he did it through the company."

"Great, get what you can and we'll pull out anything else we can back at the hub. We'll make sure to feed your reserves before we start, because I want *any* incriminating evidence extracted from the company to point everything to Deleon. I'm sure we can find something to show that he was forcing us to do his work. This is it. The end. If we can't get the law to shut down Osteolyte now, I'm sure Deleon will kill us himself."

"I can always try to doctor the evidence," she said.

"Only if we get desperate enough. I get that your Bite mod can help you alter files, but let's keep this as transparent as possible."

"Does she have any connections with the higher ups to help us twist the story in our favor?" Ralia asked.

Naoma was still too fear-struck to respond.

"We'll see about that if we need it later," I said. I didn't know how many "higher-up" connections would be hers and how many would be the Naoma created by Reef Records.

"My parents have a sky-limo," Boyband said.

I raised an eyebrow.

"You asked if I had something better than a skyshuttle."

"Oh, yeah, right."

"They have it somewhere on the property, but an and would always chauffeur them."

"I can drive it!" Ralia said. "'A sky car is a sky car.'"

I nodded. "You and Boyband can go grab the car. Pick us up here when you're done."

"Why aren't you coming?" Boyband asked. "We can leave faster if you do."

"Because you and Ralia are going to go feed. I can tell that panic burned a lot of your reserve too, Boyband. You're shaking. I'll be fine. I can wait to feed in Zingang. We don't need any risks on the ride."

Ralia tugged on my shirt. Her eyes were those of a whining pup. "Come on, Pet. This isn't necessary."

Naoma's petrified glare said otherwise.

"I don't care. You two go *now*. If we hurry, we should back it back to the hub before guk hits the wall with Techvax's announcement."

"You're sure this is all going to work?" asked Boyband.

"I get it. I'm throwing out a mess of ideas with no clear trail. To answer your question, I hope so. I hope we can make sense of all of this along the way enough to stick it all to Deleon. '*What then?*' We'll see if we make it that far." I held my hand up at an angle to grab his in a brotherly grasp. He took it, our arms made an upside down V as we shook. "You got this, kay? Ralia is a bit of a freak"—I winked at her—"but she's one hell of an Imp."

"Awe, you're gonna make me tear up, baby."

"Get some more teeth, then you can sob all you want."

I let her go and moved in front of Naoma. Ralia wouldn't go after her. My teeth were too potent for her to need to eat so soon. Naoma had no inclination of that. She was a frightened child in a world of monsters. I couldn't blame her, only give her reassurance.

I crouched beside Naoma, relaxing as she reached for my hand. It was dusty and all the light from her nails had gone out, yet it was so soft. I squeezed it with two quick pulses and felt the tensity in her grip dissipate.

"Thank you," she whispered.

I squeezed her hand again, then waved Ralia and Boyband away with my free hand. "Get moving."

"Yeah, yeah." Boyband started towards the door.

Ralia put her palms together as if ready to pray for Naoma's forgiveness as she stood and peddled back towards the exit. "Really, hun, I am *so* sorry."

"It's alright."

Ralia smiled and jogged towards the door with her usual bounciness as if nothing had happened.

We sat together without speaking or looking at each other until we could no longer hear Ralia and Boyband's footsteps.

I let go of her, but she still held tight. Alright. We still have time. How long would they be? Ten, fifteen minutes? We just had to meet them downstairs, right? We have all that we need here, the files, any...

My rambling thoughts were forced excuses to divert my attention away from the girl at my side. Outside of her shell of the Neon Idol, she was an innocent victim. I had dragged her into this journey through hell. I didn't deserve to be at her side. Any comfort she found was just in the mask that I put up to hide the terrible person I was and had become for the sake of a man who I now hoped to kill. A man who I had always hoped to kill.

I was a murderer several times over.

I did not deserve to touch a girl like Naoma.

Why would I? Why would she? What delusion was I following to think that I had a connection, a chance with a girl who I had only known as a human being for a few days? She was not the Neon Idol that I bowed to as I listened to her algorithm-produced music along with most of the Republic. Any claim to know her then was the same insane fanaticism that her twelve-year-old fans proclaimed when her lyrics *just happened* to coincide with the difficulties they were facing in life. Even I knew her lyrics led to buying antidepressants, seeking unneeded therapy, and a list of other subscriptions that Reef Forced her to advertise.

No one would want me. I hated the Imp that I was. Even if she had the slightest attraction, I couldn't betray her by giving in. It would be a loss on her part. Faithfulness could only go as far as my teeth hunger was satisfied.

She was beautiful. Beneath the shell of the Neon Idol was a sincere girl, trying to survive in the light-tainted world, just like I was.

Two escaped corporate pawns on the run in the pursuit of freedom. It was as tragic as it was romantic.

Some things are best left as dreams that can never be fulfilled.

She leaned her head against mine. Zeg. What was she doing? Stop. No. I had to break the silence. To let dangerous thoughts continue would be a disservice to us both.

Her proximity only made it more difficult.

"It's not okay," I said, still reluctant to look at her.

She lifted her head and looked at me. "What do you mean?"

I still watched the dark hallway ahead. "What Ralia did."

"I–I get it. You... people have a need. Just like you said, when you need to feed, your humanity disappears."

"That's still no excuse." I mustered the courage to look at her. "As long as you are with us, with *me*, *no one* will hurt you."

"Don't make promises you can't keep." She smiled.

Zeg, it almost broke me. Her hope and trust were based on a single act.

"What? No need to get all dramatic. If you're too serious, you're going to make me be the same. All of this is too dreary to face it head on."

"You have a song for that?"

She chuckled. She stopped smiling for a moment, licked her thumb, then reached towards me.

I moved back. "What are you doing?"

She hooked her hand behind my neck and pulled me in.

My heart vibrated.

She rubbed her wet finger across the corner of my lip. "Just a little blood."

I suddenly remembered the pain of my missing two teeth and touched the raw holes in my gums with my tongue. It stung, but my Bite reserves had already started to heal the wound. It wouldn't take too much, but I still didn't want to use more if Naoma was near me without someone else to feed upon.

"You said those implants heal your bones. Do they restore those teeth?"

It probably looked like I was trying to pick something from my teeth with my tongue. I couldn't help but feel the holes and what the sacrifice had meant. "No."

"Why not?"

"You want the gruesome details? Our teeth become stronger than bones in order to break down typical human teeth. What Ralia ate is as potent as four, maybe five *full* sets."

She nodded with a forced smile.

"It's disgusting, I know."

She leaned in and kissed my cheek.

By the Light, was it true? Was this the way of confirming our mutual feelings? We knew so little about each other, yet more than words could say. We were freed captives.

"Thank you for giving a part of yourself to save me."

So it wasn't anything romantic, just a gesture of gratitude. What did I expect? Ripping out your teeth to satiate another imp's hunger was hardly the way to win a girl over. It–stop. You're never going to *win* a girl over–stop. Don't even *think* about getting her to like you. You're her transportation to a better life. Once she's there, away from the darkness of your world, you'll leave her. Even if she wants more, you can't offer it. Doing so would be a disservice.

"Of course."

She stared at me, an affectionate smile lingering.

I made sure to crush my feelings before they could deceive me again into thinking that this could ever work out. "Come on, let's head down. They shouldn't be much longer."

The awkwardness of my sudden turn from her affection was but a pinch compared to the devastating blow dealt by her wanting eyes. She *had* wanted more. She wanted to face that which has been on my mind.

I faced the doorway and started towards the stairwell.

Neither of us spoke until Ralia and Boyband arrived with the skylimo in front of the building.

We entered and took flight, riding as high as any sky car could physically go, just below the cloud line. Even though Ralia had been unstable not long before, I was relieved to see that she was driving. Her attempted feeding on Namoa did nothing to my trust in her. I knew exactly how she felt and prayed that I would never reach such desperate hunger with Naoma so close by. Human–imp–will could only withstand so much before it became mindless and carnally driven.

Boyband turned to look at us from the passenger seat. "I can roll up the partition if you want."

I wanted to punch him, not out of high-school-esque embarrassment, but out of anger against the world who kept forcing me to face something I could never allow to happen. Was I damned to face such a bitter temptation until I broke, wanting to love something that I was destined to eventually betray for the sake of my hellish hunger for teeth?

"It's alright." Naoma giggled.

Boyband stared at me, his smile dissipating as I was unable to hold one of my own. He settled in his seat and looked at Ralia. "Am I missing something, or why the zeg did Tevon–or Deleon, if it was his call–think it was a good idea to murder the president?"

She shrugged. "I lost contact with Tevon not long after I did with you two."

"But why did he go after her?" Boyband asked. "He was supposed to be working with the Memory Runners, right? Does their Party have a bitter rivalry with the Pharma Party or is that just another lie my parents fed to me?"

"No, Babyband, you're right."

Naoma and I cracked up. The nickname to his nickname wasn't the best attempt at humor from Ralia, but the kid's reaction sold it.

He shook his head. "Do you think Tevon was stupidly ambitious?"

"I think it's more likely that Deleon was," I said. "He probably called him there after being overwhelmed by his crusade against the core of the pharma party.

"Yeah." Boyband bobbed his head. "Maybe he figured everything was going to guk and decided to pull the plug with Liu's death."

Ralia flicked her hand at him. "Nah, Deleon's ambitious, but not that stupid. Still, you're not wrong in talking about everything going to guk. Don't forget what I said back in your parents' tower."

"That his plans were sabotaged?"

She snapped. "More like planned obsolescence. He was set up for failure once he began. The hit on Liu was the final circuit holding the system together. Only I was good enough to succeed before you shacs butchered it like they wanted."

I leaned forward. "We triggered Techvax and the Finians to come after us, Tevon triggered the Party with the presidency to come after us, but what about Ali?"

"Maybe there's another hit coming our way to finish us all off," Boyband muttered.

Ralia looked at him, then back at the sky ahead. "The last reading I had from him was en route to Zingang. Let's hope Deleon brought him back. Maybe we can save him with us before sticking it on Deleon. You boys do understand that the company will fall with Deleon. The only hope we have of claiming innocence is the Bites. I can configure them to look just like neuromanipulators."

"So we're actually taking them out?" Boyband asked.

Neither of us answered. We couldn't give any assurance until we knew the consequences of such an action. For all we knew, they had become as much a part of our brains as any other piece.

Even if it took away the hunger, what would I become? Weak. Frail. Techbone would finish me off.

Would that be so terrible?

Would it be a crime to perpetuate my existence that required murder?

Silence fell upon us after a few long minutes of Boyband arguing over music to play. I rolled up the partition, noting how low Naoma's eyelids hung.

The slightest click of it closing the other two off of us was enough to stir her.

"You good?" I whispered.

She nodded and dragged her hands across her eyelids.

I let out a faint chuckle. "Rethinking your decision to come, yet?"

She smiled and laid her head to rest against the window.

"Listen, Naoma, I really am sorry. Look, I'll have Ralia drop you off somewhere—anywhere along the way. You've got that disguise and all still, right? The world will forget about Naoma's disappearance."

"Oh, I know that, but you don't believe it."

"You think so?"

She opened one eye, smiling at me. "Even if they do, you wouldn't, would you?"

"How could I? Your music is made to stick in someone's mind like a virus."

"Come on, Petya. Are we really going to talk about *this* like that?"

"What do you mean?"

Her hand slid over to mine.

"Where do you want us to take you?"

"No, Petya. We both know that we are the same here. Both slaves of corporations. I'm staying with you to see this through."

"Please, Naoma."

She tucked her thumb under mine. The smooth side of her dull violet nail was like polished glass. Her skin was smooth and soft to perfection. She gave me a tight squeeze. She wouldn't let go.

"You're not going to toss aside all you have in some hopeless mission for our freedom."

"It's not hopeless. Difficult, not hopeless. And *I* don't have anything to return to. Everything that I had belonged to Reef Records. And know this, Pet," she moved from the window. Her hand was cold from the glass as it caressed the side of my face. "I'm not tossing anything aside if I am with you. I'm holding on to the only thing, the only person who convinced me to pursue a life worth living. One outside of Reef. One that is not a farce meant to trick the world into consumerism."

I grabbed her hand, letting our grasp fall to my side.

"Oh, Pet, I'm sorry if I'm being too forward." She forced out a nervous laugh, now unable to look at me. "I guess the *Neon Idol* still has a hold on me. I was so used to just having anyone I wanted–I mean, it's not that I want to manipulate you or anything but–zeg, I sound like a teenager now. They programmed me to give into any attraction I had because it would usually benefit Reef. I'm still trying to pull myself away from those habits, but it's hard not to, now that I feel a *genuine* connection to someone. Who cares if it's been a few days. Who cares if I've forgotten all that I was before Reef. You've been real, Petya, and pairing our connection with physical attraction, I can't help but—"

"Don't forget what we are, Naoma. What *I* am."

Saying that tore my heart in two. Though it pained me to distance myself from something I wanted so much, I could not lie to her. She could overlook my mistakes, but not the Imp that I was.

She clenched her fist. I almost thought she was going to hit me.

"Ugh, Petya, you can't keep saying that. Zeg, I love you–I mean, I love what you strive for, but you can't keep pulling away from everything because you think you are some hell-bound sinner beyond redemption. We've already said that the hunger is not your choice. The basis of that claim is our argument for your innocence under Deleon's control."

She squeezed my hands. Violet eyes held me still in a locked gaze. "Petya, you are a *good person*. You are trying as hard as you can to be one, and that is enough. Stop with the self-pity. It's starting to rub off on me. Soon enough I'll start thinking about all the people my zegging music has led to bankruptcy over buying useless products for the sake of being my biggest fan. We're both flawed, but you are as much an Imp at your core as I am the Neon Idol. We're leaving those behind. I am staying with you to see Deleon punished, then we are going to go off together like two innocent kids in a mindshow. Yes, we barely know each other, but that is the beauty of it. We know enough to see that we *need* each other to become our own people, no longer slaves to a company. I'm staying with you Petya, that is, if you'll have me at your side. I need you, flaws and all."

She reached her hand over and held mine.

I wanted nothing more than to kiss her. Pure attraction pulled me to do it but now was not the time. She had kissed me out of kindness before, but I couldn't now.

Maybe eventually.

I held her hand and enjoyed the moment for what it was.

The indigo light of the car's interior shone upon us in the dark, casting our precious moment in a cinematic tone like any lovesick art house mindshows I adored.

The glow around us brightened her violet eyes shadow with a glitter so on character for the Neon Idols, though this was much more than *that* Naoma.

I felt all that I had searched for since I left my home years before.

Belonging.

Appreciation.

Someone else's gratitude that I existed.

I had no desire to tap into a socitab, for this was that very feeling that I had falsely replicated in my addiction.

She let go and wiped a tear from my cheek.

"Is something wrong?"

I shook my head, sparing the tinted partition a brief glance. No one was watching us. I broke into a childish sob and rested my head against her chest. Tears fell, yet I smiled and sniffed with heavy sobs.

I whimpered one last sentiment. Even if she didn't know how much her touch meant, she acted as if she did. The hint of any future chance at romance was enough for me to think that I wasn't as poor a person as I believed.

"Thank you."

She pulled me close as we drifted into the night.

I awoke as the partition rolled down. Boyband turned the sound up on something projected over the dashboard. Naoma and I looked at each other, unable to suppress childish grins and the warmth that came with them.

I expected Boyband to mock us. Ralia was still focused on driving, but she did not shy away from any gossip-worthy distractions.

Both of them were silent as the woman on the projection spoke.

"We come to you live from Central Zingang with Seeven Jorgensen, spokesman for Techvax Medicine United."

Both wore the best of dress, though Seeven was in pure dismay. The interviewer tried to match his emotion, but the eagerness of her eyes betrayed her rouse. It was apparent that she would be earning plenty of lumens and attention from this story. I knew so, having been its cause.

"Thank you, Helen, for the opportunity to be here."

She nodded, her curly black hair bouncing as she did so.

Seeven continued to speak. *"While our company understands the competitive nature of Republic capitalism especially in an era so politically charged by the rampancy of techbone, we cannot allow such violence to happen without reciprocation."*

"While many of our viewers may have heard rumors regarding this, why don't you clarify what happened?"

He nodded. *"I left with the Techvax marketing team and our associated advertisement crew at Reef Records, though I cannot say which artists accompanied–"*

Boyband snapped and pointed at the projection. "That zeggin' shac! I thought I saw him there! Pet? Naoma?"

I squinted, not recognizing him. The company was too large to memorize everyone.

Naoma shook her head. "My memories of that are blurry dreams. It only became clear once you broke me out of—"

Boyband continued to talk after losing interest in her forgetfulness. "*He* must've been the one who took the skyshuttle! We'd be free if he hadn't escaped." He pounded his fist on the center console.

Ralia smacked his shoulder.

"What? It's my parents' car. I can do what I want."

"I'm trying to listen!"

Helen, the interviewer, nodded with exaggerated interest. "*And will the advertisement ever air?*"

"*I am unable to disclose that at this point.*"

"*And what is it that your company hopes to achieve in the pharma race for success?*"

"*I was not permitted to discuss our marketing strategy.*"

"*Is product, strategy?*'

He let out a frustrated laugh. "*Can I discuss the matter of my escape? I assure you, Helen, that it will be just as* riveting *as you would like for your program.*"

"*Of course.*"

He showed a winning smile. "*We traveled to the Red District via a skyshuttle caravan. When I found myself spared by our murderers, I fled to the first vehicle of the three and took flight. Piloting them is not too difficult if you have flown class F vehicles..*"

"*And your assailants? Who were they?*"

He lifted a finger.

She nodded.

"I arrived at the Techvax Southern Blue District branch, astounded that I had survived. I took a few hours to reorient myself before speaking with the law."

He looked at her, checking that she wouldn't interrupt him, and continued. *"I had but the briefest memory of our assailants. Even if I allowed an officer to extract the memory from my neurospace, it would only provide a poor caricature that could apply to most of the sub-Blue population."*

Naoma scoffed and opened her mouth. I calmed her with a soft hand on her shoulder.

"I have the Zingang Peace Force to thank for what I am about to show you."

Three pale blue squares of light appeared between them in the air.

"They worked with the skyshuttle company we used to track the missing vehicle. These individuals were found to have taken the vehicle and are therefore responsible for the murders of more than twenty people within minutes."

Portraits filled two of the projected blue boxes: my face and Boyband's.

"Are they not going to show that I was with you?" Naoma asked while Helen commented on how rough we looked.

"They probably couldn't afford your information," Boyband said.

I squeezed her shoulder. "I hate to say it, but I bet whoever was left at Reef gave it to them freely. If they're not giving your face away so freely like ours, they probably want you back."

She twitched, and our focus returned to Seeven.

"—now, the intrigue does not stop there. While diving further into the limited information we could find on them—and let me tell you there was oddly too little—we found another convenient connection that might help explain another recent event."

The third image filled out. This picture was not a surveillance shot like mine and Boyband's, but a professional mugshot.

Tevon grinned, beaten and bloody.

Helen gasped. "*The president's assassin–*"

"*—was directly involved with the people who murdered my associates.*"

"Zeg!" Boyband slammed his fist against the door and center console.

"Please!" Ralia shouted, a distinct struggle was audible in her voice. "I need to stay focused or we're going to crash and zeggin' die you shac!"

I rubbed her shoulder to console her while the same emotional typhoon stirred my remaining sanity.

Naoma grabbed my other hand.

My world was an image of dissolving pixels. We were all going to die as the criminal shacs that the world had taken us to be. Even if they were spared the details of us being tooth-eaters, they knew we were monsters that belonged in the Red District.

"*–tragedy that it was.*" Helen sighed. "*While we know that President Liu's assassin is in custody preparing for execution, have the other two been apprehended?*"

"*Not yet, but we expect that they will within the hour.*"

Ralia reached her hand over to cover Boyband's mouth.

"*We were able to procure their data with the grace of echvax's investors. They are currently in Zingang in a sky limo. We–*"

Boyband pried her arm from his mouth and shouted. "I'm going to rip my zegging neurospace out!"

I shook my head. "What can we expect? *Nothing* is private anymore. I thought we accepted that years ago. We should have known that they had enough to buy our tracking rights."

"Still," Ralia said, "money shouldn't have been enough with them. Deleon had me configure our neurospaces to block any outside infiltration. I can wipe the data again with a new encryption that Deleon doesn't have."

"So he had the key to our data?" Boyband asked.

"He owned us. There was little I could do to deny him of it. Now that we're AWOL, I'll give it another wipe. What is more troubling is that *only Deleon* should have had that data."

"You think someone leaked the info?" I asked. "Potentially. If someone did, it might be the same person who sabotaged his entire plight for the presidency. What I think is more realistic is that he sold our data hoping to save his sorry ass from the law."

"So what now?" Boyband asked.

"We'll figure out all the data break stuff later. We're going to ditch this car, wipe our data again, and find our way to the hub to hail-Mary this thing. I'll extract the data to prove that Deleon forced us against our will and alter it to make it look like we did as little damage as possible. Even if they can pin some deaths on us, no one can find out about our Bites. Those will be sure to earn us an execution, if the rest isn't enough."

I leaned forward. "You think we can do it, Ral?"

"Zeg it if I know, but we have no other choice." She looked back at Naoma. "Your fate is your choice, babe. We droppin' you off?"

Translating thought to message as quickly as I could manage, I sent Naoma a private message. I saw the faintest blue in her violet eyes as she read it.

Petya: Please don't waste your life on me. A few moments together is no excuse to die with the freaks that we are. Please, save yourself.

"No," she said. "I'm staying. The whole world will be after me to force me back into Reef for their zegging music. An escape with you all, especially using your data manipulation, Ralia, is my only hope for freedom. We're all getting out or dying together."

"Zeg yeah!" Boyband shouted.

Ralia smirked. Two messages hit my neurospace interface.

Ralia: I hope it works out between you two, Pet. She's pulse.

I read the other.

Noama: Call me a shac, but I have to do this for you. I need you, Petya.

Chapter Seventeen

A Brief Return to Hell

I could not help but feel guilty as she held my hand.

We walked away from the sky limo, following Ralia towards her choice of parked car. She had given us a quick tacking wipe. She said it would hold for an hour, half of that if they had better tech than she anticipated.

Boyband leaned in close to watch, eager to see how easy her mod would make hacking the van's system. Its large wheels and sharp edges were as loud as Ralia's personality. At least she had chosen the typical chrome rather than the conspicuous choice I had expected.

She walked Boyband through the process, moving in to hack into the driver's panel.

Naoma tugged me along towards the back doors, which we had to pry upward. Naoma had done what was needed yet had not gone far enough to grant us all the vehicle's conveniences.

Ralia grinned as she turned to check that we were in our seats. Boyband walked around to enter on the passenger's side, but his smile was much more mocking.

Guilt returned as Ralia accelerated towards our destination. I hoped I could resolve my inner turmoil within the remaining twenty miles towards the hub but knew that was a laughable wish.

I was ecstatic to have the literal girl of my dreams wanting to join me in my last effort to live a free life but knew her perception was distorted. She confessed that her memories were limited to her current wakefulness, even the remnants of memory that she had from her time as the Neon Idol were but odd dreams. A sick side of me rebuked my desires for that of a predator, but she was no child. She was older than me. Her maturity matched mine. She *had* a life, it had merely been stolen and replaced with an abyss, one that would offer shadows of her life when certain circumstances would trigger their appearance.

Even if she told me that I was not taking advantage, I faced a guilt that would not capitulate. Perhaps once she saw me in a hungered frenzy, she would abandon me for the Imp that I was.

She had not abandoned Ralia.

Naoma accepted our flaws. She was a saint, but even the most pious of saints should refrain from contacting demons.

When the tragedy of our sporadic love would come, I hoped it would strike me, freeing her from whatever illusion she adored.

She lifted my chin and smiled. I smiled back but could not hold it for long.

"Ten more minutes," said Ralia.

Boyband rubbed his hands together. "How are we doin' this?"

She checked her rearview mirror, the side of the car, then changed lanes. "We'll have to be quick, but that goes without saying. Even if the tracking wipe gives us an hour, someone in the hub will figure out what is happening before too long. Simple enough, we need to eliminate any threats in our way, find Deleon, and pair his data with ours for a leak. If we can piece the evidence together in time, we should have enough proof of his control over us in order to at least prevent the law from killing us on sight. Once they settle in and give us some time for an alibi, I'll work out doctoring the data to make it look like we were programmed just as much as Naoma."

"Got it," Boyband said. "Eliminate threats, find that shac Deleon, let you do the rest."

"Pretty much," she said. "Questions?"

"Why not send the data out right now?" Naoma said.

"I don't have the equipment to alter everything now. If we get our hands on some of my stuff back at the hub, it'll be a lot easier. While I can get enough to make them stop and think, Deleon's confession is going to be what sells our defense."

"And how can you be sure he'll confess?" she asked.

"Technological manipulation, babe. Even if I need to alter the truth of his words, I'm sure I can use the zeggin' Bite mods he made against his neurospace."

Noama shook her head.

Ralia watched her through the rear-view mirror. "Don't believe me?"

"No, I *do*, and I guess that's the root of the issue. If you can make someone say anything you want, who can we trust? I get it that you have some special modification associated with your tooth-hunger-thing, but there have to be more people out there with that kind of tech. Who...what can we believe anymore?"

"Oh, hun, honesty went extinct during the technological revolution. Technological sentience only made things more complex. Today, the truth is defined by whoever can sell the best story."

"And if your boss sells a better story?"

Boyband chuckled, though his tone lacked confidence. "This is all a poor zeggin' joke, isn't it?"

Ralia hit his shoulder with the back of her hand. "Well, I'm sorry we all didn't have a nice few days to sit down and plan things out. It would have been nice if good ol' Deleon could have handed us a thorough plan, but–oh, wait, *he's* the zeggin' problem here. He's our target."

"Sorry, I just meant–"

"I know what you meant, babyband. Trust me, I'm just as frustrated as you are. This plan is utter guk."

"Sorry to make matters worse," Naoma said, "but where will I be during all of this?"

Ralia raised her eyebrows at me through the rearview mirror. I already knew Naoma had become my responsibility, yet was no closer to knowing how I would keep her safe.

"They won't harm their best advertisement," Boyband said.

"I'm not talking about Techvax or anyone they bring," Naoma said. "What about Deleon's guards? Anyone that opposed you for turning against the company?"

"We'll head to our quarters and snag one of Ralia's suits for you," I said.

"What kind of suit?"

"Form fitting armor," Ralia replied. "Plenty of little tricks to help you and your modification deficiency, unless you have some mods that can help you out?"

She shrugged. "Maybe a vocal implant, but if there is anything useful, it's hidden away with my other memories."

"I like that, girl. If there's a surprise, pray to the light that it's a good one. Back to what I was saying, I should have some grade C for you, it protects against blue light weapons and has charged shields you can activate for indigo. If we're going against violet light, well... let's hope we aren't. It's got some light shots built in with a light dagger, but we'll keep you in the back so those are kept for emergencies only. Armor up, then zeg the hell outta Del, pulse?"

"Pulse!" Boyband and I said.

I looked at Naoma, trying to lift her smile with one of my own.

She reached for my hand. "Pulse."

We parked in an abandoned lot just up the road from the hub.

Reaching our old home was a bittersweet comfort. It had been a stretch of normalcy, but one too painful to appreciate. Perhaps working for Deleon would be a relief compared to whatever torture we would be subject to if we were caught and not given immediate execution. We were too far along. Even if given the choice, I now had a new brother. I had Naoma at my side.

I had no desire to replace my new life with the former, though I felt this one was bound for destruction.

Ralia sent out sporadic EMP blasts as we made our way towards our quarters.

"Your boss doesn't have any guards?" Naoma said. "I still struggle to see why you never left."

"That's the problem," I said. "He always has a few around the building's circumference."

Ralia's eyes flashed as she searched for any security devices to disable. "And the guards weren't the problem. Deleon had plenty of external connections that kept us in his grip. Now that someone's out for him, the attention won't be centered on us. This is our best chance to leave for good, but only if he can take the fall for everything. I would rather risk this than spend my life as a fugitive."

"Any guards yet?" Boyband asked.

She shook her head, paused before opening the door closest to our rooms, then entered as the lights stopped flashing in her eyes.

I flicked the lights on. A light blue and an artificial white filled the slim hallway.

She stopped and pointed to the door at the end of that hall.

"What's there?" Naoma asked.

"A corridor that leads to the rest of the building. These doors here lead to our personal rooms. Do you boys need anything from yours?"

We shook our heads.

She waved for us to follow as she grabbed the handle to the first door on the right. The light on the locking mechanism went out and the door opened.

"Is it touch locked?" Naoma asked.

"Nah. Facial recognition, but I disabled it on the off chance that it'll notify someone that I'm entering the room. We've probably been detected by now, but any little precaution helps. The lock here is pretty poor tech, anyway. Deleon didn't care much for our privacy and worked around these locks all the time."

She flipped the lights on and waved for us to enter, closing the door quietly as we entered the room.

Blue light filled the room except for a white light bar across the top of a cracked mirror, beneath which various makeup products were in disarray. Piles of clothes were shoved into corners, most articles being torn, bloodied, or both.

"Zeg," Boyband breathed. "They must've raided your room! Did you have anything valuable in here?"

I couldn't hold back my laughter.

"Piss off, Pet," she said as she opened the sliding metal doors to her closet. "Sorry if I'm a mess and don't spend my time sulking in my room like you."

I grinned, knowing that although the comment was painfully true, she meant it out of love.

Ralia looked back at Naoma as a rotating rack extended from the closet. "Girl, please don't judge me off of this."

Naoma giggled. "I would be just as bad if it weren't for the ands who cleaned up anything I owned."

Naoma pulled a black jumpsuit from the rack. "You would think that if Deleon had ands for every other room—which he does—he could at least provide one for our rooms. Here you go, try this on."

Naoma grabbed the jumpsuit. "Where... can I–"

Ralia opened a door right behind her. "I get it, the bathroom is tiny, but you can do it in there or cramped with us in here. Personally, I don't care if you do it right here."

Naoma walked into the bathroom before Ralia could finish talking.

I avoided staring into Ralia's probing stare at the mercy of Boyband's laughing.

"What?" Ralia asked.

He held up a piece of paper. "Since when do we let kids in here?"

She ripped it from his hands. "*I* drew that, you little shac!"

"The zeg is it supposed to be? Petya? Come on, Ralia, you couldn't even color in the lines!"

"Please tell me that is not how you think I look," I said.

"Are you sure this isn't some keepsake from when you were five? Oh, now what is this?"

"Hey!" she grabbed his arm, but he grabbed a journal with the other.

He flipped it open and started reading aloud. "'*Phenmir stood with aching knees, holding an infant's corpse in his bloodied hands.*' Ral, you freak! What garbage is this?"

She kicked his shin and tore the journal from his hands.

"Hey!" He hissed through clenched teeth. "Who's this Phenmir guy? Is someone out there worse than Deleon? Killing babies?"

Ralia avoided eye contact as she tucked the journal beneath a pile of her other belongings.

"Are you *writing*, Ral?"

She shrugged. "Gotta occupy ourselves somehow. I like fantasy."

"I think that's a terrible opening line," Boyband said. "No freak will want to–"

I kicked him in the other shin. The conversation dropped as the door opened and Naoma stepped out.

I forgot to breathe. Zeg, she was beautiful. She must have caught my dumbfounded stare, for she smiled in a shy way so contradictory to what one would expect from the world's leading pop star.

There was nothing particularly different about her, but the way the jumpsuit made her look like one of us. It was a black compared to the bright colored jumpsuit she now held in her hands.

Ralia walked up and tapped the neck of the suit and the mask-shield I knew all too well covered her head. Naoma shrieked as it covered her in an instant.

"Chill, babe." Ralia tapped the neck for it to retract.

Naoma gasped, her hands rushing to her mouth, only to fall away as she realized that all was well.

Ralia giggled. "Flip it on when we get moving. It'll save your head from indigo and violet level shots, but I'm not too worried about that.

We'll keep you close and protected. I just don't want your identity spoiled–well, I guess we'll be killing anyone who could use that against us so... still just keep it up."

Naoma nodded. "You're just going to..."

"Kill anyone who comes after us? Chill, girl, we'll only take out threats, immediate and long term."

"What do I have to protect myself?"

Ralia tapped Naoma's wrist to reveal a dagger. "I think I've got a light pistol somewhere–"

Footsteps pattered outside the door. They were well beyond the door but were drawing closer. They were not stomps, but calculated steps that would likely be unheard if it weren't for our Bite-modified senses.

"What?" Naoma looked at us as we followed the sound with eyes on the door.

I raised a finger to my lips, while the other two walked towards the door with unrelenting focus.

Naoma's confused glare changed to focus on the door.

I looked at her, tapped my ear, then pointed at the door.

She nodded.

I stepped closer to Ralia and Boyband, pulling Naoma by the shoulder and giving her a slight push back. Ralia sent a message to Boyband and me.

Ralia: Can't break into their neurospace. I can see that they're send-ing messages to each other, but nothing about the content itself. Should we ambush them?

Petya: Are you two ready?

They nodded, eyes still fixed on the door.

Petya: Stay in the back. We'll have someone tail you after we deal with the people outside the door.

Naoma: How many are there?

Petya: Don't know. We'll find out.

Ralia grabbed a mod from her desk and plugged it into the back of her head.

Ralia: This'll help boost my hack mod for Deleon's system. The charge burns out fast. I forgot to dock it, but this should be enough.

She reached for the door as if walking into a sleeping child's room. As soon as I could see a crack of the blue light in the corridor, she swung it black and prowled a figure in the cramped corridor.

Her body darted towards the center of the front most guard, armorer in black with a light pistol aimed at us.

I repeated her attack, activating my mask as I speared the body of the guard right next to her. With plenty of soon-to-be corpses within the vicinity, I let my Bite burn all that it needed to eliminate each enemy with effectiveness and speed.

I jabbed the throat of my first opponent, barely feeling the armor break as my hand tore through the flesh and spine. The bitter thrill of Deleon's missions returned to me. I felt comfortable in such familiar circumstances, though I had grown much more conscious of the damage done by my hands. I had never seen any of Deleon's guards wearing such armor. For all I knew, these people could have been searching for Deleon to eliminate him just like we were.

I turned back to see Boyband already eating the teeth of one of his victims, whose helmet had busted all around the mouth area from a relentless barrage of Bite-fuelled punches.

I stood, looking for my next target, while Ralia dealt with her third or fourth.

"Ascend and we shall join."

I looked around, searching for the source of the voice.

"What?" I asked. No one seemed to notice the voice.

"You were violet, now you are indigo. We shall join in blue."

I shook my head and ran towards the next guard, hoping to remove the nonsensical thoughts from my mind. Even though I kept my body occupied as I broke a guard's legs, my mind dwelt on the voice and its command to "ascend."

The anti-spectrum.

As I toppled the guard, I saw *it* again down the corridor. The humanoid swine in traditional Chinese clothing. It was clearer than ever.

I punched through the guard's helmet, tore out some teeth, and threw them in my mouth after retracting my mask. With a honed focus, I looked back up.

As expected, the swine had disappeared.

Ascend. The anti-spectrum. Was this ghost connected to our Bite levels? If *it* wanted me to ascend to blue to "join" with it, should I obey?

My shoulder shot back with the impact of a blue shot. Cheap shacs had no idea what they were facing. If they had prepared higher light shots, I would have worried. Still, a different worry penetrated. They didn't know what we were. They *weren't* Osteolyte's–Deleon's–guards.

A third party had joined us in a final conflict. Whether they were the law, the group who sabotaged Deleon's efforts, or both, I could not let them achieve their goal, whatever it might be.

We had to reach Deleon with more urgency than ever. His data could free us from our crimes. His knowledge would explain what was happening.

If anyone could tell me why a humanoid swine beckoned me to ascend the Anti-spectrum, it would be Deleon.

In the few seconds of my paralyzed contemplation, Ralia had taken out the guard who shot me. Boyband was the furthest ahead with more kills that I would have expected from such a new Imp orientee.

I spared a glance behind. Naoma was safe. We had to move beyond the corridor to reach one of the facility's transport terminals.

Even looking upon the facility from the outside, it was impossible to tell how large it was. I assumed most of the terminals were nothing more than elevators. Our access was limited to the upper and lower two levels. Deleon denied anything beyond that, not only our access to it, but its existence. His claims that the upper stories were nothing more than remnants of the old building's owners grew less reliable by the day.

I walked towards Boyband and Ralia while they ate from their final victims.

Naoma faced them. I did not need to ask her to know that her eyes were nowhere near the impish feast at their feet.

"Zeg, that's good," Ralia moaned as she stood and wiped her mouth with her sleeve. A streak of shining wetness remained on it.

She pulled Boyband up to his feet right before he began to eat his third set of teeth.

"Piss off! I'm not done yet."

She looked back at me, not yet re-donning her mask.

"What? I'm not his dad."

"Come on, Pet."

"Yeah," he said. "Come on, Pet! Let me keep going."

I shook my head and patted his back. "'*Don't have time, kid,'* is what I think Ralia wanted me to say. She's right. These aren't Osteolyte guards. We've got to hurry to Deleon before we're out of time."

"What makes you think that? I don't care how long you've worked here. You said you don't know all of Deleon's secrets."

"I don't."

"Then how do you know they're not his secret force?"

I pointed at Ralia.

"Blue shots are a waste on us. Deleon knows that."

I snapped my fingers. I wasn't sure she had made the same conclusion, frankly I was relieved that she did, but it wouldn't have been the first time Boyband made me look like an idiot. Ralia was smart. Much smarter than me. If I ever wanted Boyband to be the same, I had to put him in these circumstances.

"They're already here then?" Naoma asked.

I waved her forward. Part of me was happy that she was so quick to come but realized that she was only ranking her fears. She had to be terrified of us, but whatever these guards were made her more afraid.

Was she more afraid to die or to return to pop slavery?

Was her expression a mere showing of her preference for death over captivity?

No. She hugged me.

Even when I thought I knew the start of true affection, all sense within me warned me that I was a mere convenience for her survival.

No one would want an imp.

A socitab sounded really nice right about now.

Ralia was whispering to Naoma, keeping watch from behind her. I couldn't quite hear them, but a quiet laugh from Naoma was enough to soothe my tension, if only for a moment.

"Down to the right," Boyband whispered.

"I hear them," I replied.

I sent a message in the group chat as the footsteps grew louder. We continued to approach, only holding back as we neared another corner.

Petya: Ral, you have a reading on Deleon's location?

Ralia: He's gotta be where he always is, or at least nearby. Even he told us that his best defense was in the center of the hub. You remember how to get there?

Petya: Of course.

Devóne: I don't.

Ralia: Gotta change your name in the chat to Boyband. I almost lost it when I saw your name. I forgot you had another one.

Petya: Focus Ral. No worry BB. Let me lead the way.

Ralia: BB, I like that haha.

Boybrand: Sure you don't want to be by your girl, Pet?

Ral: BB, change the brand in your name to band you illiterate shac.

Boyband: Piss off, grandm–

I focused out of my Neurospace before the message could load. Ralia had hit a small EMP, taking out the artificial hall lights.

"Hold tight, Nay," I heard Ralia whisper as we dashed into the darkness.

Seeing in the dark was one of the few abilities that our Bites granted that did not require us to burn from their reserve.

Guards in tight formations and rigid stances pointed their light pistols every which way, stirring at the slightest sound. Before we made our first move, Ralia tossed some scraps in the hallway down towards them. I held my breath, hoping that she wouldn't laugh as they panicked.

I shot a quick message just before making the first attack.

Petya: Keep one of them alive. We need Boyband to force one of them to say who they are. I want to hear their side before we hear it from Deleon.

Boyband: Pulse

Ralia: Pulse. Stay behind the corner, Naoma.

Naoma: Pulse.

They stirred as the balls of my heels kissed the ground with the elegance of a ballerina. With their light pistols aimed at eye level, they never expected me to slide into their ankles.

I knocked three of the five down. Ralia and Boyband took the other two while I finished the others on the ground. Each of my three shot in rapid repetition. None of the shots hit us, but they illuminated the hallway with blue flashes. I finished one with a throat punch, feeling his bones crush and mush with his neck muscles, while the other two continued to fire and move into better positions.

I flipped my mask back on before any of them hit my head. Ralia broke one of their necks after killing her first target. I ran towards the other and slammed his helmeted head into the ground with enough force to shock him, but not enough to inebriate.

I heard Boyband's mask flip up as he fed on the teeth of his target. Ralia walked towards me and whispered for Naoma to come forwards while Boyband finished feeding.

"Retract the helmet," I demanded. I pressed my knee into his back and pulled his arms back to gain leverage. Applying only enough pressure to keep him still, I lowered his arms towards his body until he stopped grunting and whining.

Ralia sent another EMP blast to take out the lights in all the other surrounding hallways, though I knew the guards would persist after an inevitable distress signal.

The guard gasped as his helmet retracted but struggled to do so completely with the multiplicity of dents.

"Boy!" I said in a harsh whisper. The others would have heard us by now. I don't know why we held up the quiet hesitation. "Here. Now."

He dropped the corpse, though its continual moaning led me to question whether he had finished the job. Ralia moved over to stomp his head in before I could ask her to. I was glad that Naoma was behind me. Our murders were horrible enough without having to face her reactions.

Boyband crouched and turned the guard's head towards him.

The guard moaned.

"Careful," I said. "After eating, you'll be a lot stronger than you expect."

The guard whined. "You freaks are eating us? Please, please—agh!" I pulled his arms back.

"Answer our questions, don't ask your own," Boyband said. He looked at me. "What do you want me to ask?" He turned to *coerce* the guard with his Bite-spell before I could answer. "*Who do you work for?*"

"Ah, come on, really?" Ralia said. "Isn't that a little on the nose?"

"Haven Health," the guard said in a dry tone.

"It worked," Boyband said.

"Haven?" Ralia crouched beside Boyband. "Come on, isn't that too obvious?"

"*Why are you here?*" Boyband asked.

The guard replied in the same monotone. "*Eliminate competition.*"

Ralia let out a frustrated laugh. "So this isn't as basic as the law coming for Deleon—well, I guess the president *is* the law—but it's even more simple than we thought?"

"What were you expecting?" Naoma asked, her voice clear but still at a safe distance.

"Some outside competitor, maybe BB's parents' cult, getting some revenge in. I—I don't know. We put all this time in trying to find who was hunting down jelly fiends, who blew up Deleon's big hit, but ended up realizing that it was the same enemy we had all along."

Boyband asked the guard another question. "*Are you Techvax?*"

"*We are Haven Health.*"

"They can't be the ones that sabotaged Deleon's job," I said. "Don't you remember that *Tevon* killed President Liu? There is no way Deleon made that call before he had more control."

Ralia shrugged. "Maybe it was someone under Liu that wanted her out of the way."

"Take a step down the ladder," I said.

"Does Techvax work for Haven Health?" Boyband asked the Guard.

"Techvax is a Finian organization."

"Do the Finians work for Haven Health?"

"Yes. No. I do not know. Yes. No."

"You're breaking him!" Ralia chuckled.

"Did your organization manipulate Osteoltye's mission?"

"We followed directives."

"Did your director call for the assassination of President Liu?"

"UNKNOWN DATA CORRUPT FILE BREACH." The guard vomited. Small metal pieces came out of his nose and mouth as he began to seize.

"Zeg!" Ralia backed away. "You asked the right question, BB! Zeggin' neurospace aborted the body?"

Boyband stood, flicking the vomit from his gloves.

I did the same, relieved that I only had a few drops on me. "Enough stopping. We're going straight for Deleon. Stay close, Naoma."

"What the *zeg* did that mean?" she asked.

"Dumb it down for us–for her, Ralia," Boyband said.

"His responses were off and altered to only let through certain pieces of information. From what I figure, Haven *is* behind this, rather a *part* of Haven."

"Someone below," Boyband said. "Techvax, right?"

"I don't think you were listening, hun. Techavax is a Finian organization. Leave it at that. Maybe they worked with our culprit, but we'll figure that out later. While Liu led Haven, someone below wanted her out of the way. At least, that is what I think the guard was trying to say. This whole job *was* an elimination of competition. Whoever did it all did not only zeg Deleon and his operation, but the Finians–through you three–and the higher ups in Haven. Just like Deleon, someone was out for the presidency. If we can't find them on our own, I'll bet you that the mastermind behind this will be whoever takes Liu's place. Without the competition of Osteotyle, Techvax and the Finians, and Haven's failing Okrepinate, someone is going to step forward with *something* from Arabasia."

"Neon Essence," Boyband said.

She nodded. "Your parents' hit job wasn't anything random. I'm sure they were the ones who led Deleon to the hit. Whoever did this all is very calculated. We are too far behind to stop it all, but we can do our best to get out of the way. Deleon holds the key to that."

"They must have thought we died somewhere along the way," I said. "Like I said, they didn't seem too prepared to face us with blue shots. If we don't hurry, we'll crash with all of this."

Boyband started jogging.

"Hey!" Ralia said.

He didn't look back. "You said let's hurry, so let's do it!"

The kid was excited and scared, but I, too, was afraid. Afraid that revenge drove Boyband more than logic.

I made sure Naoma followed us before running to the head of our party.

Each guard we faced was an obstacle. Seeing them as a living being only weighed down our pursuit. None of them proved a real challenge. I tried to remain focused, lest my cocksure attitude be the hubris at the end of this *final* assignment. I had dreamt about freedom for years. Even when it seemed close, I never let myself believe that it was. This time, it had the potential to prove true. Still, I wouldn't trust my anticipatory joy. Fortunately for me, a chain of violent murders in the name of self-defense was a simple solution for diminishing one's joy.

"I can't read any more of them." Ralia said as we finished off a trio of guards, each as naïve as their previous allies.

I looked back, my heart warming as I saw Naoma approaching us.

"Wait," Boyband asked. "How the zeg have you been following us?"

Ralia chuckled. "I forgot to turn on the night vision mod on her mask when we started. Oopsies. We're all good now, though, right Nay?"

"Right. We're pulse" Her laugh was unsure. She had a strong tone, but I suppose anyone's voice would sound deep compared to Ralia. The strong sway of her voice made her music all the more seductive.

Zeg. Focus, Petya.

"Eat up as much as you can," Ralia said. "If anything is in Deleon's wing of the hub, I want to be ready. Even if there is no one besides him in there, I don't want more complaining from you, BB."

She began to eat, ignoring Boyband while he tried to defend himself.

I was filled enough, rather, I found something else much more interesting.

Naoma walked towards me, changing her pace from hesitant to confident as I retracted my mask.

She reached for my hand. I looked down at the blood from my hands as it smeared across hers. My guilt spread across her and would continue to do so the further we went.

"What's wrong?" she asked.

I shrugged, forced a single laugh, and looked at her hands, unable to lock my eyes with hers.

"Pet?"

She beckoned me. I looked up. Piercing was too simple a description for her eyes. They were purple magnetic rings. They were everything that I wanted, yet despite any justification, would never deserve.

She squeezed my hand. "None of this...bothers me."

"Zeg, you're a terrible liar."

"Really, I get it. You do what you have to. Even if I don't like it, you better not stop. You made a promise to get me out of here."

"You could've left."

"You shac, you know what I mean. I want a real life. I want to see you having one too. We don't need to make any long-term commitments, but I want to try that life out with *you*, Petya."

I smiled, an old timidity pulling back the joy I wanted to feel.

"You *are* good enough. I might not remember a lot from my life as the Neon Idol, but I know how to read manipulation. I know how to read a bad person in someone who thinks they are good. You're just the opposite. You're good enough for a broken girl that is trying to figure out a new world with her mind *finally* working for herself. You're good enough for me."

She pulled me close, her hands on the back of my neck as she stood on her toes.

I leaned down, letting her upper lip slide in between mine. I wanted to remain there, listening to one of her longing love songs that I had put on during countless lonely nights.

The sounds of teeth crunching was most unromantic, but it meant nothing to me.

This was bliss.

She pulled away. I looked at the other two as they fed. Neither of them watched us.

Naoma tilted her head towards them. "Do your work. It's no problem. Hurry up though, let's finish this zegging thing.

I smiled at her and proceeded to eat the teeth of the remaining corpse.

The sweetest tooth pulp was bland compared to Naoma.

Chapter Eighteen

Beacon of the Rising Tide

"Petya," Deleon laughed through swollen lips, spitting blood out as he did so. Only a few teeth remained in his smile.

We stopped as we entered, raising our hands in surrender to the four guards that surrounded him. It was a ruse, but one that would work long enough to figure out our approach.

The back two guards each held a light rifle the size of their torso against their chest. Violet light pulsed in lines across their chrome encasings. The front two had violet rifles holstered against their right thighs, each a smaller alternative to the violet claymores they held by the hilt with the tip in the ground, burnt holes in the ground beneath them. I had no doubt they could burrow down if pressed deeper. It was a foolish way of holding them, yet it did not diminish the threat they posed.

"Did you know we were coming?" Boyband asked.

Deleon laughed, wincing and grunting as he did so. "I had hoped that you survived with all the guk that happened. Listen, I'm sorry about all of this. It wasn't my plan to—"

"Shut up, shac," Boyband said. He pointed to the guards. The back two had their gargantuan rifles aimed at us. "You all figured we were coming, then?"

"They're just keeping me still until their boss comes." Deleon said. "They're not a talkative bunch."

One of the front swordsmen swung his light blade to rest on his shoulder as he took a step forward. Though the violet edge could cut through anything in the room, yet it had no effect on the guard's armor.

"Who's the boss?" Ralia asked.

"Don't know yet, but I'm guessing we'll all figure it out soon! Now," he pointed at Naoma. "Who is that?"

She remained in place with her mask up.

I looked at Ralia. She was busy analyzing the room. I followed her example.

"Hihow! I asked a question!" Deleon moved in his seat but couldn't raise his hands. They were bound by bands of indigo light, as were his legs.

I tapped into the neurospace chat.

Petya: Eliminate the guards and get out of here with Deleon before the "boss" arrives?

Ralia: Agreed.

Boyband: How are we doing it?

I raised my hands again as the front most guards walked towards us. The back two kept their rifles focused—one on me, the other one Ralia.

Petya: They're holding back. If they wanted us out of here, they would've killed us by now.

Ralia: I scanned the door. It's locked. They want us in here for the boss, who has to know we are part of this all now.

Boyband: How are we going to survive this? Even if they hold back from killing, I don't think they'll shy away from injuring us, if not killing a few of us.

Ralia: They've got a violet lining that'll protect them from any small stunners.

Petra: Zeg it all. Distract the front two. Ral, make sure to keep Naoma out of the way.

Ralia: Got your babe, babe.

The other two had their feast. I was near full but readied my agility mod to deplete everything I had remaining.

I dashed forward, passing the sword-wielding guards before they could react.

Seconds felt like minutes.

The left guard pulled the trigger of his gun. My head was a foot away. I could see the light charging in the barrel. In my periphery, I saw the same thing happening to the light rifle of the right guard.

Violet light, stronger than any shield I could activate, aimed at me from two cannons of rifles that could level the building if shot enough.

Agility modded. Bite-charged imp. Indigo level on the anti-spectrum. All of these words made me seem worthy of god-like speed, yet such a claim was beyond my reach.

I had a talent given to me by a tech implant.

I was terrified.

I swung my upper torso down, landing with palms on the floor and kicking up to the right.

If I ever managed to escape Deleon's glorified enslavement, I could fare well as an acrobat. With ands, it was a dying profession, yet the thought gave me enough confidence to continue.

My feet hit the bottom of the rifle, turning the aim up above the right guard's head when it shot. I managed to deflect the shot before it hit me yet aimed too poorly for it to land on the right guard.

My movement continued as if flowing in a stream. I pushed off from the floor, rolled into the left guard, and pulled him down by the throat.

The right guard was armed, but mentally lacking. His shot landed in the center of the left guard's torso. The shot obliterated the armored body. Little holes shot through, landing on me like a light shotgun spray. Perhaps I had overestimated the durability of their armor. It stung and pierced my flesh but was far too superficial to cause me to worry.

The right guard's recharge time was his own death sentence.

I seized the left guard's sizzling corpse by the throat once again and hurled the whole body at the right guard, knocking him to the floor.

I sprang to my feet and dashed ahead. Before the right guard could stand and aim his light rifle, I speared my hands together like a diver into the center of his chest, prying them apart with all the strength I could muster. The head fell with the left portion as the legs clung to the right. I wanted to feed already but left the desiccated guards aside as I turned to check on the others.

My vision pulsed. It was *too* concentrated, *too* blood-thirsty for analysis. I peddled back to allow myself a second of rest as I eased off of my Bite reliance.

Clear images formed before me. While my engagement had been thrilling, a reminder of the fiend that I could become, their fight had been much more disappointing.

Each of the front guards rested on their knees, moaning as they held their own swords in the center of their chest.

I shot Boyband a glare, trying to calm my breathing.

He shrugged and pointed at them. "Sorry you had a hard time with your guards, Pet. The coercion mod worked easily enough for these two."

Their bodies swayed and collapsed. The light blades cut through their bodies, then into the ground as they continued to burn.

I watched the pulsing violet, if only to delay our interaction with Deleon by a few more seconds. This whole journey had been a painful circle of loss, deception, and confusion at the hands of the failed man before us. Wasted time paled little in comparison to the abominations wrought by our hands under his command all for the sake of a power that he would never achieve.

"Well then." He tried to sit up higher in his seat but his movement was limited to his hands, feet, and head under the strict violet bindings.

"Well then, what?" Boyband barked back. "What are we supposed to say to that?" He stepped up to Deleon and smacked him across the face.

Deleon cried out. His cheek was bleeding and swelling already.

"Hold on, BB." Ralia grabbed Boyband's shoulder and pulled him towards her.

I struggled to concentrate. Everyone in the room knew what I needed. I backpedaled, eyes still fixed on Deleon and Ralia. I turned away to rip off a guard's helmet and devoured her set of teeth.

"Can I talk to the dickhead now?" Boyband shouted.

Deleon laughed, grunting with each inhale. He spat a glob of bloody phlegm onto the blue rug beneath him.

Ralia squeezed Boyband's shoulders. "No more hitting, hun. The more you break his mouth, the harder it will be to understand him."

I checked to make sure Naoma kept her mask up. Seeing that she had, gladdened me. I could be spared from seeing her reaction to my feeding.

"Why'd you kill my zegging parents?" Boyband's breathing was pressured, but it was clear that he was trying to contain it.

Deleon shook his head. "So *that* is what brought you here? That is what turned you against me? Petya, don't forget our deal."

"I have other means. Judging by your circumstances, I don't think you could have fulfilled your promise, anyway."

"Hey! Dickleon! Answer my question. Why did you out my parents?"

"If you're here, I'm guessing that you have figured that out by now. Who restored your memories?"

"What?"

He chuckled. "What do I have to lose? Might as well be truthful if we're going to help each other out. I took you in after the murder. The whole 'me finding you' thing was an implanted memory. Sorry, but I knew it would be the only thing to convince you to help. Now that you've seen what you can do, you know that what I did was right."

Boyband clenched his fists but held back. "I don't care if you zegged with my mind. Tell me about the murder!"

"Funny enough, I was never able to complete the job. I had it all lined up, but *that* was when it all spiraled out of control. You were never a part of the original plan. The memory edits were added after. Still, I held onto you hoping that we could turn your revenge into utilizing their connections, but I guess I still look like the guilty party." He shook his head and shrugged. "I didn't do the hit."

"Of course you did! Osteolyte did it under your command."

"Like I said, kid, I had the plan set up, but the data was breached. I wanted what they had. Someone else found out why I wanted it and decided to pull off the hit in our name. I have no idea how they did it, let alone who had the ability to do it so cleanly, but here we are. With you, I was hoping we could turn this all against *them*, whoever they are. I figured if we could find the guilty party, we could find a way for the company to fall into my–your hands to prevent the need to repeat such an action."

He leaned forward. Blood in between each of his teeth in a wide grin. "Hey, listen, maybe we *still can*. I saw what you all did. I knew you were all capable. You'll only get better with things like this when you ascend to the next level of the anti-spectrum. *I can help you with that.*"

"I'll get revenge on my own, you prick. Even if you didn't pull off the hit, you had the intent. You even said so!"

"Well, I–"

"Let's extract what we need, Ral," I said.

"What else could you hope to gain?" Deleon said. Desperation quivering in his voice.

"Do you know who sabotaged this?" Ralia asked. Her eyes were flashing as she prepared her neurospace.

"I told you I don't but thank the light you see that this wasn't all my fault!"

Ralia stepped towards him. "Oh, Del, we don't think that greatly of you. I knew you would have waited before killing the president. I know you put research into Reef Records, but the only real success we had was in finding Techvax's influence, thanks to me."

"Why were they even important?" Ralia asked.

"Who's that?" Deleon asked.

Ralia put her fingers to her lips. "Techvax was tied to the Finians, right? Do you harbor some hatred against them, Del?"

"No! Don't you remember why you started on this? The Exos sapiens." He stared at us, looking for a reaction. "The 'jelly fiends?'"

"Neon Essence?" I asked. "The jellies make it and you wanted to preserve them from Techvax to extract it?"

"Oh-ho-ho, Petya, you are close. Close enough to zeg this all over if you don't see what is *actually* happening." He cocked his head at Ralia. "No need to extract. I'll tell you what you need to know. Once you see *why* I did what I did, you'll see why you have to join with me. Techvax is a distraction. Now that you found a name for them, they're easier to eliminate. Why was I so confident that I had the tech to dominate Haven? Why else would they send *these* guards to finish me off?"

"Just tell us you zegging shac!" Boyband shouted. "Can I hit him, Ral? I really want to!"

She stepped forward.

"Hey! Hey! What are you–gah!"

She ripped his two front teeth out and handed them to Boyband. "A little snack to hold over your hatred.

He chewed on them slowly with an open mouth. "Talk, Deleon."

"Zeg! Ah, did you really have to? Ugh." He spat out bloody phlegm and took a deep breath. "Petya, I know you have a lot of hatred for your country's government, but you need to set aside old grudges to see *why* they attacked Arabasia."

"Neon Essence," I said. "We dug into the Luxists."

"Ah, I see. Tread carefully when–"

"Are we treading carefully by listening to your side?" I asked.

He shrugged. "I suppose you are right. All arguments deserve a fair consideration of both sides. Yes, Neon Essence is at the core of this debate, not because it derives from Exos Sapiens, but because it interacts with something of particular note at their core. We'll refer to this as a light soul. When the human body has succumbed to techbone, the human is no longer present, only the light soul. Why do these light souls only perpetuate with techbone deaths and not with others? Light souls are the cause of techbone.

"What, no gasps for the big reveal? Maybe I need to do a little more explaining. Light souls began to find their ways into human bodies around the same time that we discovered the physical light that powers our society. Perhaps these are connected more than we know. That may be something the Luxists claim to know, but I don't. Light souls do not *cause* the condition we call techbone on their own, but it is the training of light souls caused by forced integration with physical light. Why is techbone caused by tech implants? Why do only some people develop the condition? If an individual that is blessed with a light soul happens to force physical light into their body with a tech implant, the light soul begins to devour the human skeleton, depriving the body of its regenerative abilities until it crumbles into a flesh mound. The light soul craves that which it does not have."

Light soul? I didn't ask and continued to listen.

He sighed. "Look at it this way. A light soul is like a human given a hot pepper that is physical light. It enjoys it, but *needs* the pain extinguished. It needs 'water' and finds its thirst quenched in human bones. Neon Essence is the heat and relief paired to perfection. It is physical light in its complete form. When Neon Essence is paired with a light soul, it no longer craves the bones. This is a perfect union. Killing the light souls through Techvax's so-called vaccination *would* in theory prevent techbone."

"Then why not go with that?" Boyband said. "No Essence needed."

"Because it eliminates the power that can be harnessed through the synergistic pairing of light soul and Neon Essence."

"And that is?" I asked.

"Don't you see? *That* is the reason my work must be perpetuated. If we allow Techvax to succeed, we lose any chance at seeing the future of Neon Essence combined with the light souls. So little is known about this. Only *I* have had the faintest glImpse at its success."

He stared at us, waiting for a response. His impatience got the best of him. "Need some help to reach the grand conclusion? The power Neon Essence is measured on the *anti-spectrum*."

"You put it in us?" Ralia asked.

"Oh, how I wish I could clap! Don't you see how you are superior to *any* modified human? You are a taste of the future."

"That's a load of guk," Boyband scoffed. "If that was Neon Essence, it would make a 'perfect union' like you said with our light souls. The problem is, we *still* crave teeth. Our light souls *still* need human bones to operate."

"I know Techvax works because I killed your light souls when I took you in, at least those of you that had them. Ralia and Tevon never did. I had to try out something beyond the natural pairing. Tell me, have you ever had any... supernatural experiences with your Bites?"

"The zeg are you talkin' about?" Ralia said. "All of it is super-zeggin'-natural."

"No, no, no I mean–"

"The zeggin' monkey?" Boyband asked. "Did you put a zeggin' monkey's light soul into my body?"

"I could die a happy man! No, I want to see this come into fruition but–gah! Yes! Yes! That! And you, Petya?"

"The humanoid swine." I uttered, trying to make sense of what was happening.

"Zhu! Sun! And you Ralia?"

"The orc, yeah, so what if I've seen it? It's just been an apparition, like a hallucination."

"Sha! They have begun to show themselves. As you ascend the Anti-spectrum, I–I don't know what this will hold! Great–"

"So *that* was your actual experiment?" I shouted. "Pumping freak-ish ghosts into our minds?"

"I knew long ago that the light soul and Neon Essence pairing would work. That was my first project under the Osteolyte title. *That* was how I was going to find success. *That* truth is why someone sabotaged my work. They thought they had it all, but not the second arc of my project. You wonderful subjects. Tevon and Ali had them as well. It comes as a part of the hypothalamic implant."

"Wait, what happened to Ali?" I asked.

"Executed with Tevon, I presume, but that is beside the point. These 'freakish' ghosts are our greatest discovery, rather a discovery of the Luxists. Straight from Arabasia in the center of old China. Gui, *living* Chinese mythology that I have reason to believe is the very origin of light's physical evolution. Why do you need teeth? Because these beings are much mightier than any typical light soul. Without the hypothalamic implant, they would cause your bones to crumble within seconds. We are on the cusp of such great discoveries. Now, don't you see why you must accompany me? If we are to gain the resources we need to support this research, we need the presidency. We need it to join with Medislavia in their war against Arabasia. Neon Essence. The Gui and their history. All of it resides within Arabasia."

Boyband glanced back at me. He knew how disdainful I would become hearing the equivalent Medislavian propaganda.

"You're insane," I said. "You're condoning tyranny in order to achieve some *dream* of yours. The zeg is wrong with you, Deleon?"

"Petya, couldn't you see that I had something beyond a mere claim for success? I sent you all out to eliminate Techvax while I focused on the rest. Sure, at that point I didn't have a concrete idea of who my opponent was, but Ralia did well to solidify that information."

"Don't drag me into this," she said.

I almost stepped up to hit him myself. "I'm not talking about your failure. Your entire motive is far beyond what you preached. This is no cure. If you wanted to cure techbone, you would have had the means to do so years ago, based on what you are saying. I just don't even know what to do with you at this point."

I looked at Ralia, who shared my same frustrated glare. Naoma remained still.

Boyband spoke. "If we are even to believe any of this—"

"Why wouldn't you?" Deleon interjected. "You've seen the Gui. The monkey is already in you, Devóne. We have much more than just this. I am not alone in my endeavors."

"The violet suits," I said. "They're not yours, are they?"

"A part of something much greater."

"The Ten Beacons," I said. "Like those girls that saved us in the Indigo District described."

"The other nine would be thrilled to see how far you have come."

"Who?"

"The Gongtide. In a world run by the peak of technological advancements, we are swift to believe that physical light, even Neon Essence, is a proponent of electricity. The world is more spiritual than that."

His smile dropped as voices and footsteps sounded beyond the doors.

"Petya!" Deleon shouted. We had no chance of hiding under a shroud of silence anymore.

I shot him a glare.

"Please, all of you. *Do not* let everything that I have found be tossed away. Protect me. Your freedom will be yours. We *need* what you have become."

He continued to plead, losing the composure of the stalwart executive he had attempted to be.

I moved to feed on one of the remaining guard's teeth but was cut off as a green light above the door lit up. *Access approved.*

A cluster of guards stepped from the open doors. Their armor was bulky and covered in violet light.

"Friends." The guard procession split. A familiar walked forward, speaking better Amerikese than I had ever heard from him. He waved at us with his metal hands. "It looks like Deleon has delivered his side of the argument. Let me show you where you *should* stand."

Ali was alive and all too well.

Chapter Nineteen

Virus

"You've done it," Deleon scoffed. "You've surprised me."

I turned back to him.

Deleon looked back at me. "I recruited all of you personally. Ali, however, was brought to me by our dear Doctor Cuttrin." He hung his head, shaking it. He looked up at Ali. "Is this his doing?"

Ali held up a hand with delicate stillness.

"You're Haven?" I asked.

"Currently? Yes. Now that Liu is out of the way."

"It was you who killed Tevon?" Ralia said.

Ali shrugged. "He followed a command and was too headstrong to consider the consequences."

"So now you're the zeggin' president?" Boyband asked.

"No, no. That position is yet to be handed over, but it is not mine for the taking."

"Cut said you were some refugee," Ralia said. "Are you here to get revenge on the immigration system like Petya?"

"While Petya and I both come from war-torn countries, our circumstances differ. You should know, Petya, that although there is corruption in Medislavia, their plight is not as malevolent as you make it out to be. Give me some time to explain my position before you make any accusations." The guards lifted violet claymores to their sides. "Devóne, we are now well aware of your ability. Do not bother attempting it with these guards. Humans are fallible, ands–however–are not as mentally frail."

"You–" Deleon began to shout but was cut quiet as a light shot hit his shoulder. "Gah!"

Ali looked into my eyes. "I do not mean to manipulate or threaten you. I want you all to join us."

"Why?" Boyband said.

"I–"

"Who *are* you?" I asked.

"To answer Devóne, I suppose I must answer you, Petya. My name is Abbas Karimi. While much of my naïvety was an act, I was surprised by the stark differences between the Republic and my homeland. Just like you, Petya, I was a 'political activist,' in Arabasia. Devóne, I recognize that you have a devout admiration for your patents, but you must realize that the Luxists are religious extremists that endanger all humanity with their obsession for Neon Essence. Deleon poses a similar threat with his fanaticism, which is why we must hone his energy with practical purposes. When I stood against the extremists of Arabasia, I was exiled and was left alone. With Arabasia against me and techbone rapidly disintegrating my body, I had only my knowledge to bargain for a second chance. I found that in a certain member of Haven Health, whom I hope to introduce you to soon."

"And what do you plan on doing with the Neon Essence?" I asked.

"Oh, there is so much to explain."

"We have time," I said.

Ali shook his head.

"If you want us, then we'll have our zegging time!" I shouted.

"Deleon's vision, but with a purpose to aid humanity rather than his fanatic cult."

"Are you going to join Medislavia in the war?"

He struggled to find words.

"Are you going to or not?""Yes, but you see–"

"No I don't!" I looked back at my companions. "I don't care what lies he spits out. I left for a reason. Medislavia's plight for Neon Essence will tear the world apart. I don't care what the new or old Haven Health stands for. I will not commit to any company who seeks to advance that war for their gain. Even if they continue with this, *I* will not be a part of it. I pray that none of you will be either."

A barrage of messages hit my neurospace.

Ralia: Piss on them, babe, I'm with you.

Boyband: Zeg em' all. Who're we hitting first?"

Naoma: I'm with you until the end. I told you then, and I'll tell you again.

Petya: Burn your reserves. We'll have a feast when they're all dead. Hang back, Naoma. Grab that dead guard's light rifle to protect yourself.

My body shook as my Bite fueled it with digested teeth.

Any remaining emotions I had in my feral mind hoped that Naoma grabbed the light rifle in time. The other two would fare well for themselves. If they were incapable of opposing these guards, so was I.

The guards move to protect Ali–Abbas. Good for him. Leave his suffering until the bitter end.

Each of my fists slammed into a different guard, flying through their throats. Sparks flew, cables broke, yet they continued to function.

I pulled back, rolling away as both claymores landed in the ground before me. If I hadn't used my speed mod, the blades would have split me in parts.

My heart felt like it vibrated. I could see Ralia and Boyband fighting guards in my periphery, but I didn't have the time to see who was winning each contest.

"*Free me,*" a husky voice spoke from the back of my mind.

What?

The swine.

Deleon's zegging Arabasian spirit.

"What can you do?"

The guards continued to swing their swords as I peddled back. They thought nothing of my question.

"*Free you.*"

I felt an opening in the same part of my mind that held my Bite reserve. I felt as if a hand reached out, devilish in its intentions, for me to make some Faustian bargain.

I reached out. "Free us."

An aura emanated from my hands. Large, burly claws of a black light came from my hands like ghostly gloves.

"*Thus commences the beginning,*" the spirit spoke. "*We have a long journey, dear friend.*"

The claws extended beyond the reach of my hand like rakes.

"*In due time, we will become truly one.*"

The black light of my claws tore through the violet claymores as the guards swung them at me. The flickering remnants of the blades fell around me as I crashed into the guards. I prepared to pounce on one of them, ready to shred them as I had their blade, but was tossed to the side. A neighboring guard had rammed its shoulder into me with the speed and strength of a skytrack train.

My mind wanted to rest, slipping out of consciousness, but my burning Bite and its swine spirit forced me onward.

I fell from a crack in the wall, matching my body's stretched-out shape, cracks reaching the floor and ceiling. Looking up, I saw two guards charging with blades at their sides. I ran towards them and slid right between them, narrowly missing their strike but tearing my clothes up in the crumbling wall.

I stood and spun back around, preparing myself as they reverted back toward me.

With the black claws held to my side, I prepared to face them head-on. Before I met their charge, Boyband slid in front of them atop a cloud of light, sweeping their legs with a ray of black light.

Before they could stand, I prowled forward and tore at them with my light claws. I screamed with rage, tossing sparking chunks of metal every which way.

My rage had deafened me from the guard approaching from behind. I only recognized their presence as Boyband lifted me on his cloud of light, pulling me from the clash between a double-bladed guard and Ralia, who shot streams of light like black water from her hands. Upon impact, the and guard's armor melted, leaving a bare robotic core that exploded as Naoma shot it with a violet blast.

I stepped from Boyband's cloud, not having enough energy to leap even though my mind wanted me to.

Ali glared back at me, brow furrowed in slight confusion. His eyes flashed as he tapped into his neurospace. The doors behind him opened, ushering forth another company of guards even more armored than the first.

I looked at Ralia, then to Boyband. Both of them breathed with heavy rage. I turned my focus back to the barrage of guards, readying my black claws.

They ignited with a flash of energy. After a second of pulsing power, they flickered and retracted to half their length.

Zeg.

"*Has our journey been cut short?*" the Swine spoke.

The guards ran after the others, while Ali raced straight for me. I screamed to keep the claws lit up as long as possible, running at him like a perishing boar in a futile attempt to survive.

Any hesitancy from the boy that I thought he was dissipated in his vile grin.

Our time together was as much a lie as the stories told in the art house mindshows he claimed to enjoy. All the time I spent trying to make him feel included was worthless against his hidden motives. Would this be the last betrayal, or the beginning of a painful road? Was Ralia who she said she was? I had experienced enough of Boyband's past to trust him, but even the most convincing truths around me crumbled.

The white light aura of a horse surrounded him as he charged me. His face turned to that of a horse blended with a Chinese dragon. I raised my claws to slash at him, but they were deflected as if I tried to strike violet light with red.

The charging white horse overcame the black swine. I have no recollection of how hard our impact was, for after we collided, I could only sense pain until my consciousness escaped me.

Chapter Twenty

A Burning Hatred of Politics

"The public is ready for your address, President Cuttrin."

The voice stirred me from a daze. A woman spoke to Cut, who sat in a pristine leather chair across from us in a grand office. His past dishevelment was cleaned away as he now wore a suit with violet light. His dark skin was without blemish and his black hair had been swept up and back.

Ralia and Naoma sat to my right, Boyband on my left.

I tried to speak, then scream. I could open my mouth, but no sound escaped. My companions went through the same experience. We settled, looking to Cut for an answer.

"I'm happy to finally have you all at my side."

Ali–Abbas–approached from behind us and stopped at Cut's side. He also wore a suit with violet light accents.

Cut patted Abbas's arm. "I know your friend here has helped clarify a little of your situation, but I would expect that with me here–" he chuckled with a joviality so unlike the man I thought we knew "—you have plenty more questions."

"President Cuttrin," the woman in the doorway said with stern urgency. "The Republic is waiting for your address."

"They can wait. I cannot address them without addressing our *new team members*." he gestured to us. "Welcome to Haven Health. I know that with the assistance of Deleon's 'Imps,' we can achieve much more than we previously believed."

Any question I had failed to leave my mouth.

"I understand that your loyalty demands mine, so why not let you in on my past? Understanding it will only help you gain confidence in what we are planning to do here. Abbas, please go begin the address for me. I'll need some time here with them."

"Of course, Mister President." Abbas left forthwith.

"Now, just you and me. I have to say, the Neon Idol was a surprising addition. Even though I sent you Imps into the Reef and Techvax trap, I did not expect Naoma to join you. We'll find you a way to work you into our business plan, Miss Naoma. Reef Records was a horrible outlet for your talent. We will allow you to be much more expressive, *under certain terms*." He muttered the last bit under his breath.

"This whole dynamic is ironic. I joined Deleon with the same intentions he had when he sent you out to sabotage the other ruling parties. I was a mere agent of Haven Health sent to investigate Osteolyte's rise in power. Rather than eliminate them as instructed, I worked with Deleon for some time, eventually years, to harness the Neon Essence, light souls, and all the associated technology. When my aides read your memory of the last few days, I was pleased to learn that he told his side of the story.

"When I joined, partnered–whatever you call it–Osteolyte, the late President Liu had her investments set to buy out Techvax's technology. Techvax was much more practical than her Okrepinate production, but once I discovered Deleon's interests, I knew Techvax had to be eliminated."

He walked towards the portrait of President Liu on the wall and stroked the violet frame. "Unfortunately, I knew President Liu was all too invested in Techvax. Why? It was a Finian corporation. I'm sure you learned that by now. With the upcoming election, she wanted to increase her diminishing support by investing in the Finians and their research. With that in mind and Techvax as something that had to be eliminated, I made use of Tevon–may he rest in the light–to remove her from the position so that I could ascend to the presidency upon her passing. Tevon was more than willing to work with '*Ali*' to assassinate the president. Tevon was a mighty man, but too dull for what I need you all to accomplish."

He walked towards the door, his eyes flashed in his neurospace for a moment, and he gave us one last apologetic look. "The Republic needs me, dear Imps. I understand your confusion and frustration. In time, you will set these aside while we utilize Deleon's findings to raise the Republic of Capital and its technology to the throne of nations."

He bowed and left.

Our silent screams perpetuated. Fear shining in each other's eyes, we waited for an escape.

A screen turned on in the air before us. Abbas stepped aside from behind a violet podium to allow Cut to take his place. The camera zoomed in, altering his wrinkles to make him appear five years younger.

He spoke with a confident smile, the flag of the Republic of Capital billowing in an artificial wind behind him.

"Dear citizens of the Republic, it is with dire sincerity that I turn to you. Techbone is taking more lives than ever before. With the death of our dear President Liu and foreign hatred brewing, it would seem that all humankind is turning against one another."

He straightened. "For this reason, we must take a position in order to preserve the republic and its citizens. Today, I–as the President of the Republic of Capital and CEO of Haven Health–will sign a treaty with Medislavia against Arabasia."

The screen disappeared. Two months remained until the election, though I feared that would not affect Cut's plight.

We were together in our suffering. Granted a false freedom just as we had under Deleon's command. Despite the illusion of stability, and whisper of peace disappeared from me.

In my mind, I spoke to the ancient spirit that called me.

"Swine."

"Yes?"

"I am ready."

End of Book 1

Afterword

Thank you for taking your time to read this book! As an independent author, your opinion of this book can make a big difference. Please take a few moments to review this book on Goodreads, Amazon, and anywhere else you would like. If you enjoyed reading this, please tell your friends and family about it and don't forget to check out my epic fantasy series, *Paladins of the Harvest.*

Acknowledgements

When my editor told me that this book knocked her ****ing socks off, it felt the same as when I qualified for the Boston Marathon. I am proud of my *Paladins of the Harvest* series, but this book was something special. Thank you Sarah for helping me reach this point. Feeling that my books are worth something is all this is about.

Thank you to Sima, my wonderful wife, for helping me write some romance into this book. Your romantasy reading paid off.

If you did not read the dedication of this novel, please do so. This is written for refugees like Petya, who endured horrible circumstances for the sake of finding a safe home away from war. This is for the Russians and Ukrainians who seek sanctuary. Please consider donating to a charity that supports refugees. Petya's description of his past was taken from real stories from real immigrants who were held in detainment because they were Russian citizens. They wanted freedom and safety and were treated like rats.

I hope this book made you feel happy, sad, and somewhat uncomfortable (besides the eating of teeth, of course). All stories have a purpose beyond entertainment. Let Toothsucker be the one that turns you to help your neighbor.

Now onto some lighter topics.

I doubt they will ever see this, but thank you to the band *Let's eat Grandma,* whose music inspired Naoma and many of the feelings in this book.

Thank you to dolphins for existing and to God for creating them. A lot of research went into creating the Finians. Yes, they actually get high on pufferfish toxins.

Lastly, thank *you* reader, especially those who have read my other books. I can't wait for you to see what is in store.

About the author

Kaden Love currently resides in Salt Lake City, Utah with his wife (and illustrator), Sima. When he isn't reading, he juggles running marathons to audiobooks, writing, and living out his own adventures.

@kadenloveauthor on Instagram, X (Twitter)

@svetlingpress on Instagram

Kadenrlove.com